P9-EFJ-395

SUDDEN FICTION

SUDDEN FICTION

American Short-Short Stories

Edited by Robert Shapard and James Thomas

With a *Frontistory* by Robert Coover

And *AfterWords,* about the short-short story form,
by forty of America's finest writers

➜ P

GIBBS M. SMITH, INC. — PEREGRINE SMITH BOOKS — SALT LAKE CITY

This is a Peregrine Smith Book

Copyright © 1986 by Gibbs M. Smith, Inc.

Published by Gibbs M. Smith, Inc.
P.O. Box 667, Layton, Utah 84041

Book design by Smith and Clarkson

Printed and bound in the United States of America
90 89 88 87   5 4 3 2

Library of Congress Cataloging-in-Publication Data

Sudden fiction.
   "A Peregrine Smith book."
   1. Short stories, American. I. Shapard, Robert,
1942-   . II. Thomas, James, 1946-
PS648.S5S8   1986   813'.01'08   86-10039
ISBN 0-87905-248-1
ISBN 0-87905-265-1 pbk.

Acknowledgment of permissions to reprint those stories
in this book which have previously appeared elsewhere
may be found in the back beginning on p. 259

We are indebted to the following readers, who helped us shape this book: François Camoin, Jim Clark, Jon Maney, Revé Shapard, Denise Thomas; and especially James B. Hall, who was so generous with his ideas and advice.

A SUDDEN STORY

ONCE UPON A TIME, suddenly, while it still could, the story began. For the hero, setting forth, there was of course nothing sudden about it, neither about the setting forth, which he'd spent his entire lifetime anticipating, nor about any conceivable endings, which seemed, like the horizon, to be always somewhere else. For the dragon, however, who was stupid, everything was sudden. He was suddenly hungry and then he was suddenly eating something. Always, it was like the first time. Then, all of a sudden, he'd remember having eaten something like that before: a certain familiar sourness . . . And, just as suddenly, he'd forget. The hero, coming suddenly upon the dragon (he'd been trekking for years through enchanted forests, endless deserts, cities carbonized by dragon-breath, for him suddenly was not exactly the word), found himself envying, as he drew his sword (a possible ending had just loomed up before him, as though the horizon had, with the desperate illusion of suddenness, tipped), the dragon's tenseless freedom. Freedom? the dragon might have asked, had he not been so stupid, chewing over meanwhile the sudden familiar sourness (a memory . . . ?) on his breath. From what? (Forgotten.)

TABLE OF CONTENTS

AFTERWORDS

Fred Chappell   Paul Theroux   John L'Heureux
Gordon Weaver   Charles Baxter   Lydia Davis
Alvin Greenberg   H. E. Francis   Charles Johnson
Leonard Michaels   William Peden   James B. Hall
Jack Matthews   Stephen Minot

Joe David Bellamy   Robert Kelly   Stuart Dybek
Philip Stevick   Philip F. O'Connor   Gary Gildner
Russell Banks   Steve Heller   Joyce Carol Oates   Mark Strand

Barry Targan   Stephen Dixon   Arturo Vivante
Hortense Calisher   C. Michael Curtis   Tobias Wolff
Robert Fox

Grace Paley   Alice K. Turner   DeWitt Henry
Frederick Busch   Gordon Lish   François Camoin
Joy Williams   Jonathan Penner   George Garrett

INTRODUCTION

ALL THE WORKS IN this collection are from one to five pages long, and all are by American authors. A few are familiar, but the great majority have been published within the last five years.

Because they are so new, and sometimes so unlike the modern notion of story, it was by no means clear at the outset exactly what to call these works. Short-short stories? Fictions? Or something else entirely? Almost nothing has been said about them yet by literary critics, so we asked the editors who publish them, and especially the writers who write them, *What are these things?* And, *Why are we seeing so many of them now?* With our queries, we sent an early version of this book under the working title, *Blasters*.

Blasters? Yes. We weren't so sure about the term, but it was handy, and certainly, we thought, memorable. Included with our working copies was an introduction, our own view of these works. From the beginning we were open to any fiction that was very short, be it prose sketch, prose poem, or some unnamed category, but we soon found that many of the best of these works, those with the most satisfying wholeness, often the most striking, belonged within the realm of story. This was disturbing, because we knew that some readers would dismiss these short-short works, in spite of their richness and variety, as fragments of the only kind of story that to them really mattered — the modern short story.

Brander Matthews claimed to be the first to identify the short story as a separate genre from the novel in 1901, in fact the first to name it, although it had been developing throughout the nineteenth century — so successfully in America that in the opinion of many it became a national form: as opera was to Italy, the short story was to America. With this as the model, it seems reasonable to assume that something called the short-*short* story must be an even younger form than the short story. Short-*shorts* must be a sub-category. Or maybe a sub-sub-category.

But of course that is all backwards. The name *short-short story* may be relatively new, but its forms are as old as parable and fable, myth and exemplum. The most often cited example of a classical short-short, Petronius' "The Widow of Ephesus," is no rude prototype. Given an updated setting it could easily pass as a contemporary short-short. In our view, in fact, the modern short story was an adaptation of many older story techniques, including those of short-short forms, to the overwhelming popularity of realism and its expansive embodiment, the novel.

It may well be that the new popularity of the short-short story began in the spirit of experiment and wordplay in the 1960s, with works that are more often called *fictions*. In this collection, for an example of the difference between fictions and stories, compare Gordon Lish's "The Merry Chase" with John Updike's "Pygmalion." Fictions, prose sketches and prose poems, as well as stories, all appeared in Robert Coover's *TriQuarterly* "Minute Stories" issue, ten years ago. Since then, as very short works have become increasingly popular in a wider variety of literary magazines, stories have become the dominant form, especially in the last five years, and that is reflected in this anthology. We hoped that the editors and writers we sent working copies to would confirm this trend, and our philosophy of the form, or offer alternate views to consider.

We expected, at least, a number of polite replies.

What we got was an uproar. It should not have surprised us that almost everyone we wrote had given thought to these things and was ready to argue in brief and at length about short-shorts — about their traditions, their present developments, the motives for writing and reading them, how they compare to sonnets, ghazals, folk tales, parables, koans, other forms. Almost no one agreed entirely on anything. They ascribed the popularity of the new short-shorts to the demands of editors; to a reaction to the overabundance of information in our time; to a continuing rebellion against the conventional scale of the modern short story with its requisite descriptive exposition and character development; to our awareness of mortality. They sent "best" lists of short-shorts and writers, and sent manuscripts, their own and others'. They argued about length: two thousand words weren't enough, some said, while others were vehement that one thousand words should be the limit (we split the difference). Only one claimed that what we had sent were fragments of longer stories. Almost all of them accepted the short-short story as a form of its own.

We felt that altogether their responses were fascinating snap-shots, soundings of the form and of our time. We present them to you in the section called "AfterWords" and invite you to enter into the crowd of voices, argue with them, take thought. As a general guide we have divided the "AfterWords" into four sections. The writings in the first two, "The Tradition" and "Toward a New Form," have to do with theory, if sometimes casually so; the third section, "A Practicum," includes notes on the writing of stories, particularly short-shorts, and on the use of short-shorts for university writing courses.

But for all these various insights, indeed because of them, we were more scattered, farther than ever from any single answer to our original question, *what are these things?* One issue, however, became the focus, the lightning rod which was struck and struck again. There were no middle grounds, no hedgings, no uncertainties — about our working title, *Blasters*.

Why were people so drawn to take a stand, for or against? After all, a name is only a name.

But among those writers who see the contemporary short-short as an emerging, entirely new form are those who insist that the form can only be established, can only be born, when its proper name has been chosen. Others explicitly or implicitly agreed: we create our world through language, through naming. Thus our working title became the grounds of a fundamental issue, how these works should be characterized or described.

Not all took the matter so formally, or seriously. Several in favor of *Blasters*, like John L'Heureux, thought that art, especially among academics, could do with a little more vulgarity, casualness, simple mundanity. People could use a little shaking up. What was wrong with having fun?

On the other side, the majority, there was no small amount of umbrage if not outrage. Several, including François Camoin, thought our title sounded like something to do with laxatives. H. E. Francis said it sounded like a sales gimmick; Barbara L. Greenberg was sure it would repel some men and most women. Paul Theroux loathed it, John Updike said it was awful. To Alice K. Turner of *Playboy* it sounded "like children's bubble-gum in red and purple flavors." But many of our critics were generous in offering alternate terms, including *quick fictions*, *mini*, *micro* and *flash fictions*; *shorter stories* and *shortest stories*; *skinny fictions* and *auto-rich fictions*, and many a variation on *The North American Review*'s Four Minute Story. None of these especially appealed to us.

Yet *Blasters* was clearly doomed. We were skeptical ourselves from the beginning, and had not used the working title too rigidly in making selections. Now the majority rightly pointed out that many of the best of these works, some highly entertaining and even powerful ones, simply didn't *blast*. The quieter, more subtle stories would not be served at all. *Blasters* suggested a too heavy, too singular emphasis on surprise, a startling effect as be-all and end-all. Thus there was a near-consensus on what these works were not.

We had begun to wonder if Jonathan Penner wasn't right to want to defend "these tiny kingdoms" against the imposition of any name at all, when Robert Kelly's letter arrived: "I think this entity of the short-short (*Sudden Fiction* — I like that a lot, not blasters, no, they don't all blast, but they all are suddenly just there . . .) is the major event of recent days."

Sudden. Without warning, from the Latin *subire*, to steal upon. Unforeseen, swift. *Sudden*. Yes.

We tried it out among the many correspondents. Almost everyone liked it, not only for the sound of it, but for its representation of the form. One author even said *sudden* was exactly how her short-short stories felt when she was writing them. Robert Coover wrote that the new title had inspired "A Sudden Story," which serves as our frontispiece — or rather, frontistory.

So, for the present — at least for the present book — the debate ends, though we have kept for your enjoyment some of the responses to our original title in the fourth of our "AfterWords" sections, called "Skippers, Snappers and Blasters." And finally, or rather to begin with, to get to the heart of the matter you must turn to the stories within, for these works exist regardless of any name we give them, and thoughtful readers have always known that the essence of story lies little in theory and not at all in length — Randall Jarrell has noted that stories can be as short as a sentence — but in wishes, dreams, and sometimes truth.

Their fundamental quality, our American writers say, is life. Highly compressed, highly charged, insidious, protean, sudden, alarming, tantalizing, these short-shorts confer form on small corners of chaos, can do in a page what a novel does in two hundred. If they can stop time and make it timeless, they are here for you, above all, as living voices.

THE STORIES

MOTHER

ONE DAY I WAS listening to the AM radio. I heard a song: "Oh, I Long to See My Mother in the Doorway." By God! I said, I understand that song. I have often longed to see my mother in the doorway. As a matter of fact, she did stand frequently in various doorways looking at me. She stood one day, just so, at the front door, the darkness of the hallway behind her. It was New Year's Day. She said sadly, If you come home at 4 A.M. when you're seventeen, what time will you come home when you're twenty? She asked this question without humor or meanness. She had begun her worried preparations for death. She would not be present, she thought, when I was twenty. So she wondered.

Another time she stood in the doorway of my room. I had just issued a political manifesto attacking the family's position on the Soviet Union. She said, Go to sleep for godsakes, you damn fool, you and your Communist ideas. We saw them already, Papa and me, in 1905. We guessed it all.

At the door of the kitchen she said, You never finish your lunch. You run around senselessly. What will become of you?

Then she died.

Naturally for the rest of my life I longed to see her, not only in doorways, in a great number of places — in the dining room with my aunts, at the window looking up and down the block, in the country garden among zinnias and marigolds, in the living room with my father.

They sat in comfortable leather chairs. They were listening to Mozart. They looked at one another amazed. It seemed to them that they'd just come over on the boat. They'd just learned the first English words. It seemed to them that he had just proudly handed in a 100 percent correct exam to the American anatomy professor. It seemed as though she'd just quit the shop for the kitchen.

I wish I could see her in the doorway of the living room.

She stood there a minute. Then she sat beside him. They owned an expensive record player. They were listening to Bach. She said to him, Talk to me a little. We don't talk so much anymore.

I'm tired, he said. Can't you see? I saw maybe thirty people today. All sick, all talk talk talk talk. Listen to the music, he said. I believe you once had perfect pitch. I'm tired, he said.

Then she died.

CAN-CAN

I'M GOING TO GO for a drive," he said to his wife. "I'll be back in an hour or two."

He didn't often leave the house for more than the few minutes it took him to go to the post office or to a store, but spent his time hanging around, doing odd jobs — Mr. Fix-it, his wife called him — and also, though not nearly enough of it, painting — which he made his living from.

"All right," his wife said brightly, as though he were doing her a favor. As a matter of fact, she didn't really like him to leave; she felt safer with him at home, and he helped look after the children, especially the baby.

"You're glad to be rid of me, aren't you?" he said.

"Uh-huh," she said with a smile that suddenly made her look very pretty — someone to be missed.

She didn't ask him where he was going for his drive. She wasn't the least bit inquisitive, though jealous she was in silent, subtle ways.

As he put his coat on, he watched her. She was in the living room with their elder daughter. "Do the can-can, mother," the child said, at which she held up her skirt and did the can-can, kicking her legs up high in his direction.

He wasn't simply going out for a drive, as he had said, but going to a café, to meet Sarah, whom his wife knew but did not suspect, and with her go to a house on a lake his wife knew nothing about — a summer cottage to which he had the key.

"Well, goodbye," he said.

"Bye," she called back, still dancing.

This wasn't the way a husband expected his wife — whom he was about to leave at home to go to another woman — to behave at all, he thought. He expected her to be sewing or washing, not doing the can-can, for God's sake. Yes, doing something uninteresting and unattractive, like darning children's clothes. She had no stockings on, no shoes, and her legs looked very white and smooth, secret, as though he had never touched them or come near them. Her feet, swinging up and down high in the air, seemed to be nodding to him. She held her skirt bunched up, attractively. Why was she doing that of all times *now?* He lingered. Her eyes had mockery in them, and she laughed. The child laughed with her as she danced. She was still dancing as he left the house.

He thought of the difficulties he had had arranging this *rendezvous* — going out to a call box; phoning Sarah at her office (she was married, too); her being out; his calling her again; the busy signal; the coin falling out of sight, his opening the door of the phone box in order to retrieve it; at last getting her on the line; her asking him to call again next week, finally setting a date.

Waiting for her at the café, he surprised himself hoping that she wouldn't come. The appointment was at three. It was now ten past. Well, she was often late. He looked at the clock, and at the picture window for her car. A car like hers, and yet not hers — no luggage rack on it. The smooth hardtop gave him a peculiar pleasure. Why? It was 3:15 now. Perhaps she wouldn't come. No, if she was going to come at all, this was the most likely time for her to arrive. Twenty past. Ah, now there was some hope. Hope? How strange he should be hoping for her absence. Why had he made the appointment if he was hoping she would miss it? He didn't know why, but simpler, simpler if she didn't come. Because all he wanted now was to smoke that cigarette, drink that cup of coffee for the sake of them, and not to give himself something to do. And he wished he could go for a drive, free and easy, as he had said he would. But he waited, and at 3:30 she arrived. "I had almost given up hope," he said.

They drove to the house on the lake. As he held her in his arms he couldn't think of her; for the life of him he couldn't.

"What are you thinking about?" she said afterwards, sensing his detachment.

For a moment he didn't answer, then he said, "You really want to know what I was thinking of?"

"Yes," she said, a little anxiously.

He suppressed a laugh, as though what he was going to tell her was too absurd or silly. "I was thinking of someone doing the can-can."

"Oh," she said, reassured. "For a moment I was afraid you were thinking of your wife."

EVEN GREENLAND

I WAS SITTING RADAR. Actually doing nothing.

We had been up to 75,000 to give the afternoon some jazz. I guess we were still in Mexico, coming into Miramar eventually in the F-14. It doesn't matter much after you've seen the curvature of the earth. For a while, nothing much matters at all. We'd had three sunsets already. I guess it's what you'd call really living the day.

But then,

"John," said I, "this plane's on fire."

"I know it," he said.

John was sort of short and angry about it.

"You thought of last-minute things any?" said I.

"Yeah. I ran out of a couple of things already. But they were cold, like. They didn't catch the moment. Bad writing," said John.

"You had the advantage. You've been knowing," said I.

"Yeah, I was going to get a leap on you. I was going to smoke you. Everything you said, it wasn't going to be good enough. I was going to have a great one, and everything you said, it wasn't going to be good enough," said he.

"But it's not like that," said I. "Is it?"

He said, "Nah. I got nothing, really."

The wings were turning red. I guess you'd call it red. It was a shade against dark blue that was mystical flamingo, very spacey-like, like living blood. Was the plane bleeding?

"You have a good time in Peru?" said I.

"Not really," said John. "I got something to tell you. I haven't had a 'good time,' in a long time. There's something between me and a good time, since, I don't know, since I was twenty-eight or like that. I've seen a lot, but you know I haven't quite *seen* it. Like somebody's seen it already. It wasn't fresh. There were eyes that had used it up some."

"Even high in Merida?" said I.

"Even," said John.

"Even Tibet, where you met your wife? By accident a beautiful American girl way up there?" I said.

"Even," said John.

"Even Greenland?" said I.

John said, "Yes. Even Greenland. It's fresh, but it's not fresh. There are footsteps in the snow."

"Maybe," said I, "you think about in Mississippi when it snows, when you're a kid. And you're the first up and there's been nobody in the snow, no footsteps."

"Shut up," said John.

"Look, are we getting into a fight here at the moment of death? We going to mix it up with the plane's on fire?"

"Shut up! Shut up!" said John. Yelled John.

"What's wrong?" said I.

He wouldn't budge at the joy stick or the controls. We might burn but we were going to stay level. We were on a 50,000 feet hold. We weren't seeking the earth at all.

"What is it, John?" I asked.

John said, "You son of a bitch, that was *mine*—that snow in Mississippi. Now it's all shot to shit."

The paper from his kneepad was flying all over the cockpit, and I could see his hand flapping up and down with the pencil in it, angry.

"It was *mine, mine,* you rotten cocksucker!" There were squares of paper sucked to the radar. "You see what I mean?"

The little pages hung on the top, and you could see the big moon just past them.

"Eject! Save your ass!" said John.

But I said, "What about you, John?"

John said, "I'm staying. Just let me have *that* one, will you?"

"But you can't," said I.

But he did.

Celeste and I visit the burn on the blond sand under one of those black romantic worthless mountains five miles or so out from Miramar base.

I'm a Lieutenant Commander in the reserve now. But to be frank, it shakes me a bit even to run a Skyhawk up to Malibu and back.

Celeste and I squat in the sand and say nothing as we look at the burn. They got all the metal away.

I don't know what Celeste is saying or thinking, I am so absorbed myself and paralyzed.

I know I am looking at John's fucking triumph.

His poem.

THE KING OF JAZZ

WELL I'M THE KING of jazz now, thought Hokie Mokie to himself as he oiled the slide on his trombone. Hasn't been a 'bone man been king of jazz for many years. But now that Spicy MacLammermoor, the old king, is dead, I guess I'm it. Maybe I better play a few notes out of this window here, to reassure myself.

"Wow!" said somebody standing on the sidewalk. "Did you hear that?"

"I did," said his companion.

"Can you distinguish our great homemade American jazz performers, each from the other?"

"Used to could."

"Then who was that playing?"

"Sounds like Hokie Mokie to me. Those few but perfectly selected notes have the real epiphanic glow."

"The what?"

"The real epiphanic glow, such as is obtained only by artists of the caliber of Hokie Mokie, who's from Pass Christian, Mississippi. He's the king of jazz, now that Spicy MacLammermoor is gone."

Hokie Mokie put his trombone in its trombone case and went to a gig. At the gig everyone fell back before him, bowing.

"Hi Bucky! Hi Zoot! Hi Freddie! Hi George! Hi Thad! Hi Roy! Hi Dexter! Hi Jo! Hi Willie! Hi Greens!"

"What we gonna play, Hokie? You the king of jazz now, you gotta decide."

"How 'bout 'Smoke'?"

"Wow!" everybody said. "Did you hear that? Hokie Mokie can just knock a fella out, just the way he pronounces a word. What a intonation on that boy! God Almighty!"

"I don't want to play 'Smoke,' " somebody said.

"Would you repeat that stranger?"

"I don't want to play 'Smoke.' 'Smoke' is dull. I don't like the changes. I refuse to play 'Smoke.' "

"He refuses to play 'Smoke'! But Hokie Mokie is the king of jazz and he says 'Smoke'!"

"Man, you from outa town or something? What do you mean you refuse to play 'Smoke'? How'd you get on this gig anyhow? Who hired you?"

"I am Hideo Yamaguchi, from Tokyo, Japan."

"Oh, you're one of those Japanese cats, eh?"

"Yes, I'm the top trombone man in all of Japan."

"Well you're welcome here until we hear you play. Tell me, is the Tennessee Tea Room still the top jazz place in Tokyo?"

"No, the top jazz place in Tokyo is the Square Box now."

"That's nice. OK, now we gonna play 'Smoke' just like Hokie said. You ready, Hokie? OK, give you four for nothin'. One! Two! Three! Four!"

The two men who had been standing under Hokie's window had followed him into the club. Now they said:

"Good God!"

"Yes, that's Hokie's famous 'English sunrise' way of playing. Playing with lots of rays coming out of it, some red rays, some blue rays, some green rays, some green stemming from a violet center, some olive stemming from a tan center—"

"That young Japanese fellow is pretty good, too."

"Yes, he is pretty good. And he holds his horn in a peculiar way. That's frequently the mark of a superior player."

"Bent over like that with his head between his knees—good God, he's sensational!"

He's sensational, Hokie thought. Maybe I ought to kill him.

But at that moment somebody came in the door pushing in front of him a four-and-one-half-octave marimba. Yes, it was Fat Man Jones, and he began to play even before he was fully in the door.

"What're we playing?"

" 'Billie's Bounce.' "

"That's what I thought it was. What're we in?"

"F."

"That's what I thought we were in. Didn't you use to play with Maynard?"

"Yeah I was in that band for a while until I was in the hospital."

"What for?"

"I was tired."

"What can we add to Hokie's fantastic playing?"

"How 'bout some rain or stars?"

"Maybe that's presumptuous?"

"Ask him if he'd mind."

"You ask him, I'm scared. You don't fool around with the king of jazz. That young Japanese guy's pretty good, too."

"He's sensational."

"You think he's playing in Japanese?"

"Well I don't think it's English."

This trombone's been makin' my neck green for thirty-five years, Hokie thought. How come I got to stand up to yet another challenge, this late in life?

"Well, Hideo—"

"Yes, Mr. Mokie?"

"You did well on both 'Smoke' and 'Billie's Bounce.' You're just about as good as me, I regret to say. In fact, I've decided you're *better* than me. It's a hideous thing to contemplate, but there it is. I have only been the king of jazz for twenty-four hours, but the unforgiving logic of this art demands we bow to Truth, when we hear it."

"Maybe you're mistaken?"

"No, I got ears. I'm not mistaken. Hideo Yamaguchi is the new king of jazz."

"You want to be king emeritus?"

"No, I'm just going to fold up my horn and steal away. This gig is yours, Hideo. You can pick the next tune."

"How 'bout 'Cream'?"

"OK, you heard what Hideo said, it's 'Cream.' You ready, Hideo?"

"Hokie, you don't have to leave. You can play too. Just move a little over to the side there—"

"Thank you, Hideo, that's very gracious of you. I guess I will play a little, since I'm still here. Sotto voce, of course."

"Hideo is wonderful on 'Cream'!"

"Yes, I imagine it's his best tune."

"What's that sound coming in from the side there?"

"Which side?"

"The left."

"You mean that sound that sounds like the cutting edge of life? That sounds like polar bears crossing Arctic ice pans? That sounds like a herd of musk ox in full flight? That sounds like male walruses diving to the bottom of the sea? That sounds like fumaroles smoking on the slopes of Mt. Katmai? That sounds like the wild turkey walking through the deep, soft forest? That sounds like beavers chewing trees in an Appalachian marsh? That sounds like an oyster fungus growing on an aspen trunk? That sounds like a mule deer wandering a montane of the Sierra Nevada? That sounds like prairie dogs kissing? That sounds like witch grass tumbling or a river meandering? That sounds like manatees munching seaweed at Cape Sable? That sounds like coatimundis moving in packs across the face of Arkansas? That sounds like—"

"Good God, it's Hokie! Even with a cup mute on, he's blowing Hideo right off the stand!"

"Hideo's playing on his knees now! Good God, he's reaching into his belt for a large steel sword—Stop him!"

"Wow! That was the most exciting 'Cream' ever played! Is Hideo all right?"

"Yes, somebody is getting him a glass of water."

"You're my man, Hokie! That was the dadblangedest thing I ever saw!"

"You're the king of jazz once again!"

"Hokie Mokie is the most happening thing there is!"

"Yes, Mr. Hokie sir, I have to admit it, you blew me right off the stand. I see I have many years of work and study before me still."

"That's OK, son. Don't think a thing about it. It happens to the best of us. Or it almost happens to the best of us. Now I want everybody to have a good time because we're gonna play 'Flats.' 'Flats' is next."

"With your permission, sir, I will return to my hotel and pack. I am most grateful for everything I have learned here."

"That's OK, Hideo. Have a nice day. He-he. Now, 'Flats.'"

REUNION

THE LAST TIME I SAW my father was in Grand Central Station. I was going from my grandmother's in the Adirondacks to a cottage on the Cape that my mother had rented, and I wrote my father that I would be in New York between trains for an hour and a half and asked if we could have lunch together. His secretary wrote to say that he would meet me at the information booth at noon, and at twelve o'clock sharp I saw him coming through the crowd. He was a stranger to me — my mother divorced him three years ago, and I hadn't been with him since — but as soon as I saw him I felt that he was my father, my flesh and blood, my future and my doom. I knew that when I was grown I would be something like him; I would have to plan my campaigns within his limitations. He was a big, good-looking man, and I was terribly happy to see him again. He struck me on the back and shook my hand. "Hi, Charlie," he said. "Hi, boy. I'd like to take you up to my club, but it's in the Sixties, and if you have to catch an early train I guess we'd better get something to eat around here." He put his arm around me, and I smelled my father the way my mother sniffs a rose. It was a rich compound of whiskey, after-shave lotion, shoe polish, woolens, and the rankness of a mature male. I hoped that someone would see us together. I wished that we could be photographed. I wanted some record of our having been together.

We went out of the station and up a side street to a restaurant. It was still early, and the place was empty. The bartender was quarreling with a delivery boy, and there was one very old waiter in a red coat down by the kitchen door. We sat down, and my father hailed the waiter in a loud voice. "*Kellner!*" he shouted. "*Garçon! Cameriere! You!*" His boisterousness in the empty restaurant seemed out of place. "Could we have a little service here!" he shouted. "Chop-chop." Then he clapped his hands. This caught the waiter's attention, and he shuffled over to our table.

"Were you clapping your hands at me?" he asked.

"Calm down, calm down, *sommelier*," my father said. "If it isn't too much to ask of you—if it wouldn't be too much above and beyond the call of duty, we would like a couple of Beefeater Gibsons."

"I don't like to be clapped at," the waiter said.

"I should have brought my whistle," my father said. "I have a whistle that is audible only to the ears of old waiters. Now, take out your little pad and your little pencil and see if you can get this straight: two Beefeater Gibsons. Repeat after me: two Beefeater Gibsons."

"I think you'd better go somewhere else," the waiter said quietly.

"That," said my father, "is one of the most brilliant suggestions I have ever heard. Come on, Charlie, let's get the hell out of here."

I followed my father out of that restaurant into another. He was not so boisterous this time. Our drinks came, and he cross-questioned me about the baseball season. He then struck the edge of his empty glass with his knife and began shouting again. "*Garçon! Kellner! You!* Could we trouble you to bring us two more of the same."

"How old is the boy?" the waiter asked.

"That," my father said, "is none of your goddamned business."

"I'm sorry, sir," the waiter said, "but I won't serve the boy another drink."

"Well, I have some news for you," my father said. "I have some very interesting news for you. This doesn't happen to be the only restaurant in New York. They've opened another on the corner. Come on, Charlie."

He paid the bill, and I followed him out of that restaurant into another. Here the waiters wore pink jackets like hunting coats, and there was a lot of horse tack on the walls. We sat down, and my father began to shout again. "Master of the hounds! Tallyhoo and all that sort of thing. We'd like a little something in the way of a stirrup cup. Namely, two Bibson Geefeaters."

"Two Bibson Geefeaters?" the waiter asked, smiling.

"You know damned well what I want," my father said angrily. "I want two Beefeater Gibsons, and make it snappy. Things have changed in jolly old England. So my friend the duke tells me. Let's see what England can produce in the way of a cocktail."

"This isn't England," the waiter said.

"Don't argue with me," my father said. "Just do as you're told."

"I just thought you might like to know where you are," the waiter said.

"If there is one thing I cannot tolerate," my father said, "it is an impudent domestic. Come on, Charlie."

The fourth place we went to was Italian. "*Buon giorno,*" my father said. "*Per favore, possiamo avere due cocktail americani, forti, forti. Molto gin, poco vermut.*"

"I don't understand Italian," the waiter said.

"Oh, come off it," my father said. "You understand Italian, and you know damned well you do. *Vogliamo due cocktail americani. Subito.*"

The waiter left us and spoke with the captain, who came over to our table and said, "I'm sorry, sir, but this table is reserved."

"All right," my father said. "Get us another table."

"All the tables are reserved," the captain said.

"I get it," my father said. "You don't desire our patronage. Is that it? Well, the hell with you. *Vada all' inferno.* Let's go, Charlie."

"I have to get my train," I said.

"I'm sorry, sonny," my father said. "I'm terribly sorry." He put his arm around me and pressed me against him. "I'll walk you back to the station. If there had only been time to go up to my club."

"That's all right, Daddy," I said.

"I'll get you a paper," he said. "I'll get you a paper to read on the train."

Then he went up to a newsstand and said, "Kind sir, will you be good enough to favor me with one of your goddamned, no-good, ten-cent afternoon papers?" The clerk turned away from him and stared at a magazine cover. "Is it asking too much, kind sir," my father said, "is it asking too much for you to sell me one of your disgusting specimens of yellow journalism?"

"I have to go, Daddy," I said. "It's late."

"Now, just wait a second, sonny," he said. "Just wait a second. I want to get a rise out of this chap."

"Goodbye, Daddy," I said, and I went down the stairs and got my train, and that was the last time I saw my father.

TWIRLER

[*A young woman stands center stage. She is dressed in a spangled, one-piece swimsuit, the kind for baton twirlers. She holds a shining silver baton in her hand.*]

I STARTED WHEN I WAS SIX. Momma sawed off a broom handle, and Uncle Carbo slapped some sort of silver paint, well, gray, really, on it and I went down in the basement and twirled. Later on Momma hit the daily double on horses named Spin Dry and Silver Revolver and she said that was a sign so she gave me lessons at the Dainty Deb Dance Studio, where the lady, Miss Aurelia, taught some twirling on the side.

I won the Ohio Juniors title when I was six and the Midwest Young Adult Division three years later, and then in high school I finished fourth in the nationals. Momma and I wore look-alike Statue of Liberty costumes that she had to send clear to Nebraska to get, and Daddy was there in a T-shirt with my name, April— my first name is April and my last name is March. There were four thousand people there, and when they yelled my name golden balloons fell out of the ceiling. Nobody, not even Charlene Ann Morrison, ever finished fourth at my age.

Oh, I've flown high and known tragedy, both. My daddy says it's put spirit in my soul and steel in my heart. My left hand was crushed in a riding accident by a horse named Big Blood Red, and though I came back to twirl, I couldn't do it at the highest level. That was denied me by Big Blood Red, who clipped my wings. You mustn't pity me, though. Oh, by no means! Being denied showed me the way, showed me the glory that sits inside life where you can't see it.

People think you're a twit if you twirl. It's a prejudice of the unknowing. Twirlers are the niggers of a white university. Yes, they are. One time I was doing fire batons at a night game, and all of a sudden I see this guy walk out of the stands. I was doing triples and he walks right out past the half-time marshals, comes up to me — he had this blue bead headband, I can still see it. Walks right up, and when I come front after a back reverse he spits in my face. That's the only, single time I ever dropped a baton. Dropped 'em both in front of sixty thousand people, and he smiles, see, and he says this thing I won't repeat. He called me a bodily part in front of half of Ohio. It was like being raped. It shows that beauty inspires hate and that hating beauty is Satan.

You haven't twirled, have you? I can see that by your hands. Would you like to hold my silver baton? Here, hold it.

You can't imagine what it feels like to have that baton up in the air. I used to twirl with that baton up in the air. I used to twirl with this girl who called it blue-collar Zen. The 'tons catch the sun when they're up, and when they go up, you go up, too. You can't twirl if you're not *inside* the 'ton. When you've got 'em up over twenty feet, it's like flying or gliding. Your hands are still down, but your insides spin and rise and leave the ground. Only a twirler knows that, so we're not niggers.

The secret for a twirler is the light. You live or die with the light. It's your fate. The best is a February sky clouded right over in the late afternoon. It's all background then, and what happens is that the 'tons leave tracks, traces, they etch the air, and if you're hot, if your hands have it, you can draw on the sky.

God, Charlene Ann Morrison. God, Charlene Ann! She was inspired by something beyond man. She won the nationals nine years in a row. Unparalleled and unrepeatable. The last two years she had leukemia and at the end you could see through her hands when she twirled. Charlene Ann died with a 'ton thirty feet up, her momma swears on that. I roomed with Charlene at a regional in Fargo, and she may have been fibbin', but she said there was a day when her 'tons erased while they turned. Like the sky was a sheet of rain and the 'tons were car wipers and when she had erased this certain part of the sky you could see the face of the Lord God Jesus, and his hair was all rhinestones and he was doing this incredible singing like the sound of a piccolo. The people who said that Charlene was crazy probably never twirled a day in their life.

Twirling is the physical parallel of revelation. You can't know that. Twirling is the throwing of yourself up to God. It's a pure gift, hidden from Satan because it is wrapped and disguised in the midst of football. It is God-throwing, spirit fire, and very few come to it. You have to grow eyes in your heart to understand its message, and when it opens to you it becomes your path to suffer ridicule, to be crucified by misunderstanding, and to be spit upon. I need my baton now.

There is one twirling no one sees. At the winter solstice we go to a meadow God showed us just outside of Green Bay. The God throwers come there on December twenty-first. There's snow, sometimes deep snow, and our clothes fall away, and we stand unprotected while acolytes bring the 'tons. They are ebony 'tons with razors set all along the shaft. They are three feet long. One by one the twirlers throw, two 'tons each, thirty feet up, and as they fall back they cut your hands. The razors arch into the air and find God and then fly down to take your blood in a crucifixion, and the red drops draw God on the ground, and if you are up with the batons you can look down and see Him revealed. Red on white. Red on white. You can't imagine. You can't imagine how wonderful that is.

I started twirling when I was six, but I never really twirled until my hand was crushed by the horse named Big Blood Red. I have seen God's face from thirty feet up in the air, and I know Him.

Listen. I will leave my silver baton here for you. Lying here as if I forgot it. And when the people file out you can wait back and pick it up, it can be yours, it can be your burden. It is the eye of the needle. I leave it for you.

[*The lights fade.*]

SUNDAY IN THE PARK

IT WAS STILL WARM in the late-afternoon sun, and the city noises came muffled through the trees in the park. She put her book down on the bench, removed her sunglasses, and sighed contentedly. Morton was reading the *Times Magazine* section, one arm flung around her shoulder; their three-year-old son, Larry, was playing in the sandbox: a faint breeze fanned her hair softly against her cheek. It was five-thirty of a Sunday afternoon, and the small playground, tucked away in a corner of the park, was all but deserted. The swings and seesaws stood motionless and abandoned, the slides were empty, and only in the sandbox two little boys squatted diligently side by side. *How good this is,* she thought, and almost smiled at her sense of well-being. They must go out in the sun more often; Morton was so city-pale, cooped up all week inside the gray factorylike university. She squeezed his arm affectionately and glanced at Larry, delighting in the pointed little face frowning in concentration over the tunnel he was digging. The other boy suddenly stood up and with a quick, deliberate swing of his chubby arm threw a spadeful of sand at Larry. It just missed his head. Larry continued digging; the boy remained standing, shovel raised, stolid and impassive.

"No, no, little boy." She shook her finger at him, her eyes searching for the child's mother or nurse. "We mustn't throw sand. It may get in someone's eyes and hurt. We must play nicely in the nice sandbox." The boy looked at her in unblinking expectancy. He was about Larry's age but perhaps ten pounds heavier, a husky little boy with none of Larry's quickness and sensitivity in his face. Where was his mother? The only other people left in the playground were two women and a little girl on roller skates leaving now through the gate, and a man on a bench a few feet away. He was a big man, and he seemed to be taking up the whole bench as he held the

Sunday comics close to his face. She supposed he was the child's father. He did not look up from his comics, but spat once deftly out of the corner of his mouth. She turned her eyes away.

At that moment, as swiftly as before, the fat little boy threw another spadeful of sand at Larry. This time some of it landed on his hair and forehead. Larry looked up at his mother, his mouth tentative; her expression would tell him whether to cry or not.

Her first instinct was to rush to her son, brush the sand out of his hair, and punish the other child, but she controlled it. She always said that she wanted Larry to learn to fight his own battles.

"Don't *do* that, little boy," she said sharply, leaning forward on the bench. "You mustn't throw sand!"

The man on the bench moved his mouth as if to spit again, but instead he spoke. He did not look at her, but at the boy only.

"You go right ahead, Joe," he said loudly. "Throw all you want. This here is a *public* sandbox."

She felt a sudden weakness in her knees as she glanced at Morton. He had become aware of what was happening. He put his *Times* down carefully on his lap and turned his fine, lean face toward the man, smiling the shy, apologetic smile he might have offered a student in pointing out an error in his thinking. When he spoke to the man, it was with his usual reasonableness.

"You're quite right," he said pleasantly, "but just because this is a public place. . . ."

The man lowered his funnies and looked at Morton. He looked at him from head to foot, slowly and deliberately. "Yeah?" His insolent voice was edged with menace. "My kid's got just as good right here as yours, and if he feels like throwing sand, he'll throw it, and if you don't like it, you can take your kid the hell out of here."

The children were listening, their eyes and mouths wide open, their spades forgotten in small fists. She noticed the muscle in Morton's jaw tighten. He was rarely angry; he seldom lost his temper. She was suffused with a tenderness for her husband and an impotent rage against the man for involving him in a situation so alien and so distasteful to him.

"Now, just a minute," Morton said courteously, "you must realize. . . ."

"Aw, shut up," said the man.

Her heart began to pound. Morton half rose; the *Times* slid to the ground. Slowly the other man stood up. He took a couple of steps toward Morton, then stopped. He flexed his great arms, waiting. She pressed her trembling knees together. Would there be violence, fighting? How dreadful, how incredible. . . . She must do something, stop them, call for help. She wanted to put her hand on her husband's sleeve, to pull him down, but for some reason she didn't.

Morton adjusted his glasses. He was very pale. "This is ridiculous," he said unevenly. "I must ask you. . . ."

"Oh, yeah?" said the man. He stood with his legs spread apart, rocking a little, looking at Morton with utter scorn. "You and who else?"

For a moment the two men looked at each other nakedly. Then Morton turned his back on the man and said quietly, "Come on, let's get out of here." He walked awkwardly, almost limping with self-consciousness, to the sandbox. He stooped and lifted Larry and his shovel out.

At once Larry came to life; his face lost its rapt expression and he began to kick and cry. "I don't *want* to go home, I want to play better, I don't *want* any supper, I don't *like* supper. . . ." It became a chant as they walked, pulling their child between them, his feet dragging on the ground. In order to get to the exit gate they had to pass the bench where the man sat sprawling again. She was careful not to look at him. With all the dignity she could summon, she pulled Larry's sandy, perspiring little hand, while Morton pulled the other. Slowly and with head high she walked with her husband and child out of the playground.

Her first feelings was one of relief that a fight had been avoided, that no one was hurt. Yet beneath it there was a layer of something else, something heavy and inescapable. She sensed that it was more than just an unpleasant incident, more than defeat of reason by force. She felt dimly it had something to do with her and Morton, something acutely personal, familiar, and important.

Suddenly Morton spoke. "It wouldn't have proved anything."

"What?" she asked.

"A fight. It wouldn't have proved anything beyond the fact that he's bigger than I am."

"Of course," she said.

"The only possible outcome," he continued reasonably, "would have been — what? My glasses broken, perhaps a tooth or two replaced, a couple of days' work missed — and for what? For justice? For truth?"

"Of course," she repeated. She quickened her step. She wanted only to get home and to busy herself with her familiar tasks; perhaps then the feeling, glued like heavy plaster on her heart, would be gone. *Of all the stupid, despicable bullies,* she thought, pulling harder on Larry's hand. The child was still crying. Always before she had felt a tender pity for his defenseless little body, the frail arms, the narrow shoulders with sharp, winglike shoulder blades, the thin and unsure legs, but now her mouth tightened in resentment.

"Stop crying," she said sharply. "I'm ashamed of you!" She felt as if all three of them were tracking mud along the street. The child cried louder.

If there had been an issue involved, she thought, *if there had been something to fight for. . . . But what else could he possibly have done? Allow himself to be beaten? Attempt to educate the man? Call a policeman? "Officer, there's a man in the park who won't stop his child from throwing sand on mine. . . ."* The whole thing was as silly as that, and not worth thinking about.

"Can't you keep him quiet, for Pete's sake?" Morton asked irritably.

"What do you suppose I've been trying to do?" she said.

Larry pulled back, dragging his feet.

"If you can't discipline this child, I will," Morton snapped, making a move toward the boy.

But her voice stopped him. She was shocked to hear it, thin and cold and penetrating with contempt. "Indeed?" she heard herself say. "You and who else?"

FIVE IVES

Esquire July 1982

JIM! ME! CALLING from The *Big* Leagues! You know, them leagues Ty Cobb and Warren Spahn was in! *Whooooo!*

I *know* it's great. Jim, you would not believe tonight. I got a nickname, I . . .

Yeah, I'll call Pop. But I can't tell him all of it. Don't want to disillusion Pop about the BIG LEAGUES.

No, it's not. . . . Just let me tell you. It is late, isn't it? Is that the baby crying? Shit, I'm . . . You shoulda been up here, Jim. Waiting to show me around. Like in Little League and high school. If it hadn't been for your knee. Yeah.

I'm *going* to tell you. Yeah, *sort* of drunk. In New York. Jim, I ain't going to get mugged. You're worse than Pop. No, I just mean — listen, I walk in this afternoon. Right? Visiting clubhouse YANKEE DAMN STADIUM, Jim. Summoned up by the Techs.

I know we didn't exactly grow up drooling to be Techs, 'cause there wasn't any then. But if the Dodgers'd held on to me, I'd still be in Lodi. Techs pick me up, this Perridge breaks his leg, and I get a CALL, Jim.

Only thing, to get here, I have to grab two buses and a red-eye. And I walk into the dressing room with zip sleep. And first thing, this Spanish guy jumps on my back. Yelling, Jibdyjibdyjibdy ninety miles an hour. Then this bald black guy with a big gut who is stepping real painfully into his pants yells across the room, "Ju-lo, get off the man's back! He don't even speak Spanish!"

"Jibdyjibdyjibdy espic Esponish!?" the guy yells. And he gets off me, like he's pissed I'm not bilingle, and he goes to his locker and I see the name, it's Julio Uribe! You remember, played second for the Orioles a couple of years and bounced around. And Jim, the fat guy is Boom Holmes! "GodDAMN my feet!" he yells, and that's my greeting to the Techs.

Except just then I meet my Peerless Leader. Berkey. Yells out from his office, "Who you!" Jesus, who'd he think I was, I'm the only guy got sent up. I go in, kind of salute, like reporting to duty, only he don't laugh. He is sitting there eating a—looks like maybe a Franco-American spaghetti sandwich, real wet, and there's a big bottle of Maalox on his desk, and he looks at me like I'm already overpaid. "Can you mbunt?" he wants to know. Is all he wants to know. I don't know whether he can manage, but he has a lot of trouble with his *b*'s.

"Yeah," I say. He's a big sumbitch but a real old sour-looking guy, Jim, looks like Mr. Wiedl used to teach us history and be pissed all the time because we didn't care about the broad sweep of the great human saga. Only Berkey I guess is pissed because the Techs just about got a lock on last place in June. Yeah.

Anyway, what Berkey does, he grabs me by the arm and drags me back out into the dressing room and hollers at everybody, "This guy can mbunt! He prombly can't play, but he can mbunt!" And he goes back to his office with his wet sandwich.

And I'm standing there. Clubhouse guy shows me my locker— I'm dressing next to Hub Kopf. Yeah, right, used to have the crippled children commercial. He is talking to Junior Wren. Yeah. And here's what they're saying:

"Your *niece*! How could you . . . ?"

"Axly it was more my half niece," says Junior Wren.

"How the hell . . . ?"

"Anyway she was adopted, I think."

"You *think*. You didn't *know*?"

"Anyway, she was in these little shorts and halter, and she had this raspberry wine . . . and I gave her a little bump. Next morning I felt so bad, I quit smoking."

Here I am, hearing this shit from guys was all-stars once, and meanwhile I am *wasted*. "I'm Reed Ives," I say. 'Cause I'm new in this whole organization, they don't know me. "I'm wasted," I say.

"Welcome to the AL," says Junior. "Have one." And he gives me a pill.

So—no, I wouldn't ever depend on it, no, but anyway, I pop this thing, and then I ask, "What is it?"

You're right, but—anyway, "Five milligrams," he says.

I never had half that! And I'm sitting there thinking, "Oh, Jesus. Five milligrams."

And the next thing, I'm on the field running all over like I've had twenty hours sleep. Playing pepper, taking grounders, little b.p. — yeah, I got ahold of a couple pretty good — and then, though, the game starts.

And I'm sitting. And I'm, you know, *VAW-AW-AW-AWM*. There's these billions of dollars' worth of Yankees out there a few feet in front of my face, and I'm jumping up, getting water, sitting back down, jumping up, taking a leak, and thirty thousand people are screaming all up above and behind me, and Junior Wren is looking over and nudging Hub Kopf, and they're giggling, and Berkey is glaring at me. 'Cause I'm not even *seeing* the game. I'm sitting there exploding, thinking, "Five milligrams!"

And Berkey grabs me, drags me off into the tunnel. I can't believe it, I'm about to fly into smithereens and Berkey is yelling, "If you tell anymbody what I'm mbout to tell you, I'll mbeat your ass."

I'm going, "Whaaaat" and he's saying, "Mbefore I was mborn my father was hunting with a preacher named Harding Earth. That preacher stood up at the wrong time and my father shot him in the temple and killed him outright. Preacher was to mblame, mbut my father swore right then that he'd have a son and name him Harding Earth mBerkey and have him mbe a preacher. He had that son, it was me. Only he never told me. Till the day he died. He told me then. He told me he had done everything in his power, without telling me, to make me grow up to want to mbe a preacher. Mbut I grew up to want to play mball. That's how much I wanted to play mball. If you don't want to play mball, I don't want you *around*."

And he leaves me, and I ease back to the bench with my brakes jammed on, and I'm sitting there dazed next to Roe Humble — yeah, he's okay — Humble says, "He give you the shoot-the-preacher story?"

And I just nod and I have no idea the status of the game and next thing, Berkey is standing in front of me, trembling. And he says, "Let's *see* you mbunt."

And he's sending me up! I don't even know who I'm hitting for. I'm in the game! Against — you know who pitched tonight for the Yankees?

Tommy damn John. My first up in the big leagues. Only, I'm not thinking Tommy John. I'm thinking, "Five milligrams!"

And here comes this pitch — well, you know, Tommy John don't waste any time, but it seems to me he's idling *very* low. I'm jumping up and down and "five milligrams" and here comes this dippy-do sinker, wandering up to the plate like its heart's not in it, and I square off to bunt, which in my present state means I am holding the bat like it's an alligator, and, dum, de dum — *sink*, the ball drops, and I miss it a foot.

Yeah. I know Pop taught us. But — and the same thing happens the second pitch. "Five milligrams!" is blasting in my head and then, 0 and 2, he wastes a fastball up and away. And you know, Jim, I like that pitch. I could even hit you, when I was nine and you threw me something up there. Went *with* it. And Jim, I got it all.

Jim, I took Tommy John out of Yankee Stadium at the 385 in right center. Two men on, we're only behind one run for some reason, and *WOOOM* I put us ahead. I'm circling the damn Yankee damn Stadium bases, and, you know, on the postgame shows they always ask 'em, "What were you thinking about, rounding the bases?" I'm thinking, "FIVE MILLIGRAMS!"

And I cross the plate, and Boom Holmes gives me a high five — Boom Holmes gives me one, Jim — which, a high five, is appropriate as shit. And he says, "I didn't know you was that STRAWNG."

And all I can think to do is, now everybody's slapping at me, is open my mouth and holler, "FIVE! FIVE!"

And Junior Wren and Hub Kopf are rolling around in the dugout, and, of course, what the hell, we don't hold the lead, Jim. But in the dressing room afterward everybody is hollering, "Five!" "The Big Five!" "Five Ives!"

"Why're you calling him Five?" this reporter asks Boom, and he says, "Well, that's ghetto talk, you know. That's some *street* talk there. Means . . . Means he got the full five faingers on it, you know," and Junior Wren and Hub and Uribe and everybody else except maybe Berkey knows the truth — they're yelling, "*Full* Five." "F.F. Ives." And . . .

Well, yeah, I guess it is a shame, sort of. Never know, yeah, whether I could've done it just straight, first time up. Yeah. But, Jim, you know, if I'd been straight I'd've *sacrificed*.

You're right, that'd been sound baseball. So, yeah. So, sorry I woke the baby — tell Sharon. I guess I better go, I'm in this restaurant somewhere. I'm *still up*, Jim. And Jim, there's this honey at the bar . . .

Yeah, maybe they don't call them honey in New York. I'll call her something else.

I took Tommy John out of the Stadium, Jim! No, not all the way out, nobody ever . . . I know. But that's the expression . . . uh-huh.

So. . . . Well, thanks. I will. I'll watch it. Yeah. Hey, Jim, don't, you know, don't tell Pop.

SONG ON ROYAL STREET

"AHH, GO BUY YOURSELF a set of legs," he snarls at the chubby black dachshund that waddles after them, barking.

"Willow Street, remember?" she says. "Could it be the same dog?"

"After thirteen years? And this one almost a puppy?"

"All right, then," she says. "It's the puppy of the same one."

They are walking the streets of New Orleans, the University district, on a night heavy with rainlike mist. The dog stops to sniff the trunk of a mimosa, and they walk on under the broad-leaved trees. The scent of honeysuckle is everywhere.

"Old age," he says. "Ain't it great?"

"Come on," she says. "Forty isn't old age."

He is conscious of added weight at the middle, flesh under the jawline. He thinks how well she has aged. The blond hair is curled now, short and becoming, and the body is fuller, a woman's body and not a girl's.

"It's just nothing is like we planned," he says. "Like I planned."

"Nothing ever is. For anybody. But has it been *so* bad?"

Tulane Stadium rises out of the mist like a cathedral in some history book, dwarfing the houses for blocks around.

"Not for you, maybe," he says. "You have the boy."

"Look," she says. "The stadium. Remember that Thanksgiving in the French Quarter motel, and then we came up here for the game?"

"I remember. Tulane lost."

"I don't remember the game."

"Ah," he says, "thank you for that."

For a moment they drift together, shoulders touching. "I miss this city," he says.

"It's not so bad," she says. "We have a happy kid, a healthy one."

"*You* have."

"Don't say that," she says. "He misses you, he does, but he understands."

Crickets chirp in the dark grass. Her heels are lower these days, he notices. Sensible shoes make her seem smaller, diminished. She barely reaches his shoulder.

"Do you believe in magic?" he asks. "There was that old Negro woman on Royal Street, oh way back, when we were just beginning. She wanted money. Remember?"

"No."

"She wanted money and I walked away. You must remember. She came up behind us then and took my hand and she sang something. You remember."

"No."

"And after, I had to sit down, I felt that sick and dizzy. You said it was nerves. You said it was not eating. You said I was making it up. Imagining things."

"I don't remember."

"After that we were never happy."

"I don't remember."

"All right," he says, "all right. Anyway, we have a healthy kid."

"That's a lot."

"That's something."

"Yes."

They turn up McAlister Drive, passing the brick dormitories, the broad-shadowed quadrangles. It is late summer. The students have all gone home. He bends his head passing under the mimosas, the low-hanging boughs.

"Was there really a black woman?" she asks.

"I had to sit down, I was that sick. And the next day we found out you were pregnant. Remember now? And then things just happened like they happened. She sang a song on Royal Street."

"I remember you were scared. Like a boy. I remember you wanted the baby dead."

"No."

" 'There are ways,' you said. 'I know people,' you said."

"No. The Negro woman. She sang a song and I got sick."

"You wanted him dead. I don't remember a woman."

They have come to a corner, the streetlamps glimmering through the heavy leaves of trees. A bus flashes past and disappears into mist and dark.

"Look," he says, "the Freret Jet. We rode that enough times. Boy, the Freret Jet. I remember that."

"I think you made that up," she says. "About the black woman."

"After she sang, you never made it," he says. "Not one time."

"I was morning sick."

"Not one time."

"She didn't take *my* hand. She never sang to *me*."

"You remember then?"

"No."

He drives his fist against a stop sign and sinks to one knee in pain. He looks up at her. "There was a woman," he says slowly. "She took my hand. On Royal Street. She sang a song."

"She never took my hand."

"It was never any good again. Not once."

"I was sick with Chris. And then Daddy died."

"Lots of people die."

"Not like that. Not so horribly."

"But never again."

"Not never," she says. "Just never for you."

"Liar," he says. "Never again in your life."

She turns to him then and her eyes burn through the mist. "All right," she says, "all right. I remember the woman. She was horrible, all wrinkles and bad smell. When she took your hand her eyes shone red in the dark like a swamp animal."

"No," he says. "She was just an old beggar."

"When she crooned, there was death in her voice. She made you a dead man, and you didn't know."

"I don't remember."

"You remember, all right. After that, touching you was a nightmare. You stunk of the grave, a dead man walking around. Look at you. You're more dead than my father."

"There was never a woman. Or not like that. I made her up, an excuse."

"No. After that I never came with you. Remember?"

"No."

"She was old and horrible and you wouldn't give her money. She touched you with her putrefying hand. She put a spell on you on Royal Street. I never made it again, not with you. Everyone else. Never with you."

"I made her up."

"No. Stop crying."

"I can't. I don't have anything, not even my boy."

"Stop crying."

"You never came, not once."

"You were afraid."

"Not once."

"When I touched you," she says, "I was touching death."

He sits down on the cold stone of the gymnasium stairs. She moves in and out of focus, like someone seen through poorly adjusted binoculars.

"The black woman," he says.

"Yes," she says, "the black woman."

"No," he says. "It was your hand, your song."

"All right," she says, "all right. We have a fine son."

"Yes," he says. "That's a lot. That's everything."

"He isn't even yours," she says.

PYGMALION

WHAT HE LIKED ABOUT his first wife was her gift of mimicry; after a party, theirs or another couple's, she would vivify for him what they had seen, the faces, the voices, twisting her pretty mouth into small contortions that brought back, for a dazzling instant, the presence of an absent acquaintance. "Well, if I reawy — how does Gwen talk? — if I *re*-awwy cared about conserwation —" And he, the husband, would laugh and laugh, even though Gwen was secretly his mistress and would become his second wife. What he liked about *her* was her liveliness in bed, and what he disliked about his first wife was the way she would ask to have her back rubbed and then, under his laboring hands, night after night, fall asleep.

For the first years of the new marriage, after he and Gwen had returned from a party he would wait, unconsciously, for the imitations, the recapitulation, to begin. He would even prompt, "What did you make of our hostess's brother?"

"Oh," Gwen would simply say, "he seemed very pleasant." Sensing with feminine intuition that he expected more, she might add, "Harmless. Maybe a little stuffy." Her eyes flashed as she heard in his expectant silence an unvoiced demand, and with that touching, childlike impediment of hers she blurted out, "What are you reawy after?"

"Oh, nothing. Nothing. It's just — Marguerite met him once a few years ago and she was struck by what a pompous nitwit he was. That way he has of sucking his pipestem and ending every statement with 'Do you follow me?' "

"I thought he was perfectly pleasant," Gwen said frostily, and turned her back to remove her silvery, snug party dress. As she wriggled it down over her hips she turned her head and defiantly added, "He had a *lot* to say about tax shelters."

"I bet he did," Pygmalion scoffed feebly, numbed by the sight of his wife frontally advancing, nude, toward him and their marital bed. "It's awfully late," he warned her.

"Oh, come on," she said, the lights out.

The first imitation Gwen did was of Marguerite's second husband, Ed; they had all unexpectedly met at a Save the Whales benefit ball, to which invitations had been sent out indiscriminately. "Oh-ho-*ho*," she boomed in the privacy of their bedroom afterward, "so you're my noble predecessor!" In aside she added, "Noble, my ass. He hates you so much you turned him on."

"I did?" he said. "I thought he was perfectly pleasant, in what could have been an awkward encounter."

"Yes, in*dee*dy," she agreed, imitating hearty Ed, and for a dazzling second allowing the man's slightly glassy and slack expression of forced benignity to invade her own usually petite and rounded features. "Nothing awkward about *us*, ho ho," she went on, encouraged. "And tell me, old chap, why *is* it your child-support check is never on time anymore?"

He laughed and laughed, entranced to see his bride arrive at what he conceived to be proper womanliness — a plastic, alert sensitivity to the human environment, a susceptible responsiveness tugged this way and that by the currents of Nature herself. He could not know the world, was his fear, unless a woman translated it for him. Now, when they returned from a gathering, and he asked what she had made of so-and-so, Gwen would stand in her underwear and consider, as if onstage. "We-hell, my dear," she would announce in sudden, fluting parody, "if it wasn't for Portugal there *rally* wouldn't be a country left in Europe!"

"Oh, come on," he would protest, delighted to see her pretty features distort themselves into an uncanny, snobbish horsiness.

"How did she do it?" Gwen would ask, as if professionally intent. "Something with the chin, sort of rolling it from side to side without unclenching the teeth."

"You've got it!" he applauded.

"Of course you *knoaow*," she went on in the assumed voice, "there *used* to be Greece, but now all these dreadful *A*rabs. . . ."

"Oh, yes, yes," he said, his face smarting from laughing so hard, so proudly. She had become perfect for him.

In bed she pointed out, "It's awfully late."

"Want a back rub?"

"Mmmm. That would be reawy nice." As his left hand labored on the smooth, warm, pliable surface, his wife — that small something in her that was all her own — sank out of reach; night after night, she fell asleep.

A FABLE

THE YOUNG MAN WAS clean shaven and neatly dressed. It was early Monday morning and he got on the subway. It was the first day of his first job and he was slightly nervous; he didn't know exactly what his job would be. Otherwise he felt fine. He loved everybody he saw. He loved everybody on the street and everybody disappearing into the subway, and he loved the world because it was a fine clear day and he was starting his first job.

Without kicking anybody, the young man was able to find a seat on the Manhattan-bound train. The car filled quickly and he looked up at the people standing over him envying his seat. Among them were a mother and daughter who were going shopping. The daughter was a beautiful girl with blond hair and soft-looking skin, and he was immediately attracted to her.

"He's staring at you," the mother whispered to the daughter.

"Yes, Mother, I feel so uncomfortable. What shall I *do?*"

"He's in love with you."

"In love with me? How can you tell?"

"Because I'm your mother."

"But what shall I do?"

"Nothing. He'll try to talk to you. If he does, answer him. Be nice to him. He's only a boy."

The train reached the business district and many people got off. The girl and her mother found seats opposite the young man. He continued to look at the girl who occasionally looked to see if he was looking at her.

The young man found a good pretext for standing in giving his seat to an elderly man. He stood over the girl and her mother. They whispered back and forth and looked up at him. At another stop the seat next to the girl was vacated, and the young man blushed but quickly took it.

"I knew it," the mother said between her teeth. "I knew it, I *knew* it."

The young man cleared his throat and tapped the girl. She jumped.

"Pardon me," he said. "You're a very pretty girl."

"Thank you," she said.

"Don't talk to him," her mother said. "Don't answer him. I'm warning you. Believe me."

"I'm in love with you," he said to the girl.

"I don't believe you," the girl said.

"Don't answer him," the mother said.

"I really do," he said. "In fact, I'm so much in love with you that I want to marry you."

"Do you have a job?" she said.

"Yes, today is my first day. I'm going to Manhattan to start my first day of work."

"What kind of work will you do?" she asked.

"I don't know exactly," he said. "You see, I didn't start yet."

"It sounds exciting," she said.

"It's my first job, but I'll have my own desk and handle a lot of papers and carry them around in a briefcase, and it will pay well, and I'll work my way up."

"I love you," she said.

"Will you marry me?"

"I don't know. You'll have to ask my mother."

The young man rose from his seat and stood before the girl's mother. He cleared his throat very carefully for a long time. "May I have the honor of having your daughter's hand in marriage?" he said, but he was drowned out by the subway noise.

The mother looked up at him and said, "What?" He couldn't hear her either, but he could tell by the movement of her lips and by the way her face wrinkled up that she said, What.

The train pulled to a stop.

"May I have the honor of having your daughter's hand in marriage!" he shouted, not realizing there was no subway noise. Everybody on the train looked at him, smiled, and then they all applauded.

"Are you crazy?" the mother asked.

The train started again.

"What?" he said.

"Why do you want to marry her?" she asked.

"Well, she's pretty—I mean, I'm in love with her."

"Is that all?"

"I guess so," he said. "Is there supposed to be more?"

"No. Not usually," the mother said. "Are you working?"

"Yes. As a matter of fact, that's why I'm going into Manhattan so early. Today is the first day of my first job."

"Congratulations," the mother said.

"Thanks," he said. "Can I marry your daughter?"

"Do you have a car?" she asked.

"Not yet," he said. "But I should be able to get one pretty soon. And a house, too."

"A house?"

"With lots of rooms."

"Yes, that's what I expected you to say," she said. She turned to her daughter. "Do you love him?"

"Yes, Mother, I do."

"Why?"

"Because he's good, and gentle, and kind."

"Are you sure?"

"Yes."

"Then you really love him."

"Yes."

"Are you sure there isn't anyone else that you might love and might want to marry?"

"No, Mother," the girl said.

"Well, then," the mother said to the young man. "Looks like there's nothing I can do about it. Ask her again."

The train stopped.

"My dearest one," he said, "will you marry me?"

"Yes," she said.

Everybody in the car smiled and applauded.

"Isn't life wonderful?" the boy asked the mother.

"Beautiful," the mother said.

The conductor climbed down from between the cars as the train started up and, straightening his dark tie, approached them with a solemn black book in his hand.

THE MOVING

1953

WE STOOD BY THE LOADED wagon while Father nailed the windows down and spat into the keyholes to make the locks turn. We waited, restless as the harnessed mare, anxious to hasten beyond staring eyes. Hardstay mine was closed for all time and idle men had gathered to watch us leave. They hung over the fence; they crowded where last year's dogtick stalks clutched their brown leaf-hands into fists.

I saw the boys glance at our windowpanes, their pockets bulging with rocks. I spied into their faces and a homesickness grew large inside of me. I hungered for a word, a nod of farewell. But only a witty was sad at my going, only a child of a man who valued strings and tobacco tags, a chap in a man's clothes who was bound forever to speak things backward. Hig Sommers stood bug-eyed, and fellows were picking at him. One knelt and jerked loose the eel-strings of his brogans.

Though women watched from their porches only a widow-woman came to say a goodbye to Mother. Sula Basham came walking, tall as a butterweed, and with a yellow locket swinging from her neck like a clockweight.

Loss Tramble spoke, grinning, "If I had a woman that tall, I'd string her with gourds and use her for a martin pole. I would, now." A dry chuckle rattled in the crowd. Loss stepped back, knowing the muscle frogs of her arms were the size of any man's.

Sula towered over Mother. The locket dropped like a plumb. Mother was barely five feet tall and she had to look upward as into the sky; and her eyes set on the locket, for never had she owned a grain of gold, never a locket, or a ring, or bighead pin. Sula spoke loudly to Mother, glancing at the men with scorn: "You ought to be proud that your man's not satisfied to rot in Hardstay camp, a-setting on his chinebone. Before long all's got to move, all's got to roust or starve. This mine hain't opening ag'in. Hit's too nigh dug out."

"Hit" = It

The men stirred uneasily. Sill Lovelock lifted his arms, spreading them like a preacher's. "These folks air moving to nowheres," he said. "Thar's no camps along the Kentucky River a-taking on hands; they's no work anywheres. Hit's mortal sin to make gypsies of a family. I say as long's a body has got a rooftree, let him roost under it."

Men grunted, doddering their heads, and the boys lifted their rock-heavy pockets and sidled toward the wagon. Cece Goodloe snatched Hig Sommers's hat as he passed, clapping it onto his own head. The hat rested upon his ears. The boys placed their hands on the wagon wheels; they fingered the mare's harness; they raised the lid of the toolbox to see what was in it. Cece crawled under the wagon, back hound to front hound, shaking the swingletree. I watched out of the tail of my eye, thinking a rusty might be pulled.

Father came into the yard with the key, and now the house was shut against our turning back. I looked at the empty hull of our dwelling; I looked at the lost town, yearning to stay in this place where I was born, among the people I knew. Father lifted the key on a finger. "If a body here would drap this key by the commissary," he said, "I'd be obliged."

Hig Sommers lumbered toward Father, his shirttail flying. Someone had shagged his shirt out. "I'll fotch it," Hig cried, stretching both hands for the key as a babe would reach.

"I'm not a-wanting it fotched," Father said. He'd not trust the key to a fellow who wasn't bright. "You've got it back'ards, Hig. I'm wanting it tuck."   took ?

Sill Lovelock stepped forward, though he didn't offer to carry the key. "They's Scripture ag'in' a feller hauling off the innocent," he vowed gravely. "I say, stay where there's a floor underfoot and joists overhead."

Father said testily, "There ought to be a statute telling a feller to salt his own steers. Ruther to drown o' sweat hunting for work than die o' dry rot in Hardstay."

Loss Tramble edged near Father, his eyes burning and the corners of his mouth curled. He nodded his head toward Sula Basham. "I'll deliver that key willing if you'll take this beanpole widow-woman along some'eres and git her a man. She's wore the black bonnet long enough."

Laughter sprang forth, gulping in throats, wheezing noses. Sula whirled, her face lit with anger. "If I was a-mind to marry," she said, grudging her words, "it's certain I'd have to go where there's a man fitten. I'd be bound—"

Sill Lovelock broke in, thinking Sula's talk of no account. He asked Father, "What air you to use for bread along the way? There's no manna falling from Heaven this day and time."

Father was grinning at Sula. He saw the muscle knots clench on her arms, and he saw Loss inch away. He turned toward Sill in good humor. "Why, there's a gum o' honey dew on the leaves of a morning. We kin wake early and eat it off."

"The Devil take 'em," Mother said, calming Sula. "Menfolks are heathens. Let them crawl their own dirt." She was studying the locket, studying it to remember, to take away in her mind. I thought of Mother's unpierced ear lobes where never a bob had hung, the worn stems of her fingers never circled by gold, her plain bosom no pin-pretty had ever hooked. She was looking at the locket, not covetously, but in wonder.

"I'll take the key," Sula told Father. "Nobody else seems anxious to neighbor you."

Loss opened his hands, his face as grave as Sill Lovelock's, mocking. He pointed an arm at Sula, the other appealing to the crowd. "I allus did pity a widow woman," he said. He spanned Sula's height with his eyes. "In this gethering there ought to be one single man willing to marry the Way Up Yonder Woman."

Sula's mouth hardened. "I want none o' your pity pie," she blurted. She took a step toward Loss, the sinews of her long arms quickening. When Loss retreated she turned to Mother, who had just climbed onto the wagon. Sula and Mother were now at an eye level. "You were a help when my chaps died," Sula said. "You were a comfort when my man lay in his box. I hain't forgetting. Wish I had a keepsake to give you, showing I'll allus remember."

"I'll keep you in my head," Mother assured.

"I'll be proud to know it."

We were ready to go. "Climb on, Son," Father called. I swung up from the hindgate to the top of the load. Over the heads of the men I could see the whole of the camp, the shotgun houses in the flat, the smoke rising above the burning gob heaps. The pain of leaving rose in my chest. Father clucked his tongue, and the mare started off. She walked clear out of the wagon shafts. Loose trace chains swung free and pole-ends of the shafts bounded to the ground.

"Whoa ho!" Father shouted, jumping down. A squall of joy sounded behind us. Cece Goodloe had pulled this rusty; he'd done the unfastening. Father smiled while adjusting the harness. Oh, he didn't mind a clever trick. And he sprang back onto the wagon again.

Loss Tramble spooled his hands, calling through them, "If you don't aim to take this widow along, we'll have to marry her to a born fool. We'll have to match her with Hig Sommers."

We drove away, the wheels taking the groove of ruts, the load swaying; we drove away with Sill Lovelock's last warning ringing in our ears. "You're making your bed in Hell!" he had shouted. Then it was I saw the gold locket about Mother's neck, beating her bosom like a heart.

I looked back, seeing the first rocks thrown, hearing our windows shatter; I looked back upon the camp as upon the face of the dead. I saw the crowd fall back from Sula Basham, tripping over each other. She had struck Loss Tramble with her fist, and he knelt before her, fearing to rise. And only Hig Sommers was watching us move away. He stood holding up his breeches, for someone had cut his galluses with a knife. He thrust one arm into the air, crying, "Hello, hello!"

THE CLIFF

ON THE WAY OUT to the cliff, the old man kept one hand on the wheel. He smoked with the other hand. The inside of the car smelled of wine and cigarette ashes. He coughed constantly. His voice sounded like a version of the cough.

"I used to smoke Camels unfiltered," he told the boy. The dirt road, rutted, dipped hard, and the car bounced. "But I switched brands. Camels interfered with my eating. I couldn't taste what the Duchess cooked up. Meat, salad, Jell-O: it all tasted the same. So I went to low tar. You don't smoke, do you, boy?"

The boy stared at the road and shook his head.

"Not after what I've taught you, I hope not. You got to keep the body pure for the stuff we're doing."

"You don't keep it pure," the boy said.

"I don't have to. It's *been* pure. And, like I say, nobody is ever pure twice."

The California pines seemed brittle and did not sway as they drove past. The boy thought he could hear the crash of the waves in front of them. "Are we almost there?"

"Kind of impatient, aren't you?" the old man said, suppressing his cough. "Look, boy, I told you a hundred times: you got to train your will to do this. You get impatient, and you—"

"—I know, I know. 'You die.' " The boy was wearing a jacket and a New York Mets cap. "I know all that. You taught me. I'm only asking if we're there yet."

"You got a woman, boy?" The old man looked suspicious. "You got a woman?"

"I'm only fifteen," the boy said nervously.

"That's not too old for it, especially around here."

"I've been kissed," the boy said. "Is that the ocean?"

"That's her," the old man said. "Sometimes I think I know everything about you, and then sometimes I don't think I know anything. I hate to take chances like this. You could be hiding something out on me. The magic's no damn good if you're hiding something out on me."

"It'll be good," the boy said, seeing the long line of blue water through the trees. He pulled the visor down lower, so he wouldn't squint. "It'll be real good."

"Faith, hope, charity, and love," the old man recited. "And the spells. Now I admit I have fallen from the path of righteousness at times. But I never forget the spells. You forget them, you die."

"I would not forget them," the boy said.

"You better not be lying to me. You been thieving, sleeping with whores, you been carrying on in the bad way, well, we'll find out soon enough." He stopped the car at a clearing. He turned the key off in the ignition and reached under his seat for a wine bottle. His hands were shaking. The old man unscrewed the cap and took a long swig. He recapped it and breathed out the sweet aroma in the boy's direction. "Something for my nerves," he said. "I don't do this every day."

"You don't believe in the spells anymore," the boy said.

"I *am* the spells," the old man shouted. "I invented them. I just hate to see a fresh kid like you crash on the rocks on account of *you* don't believe in them."

"Don't worry," the boy said. "Don't worry about me."

They got out of the car together, and the old man reached around into the back seat for his coil of rope.

"I don't need it," the boy said. "I don't need the rope."

"Kid, we do it my way or we don't do it."

The boy took off his shoes. His bare feet stepped over pine needles and stones. He was wearing faded blue jeans and a sweat-shirt, with a stain from the old man's wine bottle on it. He had taken off his jacket in the car, but he was still wearing the cap. They walked over a stretch of burnt grass and came to the edge of the cliff.

"Look at those sea gulls down there," the old man pointed. "Must be a hundred." His voice was trembling with nervousness.

"I know about the sea gulls." The boy had to raise his voice to be heard above the surf. "I've seen them."

"You're so smart, huh?" the old man coughed. He drew a ciga-rette out of his shirt and lit it with his Zippo lighter. "All right, I'm tired of telling you what to do, Mr. Know-It-All. Take off the sweat-shirt." The boy took it off. "Now make a circle in the dirt."

"With what?"

"With your foot."

"There isn't any dirt."

"Do like I tell you."

The boy extended his foot and drew a magic circle around himself. It could not be seen, but he knew it was there.

"Now look out at the horizon and tell it what I told you to tell it."

The boy did as he was told.

"Now take this rope, take this end." The old man handed it to him. "God, I don't know sometimes." The old man bent down for another swig of wine. "Is your mind clear?"

"Yeah," the boy said.

"Are you scared?"

"Naw."

"Do you see anybody?"

"Nope."

"You got any last questions?"

"Do I hold my arms out?"

"They do that in the Soviet Union," the old man said, "but they also do it sitting on pigs. That's the kind of people they are. You don't have to hold your arms out. Are you ready? Jump!"

The boy felt the edge of the cliff with his feet, jumped, and felt the magic and the horizon lifting him up and then out over the water, his body parallel to the ground. He took it into his mind to swoop down toward the cliffs, and then to veer away suddenly, and whatever he thought, he did. At first he held on to the rope, but even the old man could see that it was unnecessary, and reeled it in. In his jeans and cap, the boy lifted himself upward, then dove down toward the sea gulls, then just as easily lifted himself up again, rushing over the old man's head before flying out over the water.

He shouted with happiness.

The old man reached down again for his wine.

"The sun!" the old man shouted. "The ocean! The land! That's how to do it!" And he laughed suddenly, his cough all gone. "The sky!" he said at last.

The boy flew in great soaring circles. He tumbled in the air, dove, flipped, and sailed. His eyes were dazzled with the blue also, and like the old man he smelled the sea salt.

But of course he was a teen-ager. He was grateful to the old man for teaching him the spells. But this—the cliffs, the sea, the blue sky, and the sweet wine—this was the old man's style, not his. He loved the old man for sharing the spells. He would think of him always, for that.

But even as he flew, he was getting ideas. It isn't the style of teen-agers to fly in broad daylight, on sunny days, even in California. What the boy wanted was something else: to fly low, near the ground, in the cities, speeding in smooth arcs between the buildings, late at night. Very late: at the time the girls are hanging up their clothes and sighing, sighing out their windows to the stagnant air, as the clocks strike midnight. The idea of the pig interested the boy. He grinned far down at the old man, who waved, who had long ago forgotten the dirty purposes of flight.

NO ONE'S A MYSTERY

OR MY EIGHTEENTH birthday Jack gave me a five-year diary
with a latch and a little key, light as a dime. I was sitting beside him
scratching at the lock, which didn't seem to want to work, when he
thought he saw his wife's Cadillac in the distance, coming toward
us. He pushed me down onto the dirty floor of the pickup and kept
one hand on my head while I inhaled the musk of his cigarettes in
the dashboard ashtray and sang along with Rosanne Cash on the
tape deck. We'd been drinking tequila and the bottle was between
his legs, resting up against his crotch, where the seam of his Levi's
was bleached linen-white, though the Levi's were nearly new. I don't
know why his Levi's always bleached like that, along the seams and
at the knees. In a curve of cloth his zipper glinted, gold.

"It's her," he said. "She keeps the lights on in the daytime. I can't
think of a single habit in a woman that irritates me more than that."
When he saw that I was going to stay still he took his hand from
my head and ran it through his own dark hair.

"Why does she?" I said.

"She thinks it's safer. Why does she need to be safer? She's driving exactly fifty-five miles an hour. She believes in those signs:
'Speed Monitored by Aircraft.' It doesn't matter that you can look
up and see that the sky is empty."

"She'll see your lips move, Jack. She'll know you're talking to
someone."

"She'll think I'm singing along with the radio."

He didn't lift his hand, just raised the fingers in salute while the
pressure of his palm steadied the wheel, and I heard the Cadillac
honk twice, musically; he was driving easily eighty miles an hour.
I studied his boots. The elk heads stitched into the leather were
bearded with frayed thread, the toes were scuffed, and there
was a compact wedge of muddy manure between the heel and the
sole — the same boots he'd been wearing for the two years I'd known

him. On the tape deck Rosanne Cash sang, "Nobody's into me, no one's a mystery."

"Do you think she's getting famous because of who her daddy is or for herself?" Jack said.

"There are about a hundred pop tops on the floor, did you know that? Some little kid could cut a bare foot on one of these, Jack."

"No little kids get into this truck except for you."

"How come you let it get so dirty?"

" 'How come,' " he mocked. "You even sound like a kid. You can get back into the seat now, if you want. She's not going to look over her shoulder and see you."

"How do you know?"

"I just know," he said. "Like I know I'm going to get meat loaf for supper. It's in the air. Like I know what you'll be writing in that diary."

"What will I be writing?" I knelt on my side of the seat and craned around to look at the butterfly of dust printed on my jeans. Outside the window Wyoming was dazzling in the heat. The wheat was fawn and yellow and parted smoothly by the thin dirt road. I could smell the water in the irrigation ditches hidden in the wheat.

"Tonight you'll write, 'I love Jack. This is my birthday present from him. I can't imagine anybody loving anybody more than I love Jack.' "

"I can't."

"In a year you'll write, 'I wonder what I ever really saw in Jack. I wonder why I spent so many days just riding around in his pickup. It's true he taught me something about sex. It's true there wasn't ever much else to do in Cheyenne.' "

"I won't write that."

"In two years you'll write, 'I wonder what that old guy's name was, the one with the curly hair and the filthy dirty pickup truck and time on his hands.' "

"I won't write that."

"No?"

"Tonight I'll write, 'I love Jack. This is my birthday present from him. I can't imagine anybody loving anybody more than I love Jack.' "

"No, you can't," he said. "You can't imagine it."

"In a year I'll write, 'Jack should be home any minute now. The table's set — my grandmother's linen and her old silver and the yellow candles left over from the wedding — but I don't know if I can wait until after the trout à la Navarra to make love to him.' "

"It must have been a fast divorce."

"In two years I'll write, 'Jack should be home by now. Little Jack is hungry for his supper. He said his first word today besides "Mama" and "Papa." He said "kaka." ' "

Jack laughed. "He was probably trying to finger-paint with kaka on the bathroom wall when you heard him say it."

"In three years I'll write, 'My nipples are a little sore from nursing Eliza Rosamund.' "

"Rosamund. Every little girl should have a middle name she hates."

" 'Her breath smells like vanilla and her eyes are just Jack's color of blue.' "

"That's nice," Jack said.

"So, which one do you like?"

"I like yours," he said. "But I believe mine."

"It doesn't matter. I believe mine."

"Not in your heart of hearts, you don't."

"You're wrong."

"I'm not wrong," he said. "And her breath would smell like your milk, and it's kind of a bittersweet smell, if you want to know the truth."

THE MERRY CHASE

Don't tell me. Do me a favor and let me guess. Be honest
with me, tell the truth, don't make me laugh. Tell me, don't make
me have to tell you, do I have to tell you that when you're hot, you're
hot, that when you're dead, you're dead? Because you know what
I know? I know you like I know myself, I know you like the back
of my hand, I know you like a book, I know you inside out. I know
you like you'll never know.

You think I don't know whereof I speak? I know, I know. I
know the day will come, the day will dawn.

Didn't I tell you you never know? Because I guarantee it. I tell
you, no one will dance a jig. No one will do a dance. No one will
cater to you so fast, or wait on you hand and foot. You think they
could care less if you live or die?

But I could never get enough of it—I could never get enough.
Look at me, I could take a bite out of it. I could eat it up alive. But
you want to make a monkey out of me, don't you? You want me
to talk myself blue in the face for you, beat my head against a brick
wall for you, come running when you have the least little complaint.
What am I, your slave? You couldn't be happy except over my dead
body? You think I don't know whereof I speak? I promise you, one
day you will sing a different tune.

In the interim, first things first, it won't kill you to do without,
tomorrow is another day, let me look at it, let me see it, there is no
time like the present, let me kiss it and make it better.

Let me tell you something. Everyone in the whole wide world
should only have it half as good as you do.

You know what this is? You want to know what this is? Because
this is some deal, this is some set-up, this is some joke—you could
vomit from what a joke this is. I want you to hear something, I want
you to hear the unvarnished truth. I want you to hear it from me,
right from the horse's mouth, from the one person who really cares.

You know what you are? *That's* what you are!

You sit, I'll go — I already had enough to choke a horse.

Go ahead and talk my arm off. Talk me deaf, dumb, and blind. Nobody is asking, nobody is talking, nobody wants to know. In all decency, in all honesty, in all candor, in all modesty, you have some gall, some nerve, and I mean that in all sincerity.

I am telling you, I am pleading with you, I am down to you on bended knee — just don't get cute with me, just don't make any excuses to me — because in broad daylight, in the dead of night, at the crack of dawn.

You think the whole world is going to do a dance around you? No one is going to do a dance around you. No one even knows you are alive, they don't know you from Adam.

But if it is not one thing, then it is another.

Just who do you think you are, coming in here and lording it all over all of us? Do you think you are a law unto yourself? I am going to give you some advice. Don't flatter yourself — you are not the queen of the May, not by a long shot. Act your age — share and share alike.

Ages ago, years ago, so long ago I couldn't begin to remember, past history, ancient history — you don't want to know, another age, another life, another theory altogether.

Don't ask. Don't even begin to ask. Don't make me any promises. Don't tell me one thing and do another. Don't look at me cross-eyed. Don't look at me like that. Don't hand me that crap. Look around you, for pity's sake. Don't you know that one hand washes the other? Talk sense. Take stock.

Give me some credit for intelligence. Show me I'm not wasting my breath. Don't make me sick. You are making me sick. Why are you doing this to me? Do you get pleasure from doing this to me? Don't think I don't know what you are trying to do to me.

Don't make me do your thinking for you.

Shame on you, be ashamed of yourself, have you absolutely no decency and shame?

Why must I always have to tell you?

Why must I always drop everything and come running?

Does nothing ever occur to you?

Can't you see with your own two eyes?

You are your own worst enemy.

What's the sense of talking to you? I might as well talk to myself. Say something. Try to look like you've got a brain in your head.

You think this is a picnic? This is no picnic. Don't stand on ceremony with me. The whole world is not going to step to your tune. I warn you—wake up before it's too late.

You know what? A little birdie just told me. You know what? You have got a lot to learn—that's what.

I can't hear myself talk. I can't hear myself think. I cannot remember from one minute to the next.

Why do I always have to tell you again and again?

Give me a minute to think. Just let me catch my breath.

Don't you ever stop to ask?

I'm going to tell you something. I'm going to tell you what no one else would have the heart to tell you. I'm going to give you the benefit of my advice. Do you want some good advice?

You think the sun rises and sets on you, don't you? You should get down on your hands and knees and thank God. You should count your blessings. Why don't you look around yourself and really see for once in your life? You just don't know when you're well off. You have no idea how the rest of the world lives. You are as innocent as the day you were born. You should thank your lucky stars. You should try to make amends. You should do your best to put it all out of your mind. Worry never got anybody anywhere.

But by the same token.

Whatever you do, promise me this—just promise me that you will do your best to keep an open mind.

What do I say to you, where do I start with you, how do I make myself heard? I don't know where to begin with you, I don't know where to start with you, I don't know how to impress on you the importance of every single solitary word. Thank God I am alive to tell you, thank God I am here to tell you, thank God you've got someone to tell you, I only wish I could begin to tell you, if there were only some way someone could tell you, if only there were someone here to tell you, but you don't want to listen, you don't want to learn, you don't want to know, you don't want to help yourself, you just want to have it all your own sweet way. Who can talk to you? Can anyone talk to you? You don't want anyone to talk to you. So far as you are concerned, the whole world could drop dead.

You think death is a picnic? Death is no picnic. Face facts, don't kid yourself, people are trying to talk some sense into you, it's not all just fun and fancy free, it's not all just high, wide, and handsome, it's not just a bed of roses and peaches and cream.

You take the cake, you take my breath away—you are really one for the books—you know, you know, you know?

Be smart and downplay it. Be smart and stay in the wings. Be smart and let somebody else carry the ball for a change.

You know what I've got to do? I've got to talk to you like a baby. I've got to talk to you like a Dutch uncle. I've got to handle you with kid gloves, just in case you didn't know.

Let me tell you something no one else would have the heart to tell you. Go ahead, look! Look far and wide—because they are few and far between!

Go ahead, go to the ends of the earth, go to the highest mountain, go to any lengths, because they won't lift a finger for you—or didn't you know that some things are not for man to know, that some things are better left unsaid, that some things you shouldn't wish on a dog, not on a bet, not on your life, not in a month of Sundays?

What do you want? You want the whole world to revolve around you, you want the whole world at your beck and call? That's what you want, isn't it? Be honest with me and let's be done with it, be finished with it, over and done with it, enough, for crying out loud, enough.

Answer me this one question—how can you look at me like this?

Don't you dare act as if you didn't hear me. You want to know what's wrong with you? This is what is wrong with you. You are going to the dogs, you are lying down with dogs, you are waking sleeping dogs—don't you know enough to leave before the last dog is dead?

When are you going to learn to leave well enough alone?

You know what you are? Let me tell you what you are. You are betwixt and between.

I'm on to you, I've got your number, I can see right through you—I warn you, don't you dare try to put anything over on me or get on my good side or lead me a merry chase.

So who's going to do your dirty work? You?

Oh, sure, you think you can just rise above it all, but no one can live forever with his head in the clouds, in the woods, in a cave, with neither rhyme nor reason, without hope, without blemish, without a hitch, without batting an eyelash, without a leg to stand on, without fail, without cause, without a little bit of butter on his bread.

Pardon my French — but put up or shut up!

Oh, we could just laugh in your face.

Oh, you — you dirty dickens, you! Can't you just leave us in peace?

YOURS

1981

ALLISON STRUGGLED away from her white Renault, limping with the weight of the last of the pumpkins. She found Clark in the twilight on the twig-and-leaf-littered porch behind the house.

He wore a wool shawl. He was moving up and back in a padded glider, pushed by the ball of his slippered foot.

Allison lowered a big pumpkin, let it rest on the wide floorboards.

Clark was much older—seventy-eight to Allison's thirty-five. They were married. They were both quite tall and looked something alike in their facial features. Allison wore a natural-hair wig. It was a thick blond hood around her face. She was dressed in bright-dyed denims today. She wore durable clothes, usually, for she volunteered afternoons at a children's day-care center.

She put one of the smaller pumpkins on Clark's long lap. "Now, nothing surreal," she told him. "Carve just a *regular* face. These are for kids."

In the foyer, on the Hepplewhite desk, Allison found the maid's chore list with its cross-offs, which included Clark's supper. Allison went quickly through the day's mail: a garish coupon packet, a bill from Jamestown Liquors, November's pay-TV program guide, and the worst thing, the funniest, an already opened, extremely unkind letter from Clark's relations up North. "You're an old fool," Allison read, and, "You're being cruelly deceived." There was a gift check for Clark enclosed, but it was uncashable, signed, as it was, "Jesus H. Christ."

Late, late into this night, Allison and Clark gutted and carved the pumpkins together, at an old table set on the back porch, over newspaper after soggy newspaper, with paring knives and with spoons and with a Swiss Army knife Clark used for exact shaping of tooth and eye and nostril. Clark had been a doctor, an internist, but also a Sunday watercolorist. His four pumpkins were expressive and artful. Their carved features were suited to the sizes and shapes of the pumpkins. Two looked ferocious and jagged. One registered surprise. The last was serene and beaming.

Allison's four faces were less deftly drawn, with slits and areas of distortion. She had cut triangles for noses and eyes. The mouths she had made were just wedges—two turned up and two turned down.

By one in the morning they were finished. Clark, who had bent his long torso forward to work, moved back over to the glider and looked out sleepily at nothing. All the lights were out across the ravine.

Clark stayed. For the season and time, the Virginia night was warm. Most leaves had been blown away already, and the trees stood unbothered. The moon was round above them.

Allison cleaned up the mess.

"Your jack-o'-lanterns are much, much better than mine," Clark said to her.

"Like hell," Allison said.

"Look at me," Clark said, and Allison did.

She was holding a squishy bundle of newspapers. The papers reeked sweetly with the smell of pumpkin guts.

"Yours are *far* better," he said.

"You're wrong. You'll see when they're lit," Allison said.

She went inside, came back with yellow vigil candles. It took her a while to get each candle settled, and then to line up the results in a row on the porch railing. She went along and lit each candle and fixed the pumpkin lids over the little flames.

"See?" she said.

They sat together a moment and looked at the orange faces.

"We're exhausted. It's good night time," Allison said. "Don't blow out the candles. I'll put in new ones tomorrow."

That night, in their bedroom, a few weeks earlier in her life than had been predicted, Allison began to die. "Don't look at me if my wig comes off," she told Clark. "Please."

Her pulse cords were fluttering under his fingers. She raised her knees and kicked away the comforter. She said something to Clark about the garage being locked.

At the telephone, Clark had a clear view out back and down to the porch. He wanted to get drunk with his wife once more. He wanted to tell her, from the greater perspective he had, that to own only a little talent, like his, was an awful, plaguing thing; that being only a little special meant you expected too much, most of the time, and liked yourself too little. He wanted to assure her that she had missed nothing.

He was speaking into the phone now. He watched the jack-o'-lanterns. The jack-o'-lanterns watched him.

A WALLED GARDEN

N O, MEMPHIS IN AUTUMN has not the moss-hung oaks of Natchez. Nor, my dear young man, have we the exotic, the really exotic orange and yellow and rust foliage of the maples at Rye or Saratoga. When our five-month summer season burns itself out, the foliage is left a cheerless brown. Observe that Catawba tree beyond the wall, and the leaves under your feet here on the terrace are mustard and khaki colored; and the air, the atmosphere (who would dare to breathe a deep breath!) is virtually a sea of dust. But we do what we can. We've walled ourselves in here with these evergreens and box and jasmine. You must know, yourself, young man, that no beauty is native to us but the verdure of early summer. And it's as though I've had to take my finger, just so, and point out to Frances the lack of sympathy that there is in the climate and in the eroded countryside of this region. I have had to build this garden and say, "See, my child, how nice and sympathetic everything can be." But now she does see it my way, you understand. You understand, my daughter has finally made her life with me in this little garden plot, and year by year she has come to realize how little else there is hereabouts to compare with it.

And you, you know nothing of flowers? A young man who doesn't know the zinnia from the aster! How curious that you and my daughter should have made friends. I don't know under what circumstances you two may have met. In her League work, no doubt. She *throws* herself so into whatever work she undertakes. Oh? Why, of course, I should have guessed. She simply *spent* herself on the Chest Drive this year. . . . But my daughter has most of her permanent friends among the flower-minded people. She makes so few friends nowadays outside of our little circle, sees so few people outside our own garden here, really, that I find it quite strange for there to be someone who doesn't know flowers.

No, nothing, we've come to feel, is ever very lovely, really lovely, I mean, in this part of the nation, nothing *but* this garden; and you can well imagine what even this little bandbox of a garden once was. I created it out of a virtual chaos of a backyard—Franny's playground, I might say. For three years I nursed that little magnolia there, for one whole summer did nothing but water the ivy on the east wall of the house; if only you could have seen the scrubby hedge and the unsightly servants' quarters of our neighbors that are beyond my serpentine wall (I suppose, at least, they're still there). In those days it was all very different, you understand, and Frances's father was about the house, and Frances was a child. But now in the spring we have what is truly a sweet garden here, modeled on my mother's at Rye; for three weeks in March our hyacinths are an inspiration to Frances and to me and to all those who come to us regularly; the larkspur and marigold are heavenly in May over there beside the roses.

But you do not know the zinnia from the aster, young man? How curious that you two should have become friends. And now you are impatient with her, and you mustn't be; I don't mean to be too indulgent, but she'll be along presently. Only recently she's become incredibly painstaking in her toilet again. Whereas in the last few years she's not cared so much for the popular fads of dress. Gardens and floral design have occupied her—with what guidance I could give—have been pretty much her life, really. Now in the old days, I confess, before her father was taken from us—I lost Mr. Harris in the dreadfully hot summer of '48 (people don't generally realize what a dreadful year that was—the worst year for perennials and annuals, alike, since Terrible '30. Things died that year that I didn't think would *ever* die. A dreadful summer)—why, she used then to run here and there with people of every sort, it seemed. I put no restraint upon her, understand. How many times I've said to my Franny, "You must make your own life, my child, as you would have it." Yes, in those days she used to run here and there with people of every sort and variety, it seemed to me. Where was it you say you met, for she goes so few places that are really *out* anymore? But Mr. Harris would let me put no restraint upon her. I still remember the strongheadedness of her teens that had to be overcome and the testiness in her character when she was nearer to twenty than thirty. And you should have seen her as a tot of twelve when she would be somersaulting and rolling about on this very spot. Honestly, I see that child now, the mud on her middy blouse and her straight yellow hair in her eyes.

When I used to come back from visiting my people at Rye, she would grit her teeth at me and give her confidence to the black cook. I would find my own child become a mad little animal. It was through this door here from the sun room that I came one September afternoon—just such an afternoon as this, young man—still wearing my traveling suit, and called to my child across the yard for her to come and greet me. I had been away for the two miserable summer months, caring for my sick mother, but at the sight of me the little Indian turned, and with a whoop she ran to hide in the scraggly privet hedge that was at the far end of the yard. I called her twice to come from out that filthiest of shrubs. "Frances Ann!" We used to call her by her full name when her father was alive. But she didn't stir. She crouched at the roots of the hedge and spied at her travel-worn mother between the leaves.

I pleaded with her at first quite indulgently and good-naturedly and described the new ruffled dress and the paper cutouts I had brought from her grandmother at Rye. (I wasn't to have Mother much longer, and I knew it, and it was hard to come home to this kind of scene.) At last I threatened to withhold my presents until Thanksgiving or Christmas. The cook in the kitchen may have heard some change in my tone, for she came to the kitchen door over beyond the latticework that we've since put up, and looked out first at me and then at the child. While I was threatening, my daughter crouched in the dirt and began to mumble things to herself that I could not hear, and the noises she made were like those of an angry little cat. It seems that it was a warmer afternoon than this one— but my garden does deceive—and I had been moving about in my heavy traveling suit. In my exasperation I stepped out into the rays of the sweltering sun, and into the yard which I so detested; and I uttered in a scream the child's full name, "Frances Ann Harris!" Just then the black cook stepped out onto the back porch, but I ordered her to return to the kitchen. I began to cross the yard toward Frances Ann—that scowling little creature who was *incredibly* the same Frances you've met—and simultaneously she began to crawl along the hedgerow toward the wire fence that divided my property from the neighbor's.

I believe it was the extreme heat that made me speak so very harshly and with such swiftness as to make my words incomprehensible. When I saw that the child had reached the fence and intended climbing it, I pulled off my hat, tearing my veil to pieces as I hurried my pace. I don't actually know what I was saying—I probably couldn't have told you even a moment later — and I didn't even feel any pain from the turn that I gave my ankle in the gully across the middle of the yard. But the child kept her nervous little eyes on me and her lips continued to move now and again. Each time her lips moved I believe I must have raised my voice in more intense rage and greater horror at her ugliness. And so, young man, striding straight through the hedge I reached her before she had climbed to the top of the wire fencing. I think I took her by the arm above the elbow, about here, and I said something like, "I shall have to punish you, Frances Ann." I did not jerk her. I didn't jerk her one bit, as she wished to make it appear, but rather, as soon as I touched her, she relaxed her hold on the wire and fell to the ground. But she lay there — in her canniness — only the briefest moment looking up and past me through the straight hair that hung over her face like an untrimmed mane. I had barely ordered her to rise when she sprang up and moved with such celerity that she soon was out of my reach again. I followed — running in those high heels — and this time I turned my other ankle in the gully, and I fell there on the ground in that yard, this garden. You won't believe it — pardon, I must sit down. . . . I hope you don't think it too odd, me telling you all this. . . . You won't believe it: I lay there in the ditch and she didn't come to aid me with childish apologies and such, but instead she deliberately climbed into her swing that hung from the dirty old poplar that was here formerly (I have had it cut down and the roots dug up) and she began to swing, not high and low, but only gently, and stared straight down at her mother through her long hair — which, you may be sure, young man, I had cut the very next day at my own beautician's and curled into a hundred ringlets.

HEART ATTACK

MY SICKNESS BOTHERS ME, though I persist in denying it. It is indigestion I think and eat no onions; gout and I order no liver or goose. The possibility of nervous exhaustion keeps me abed for three days, breathing deeply. I do yoga for anxiety. But, finally, here I am amid magazines awaiting, naked to the waist, cough at the balls, needle in the vein. From my viral pneumonia days, I remember his Sheaffers desk set and the 14kt. gold point. It writes prescriptions without a scratch. In the time of the bad sunburn, my damaged eyes scanned the walls reading degrees and being jealous of the good-looking woman, the three boys, the weeping willow in the back yard.

I have a choice of *Sports Illustrated*, *Time*, *Boy's World*, others. As if by design, I choose the free pamphlet on the wall. Fleischmann's Margarine gives me some straight talk about cholesterol. I remember the ten thousand eggs of my youth, those miracles of protein that have perhaps made my interior an artgum eraser. Two over easy in the morning, a hard one every night, poached, sometimes eviscerated by mayonnaise. In many ways I have been an egg man. The pamphlet shows my heart, a small pump the size of my fist. I make a fist and stare at knuckles, white as the eggshells I wish I had eaten instead. Where did I learn that your penis is the size of your middle finger plus the distance that finger can reach down your arm. Mine cannot make it to the wrist. My heart too must be a pea in this flimsy, hairless chest.

From a door marked PRIVATE a nurse, all in white, comes to me. She sits very close on the couch and looks down at my pamphlet. She takes my damp hand in hers and tickles my palm. Her soft lips against my ear whisper musically, "Every cloud has a silver lining. . . ."

"But arteries," I respond, "my arteries are caked with the mistakes of my youth."

She points to the pamphlet. "Arteries should be lined only with their moist little selves. Be good to your arteries, be kind to your heart. It's the only one you'll ever have." She puts her tongue in my ear, and one arm reaches under my shirt. She sings, "A fella needs a girl. . . ."

"I need a doctor . . . my arteries."

She points again to the pamphlet and reads, "Arteries, though similar to, are more important than girls in several ways. Look at this one pink and flexible as a Speidel band. Over there threatens cholesterol, dark as motor oil, thick as birthday cake. Cholesterol is the bully of the body. It picks on blood, good honest blood who bothers no one and goes happily between the races, creeds, and colors."

"I have pains," I tell her, "pains in my chest and my tongue feels fat and moss grows in my joints."

She unbuttons my shirt slowly. Her long cool fingers cup me as if I were all breasts. Her clever right hand is at my back counting vertebrae. She takes off the stiff nurse's cap and nuzzles my solar plexus. Into my middle she hums, "I'm as corny as Kansas in August . . ." The vibrations go deep. She responds to me. "There," I gasp, "right there." I am overcome as if by Valium. As I moan she moves me down on the cracking vinyl couch. Her lips, teeth, and tongue fire between my ribs. She hums Muzak and the room spins until I sight the pamphlet clinging to a bobby pin. In my ecstasy, I see the diagram of cholesterol, in peaks and valleys, nipping at blood that makes its way, like a hero, through the narrow places.

When she lets me up, I am bruised but feeling wonderful. Her lips are colorless from the pressure she has exerted upon me. I start to take off my trousers. She stays my hand at the belt buckle, kisses me long. "The oath," she whispers.

"I'm cured," I say. "Forget him. Forget the urine and the blood. Look." I beat my chest like Tarzan, I spit across the room into a tiny bronze ashtray.

"I'll pack," she says. She goes into PRIVATE while I pick out a few *Reader's Digests* for the road, *Today's Health* for the bathroom. She returns carrying a centrifuge and a rack of test tubes. We embrace, then I bend to help with her things.

"Don't be cruel," she whispers, "to a heart that's true . . ."

On the way out we throw a kiss to the pharmacist and my blood slips through.

THANK YOU, M'AM

1958

SHE WAS A LARGE WOMAN with a large purse that had everything in it but a hammer and nails. It had a long strap, and she carried it slung across her shoulder. It was about eleven o'clock at night, dark, and she was walking alone, when a boy ran up behind her and tried to snatch her purse. The strap broke with the sudden single tug the boy gave it from behind. But the boy's weight and the weight of the purse combined caused him to lose his balance. Instead of taking off full blast as he had hoped, the boy fell on his back on the sidewalk and his legs flew up. The large woman simply turned around and kicked him right square in his blue-jeaned sitter. Then she reached down, picked the boy up by his shirt front, and shook him until his teeth rattled.

After that the woman said, "Pick up my pocketbook, boy, and give it here."

She still held him tightly. But she bent down enough to permit him to stoop and pick up her purse. Then she said, "Now ain't you ashamed of yourself?"

Firmly gripped by his shirt front, the boy said, "Yes'm."

The woman said, "What did you want to do it for?"

The boy said, "I didn't aim to."

She said, "You a lie!"

By that time two or three people passed, stopped, turned to look, and some stood watching.

"If I turn you loose, will you run?" asked the woman.

"Yes'm," said the boy.

"Then I won't turn you loose," said the woman. She did not release him.

"Lady, I'm sorry," whispered the boy.

"Um-hum! Your face is dirty. I got a great mind to wash your face for you. Ain't you got nobody home to tell you to wash your face?"

"No'm," said the boy.

"Then it will get washed this evening," said the large woman, starting up the street, dragging the frightened boy behind her.

He looked as if he were fourteen or fifteen, frail and willow-wild, in tennis shoes and blue jeans.

The woman said, "You ought to be my son. I would teach you right from wrong. Least I can do right now is to wash your face. Are you hungry?"

"No'm," said the being-dragged boy. "I just want you to turn me loose."

"Was I bothering *you* when I turned that corner?" asked the woman.

"No'm."

"But you put yourself in contact with *me*," said the woman. "If you think that that contact is not going to last awhile, you got another thought coming. When I get through with you, sir, you are going to remember Mrs. Luella Bates Washington Jones."

Sweat popped out on the boy's face and he began to struggle. Mrs. Jones stopped, jerked him around in front of her, put a half nelson about his neck, and continued to drag him up the street. When she got to her door, she dragged the boy inside, down a hall, and into a large kitchenette-furnished room at the rear of the house. She switched on the light and left the door open. The boy could hear other roomers laughing and talking in the large house. Some of their doors were open, too, so he knew he and the woman were not alone. The woman still had him by the neck in the middle of her room.

She said, "What is your name?"

"Roger," answered the boy.

"Then, Roger, you go to that sink and wash your face," said the woman, whereupon she turned him loose—at last. Roger looked at the door—looked at the woman—looked at the door—*and went to the sink*.

"Let the water run until it gets warm," she said. "Here's a clean towel."

"You gonna take me to jail?" asked the boy, bending over the sink.

"Not with that face, I would not take you nowhere," said the woman. "Here I am trying to get home to cook me a bite to eat, and you snatch my pocketbook! Maybe you ain't been to your supper either, late as it be. Have you?"

"There's nobody home at my house," said the boy.

"Then we'll eat," said the woman. "I believe you're hungry — or been hungry — to try to snatch my pocketbook!"

"I want a pair of blue suede shoes," said the boy.

"Well, you didn't have to snatch *my* pocketbook to get some suede shoes," said Mrs. Luella Bates Washington Jones. "You could of asked me."

"M'am?"

The water dripping from his face, the boy looked at her. There was a long pause. A very long pause. After he had dried his face, and not knowing what else to do, dried it again, the boy turned around, wondering what next. The door was open. He could make a dash for it down the hall. He could run, run, run, *run!*

The woman was sitting on the daybed. After a while she said, "I were young once and I wanted things I could not get."

There was another long pause. The boy's mouth opened. Then he frowned, not knowing he frowned.

The woman said, "Um-hum! You thought I was going to say *but*, didn't you? You thought I was going to say, *but I didn't snatch people's pocketbooks*. Well, I wasn't going to say that." Pause. Silence. "I have done things, too, which I would not tell you, son — neither tell God, if He didn't already know. Everybody's got something in common. So you set down while I fix us something to eat. You might run that comb through your hair so you will look presentable."

In another corner of the room behind a screen was a gas plate and an icebox. Mrs. Jones got up and went behind the screen. The woman did not watch the boy to see if he was going to run now, nor did she watch her purse, which she left behind her on the daybed. But the boy took care to sit on the far side of the room, away from the purse, where he thought she could easily see him out of the corner of her eye if she wanted to. He did not trust the woman *not* to trust him. And he did not want to be mistrusted now.

"Do you need somebody to go to the store," asked the boy, "maybe to get some milk or something?"

"Don't believe I do," said the woman, "unless you just want sweet milk yourself. I was going to make cocoa out of this canned milk I got here."

"That will be fine," said the boy.

She heated some lima beans and ham she had in the icebox, made the cocoa, and set the table. The woman did not ask the boy anything about where he lived, or his folks, or anything else that would embarrass him. Instead, as they ate, she told him about her job in a hotel beauty shop that stayed open late, what the work was like, and how all kinds of women came in and out, blonds, redheads, and Spanish. Then she cut him a half of her ten-cent cake.

"Eat some more, son," she said.

When they were finished eating, she got up and said, "Now here, take this ten dollars and buy yourself some blue suede shoes. And next time, do not make the mistake of latching onto *my* pocket book *nor nobody else's* — because shoes got by devilish ways will burn your feet. I got to get my rest now. But from here on in, son, I hope you will behave yourself."

She led him down the hall to the front door and opened it. "Good night! Behave yourself, boy!" she said, looking out into the street as he went down the steps.

The boy wanted to say something other than, "Thank you, M'am," to Mrs. Luella Bates Washington Jones, but although his lips moved, he couldn't even say that as he turned at the foot of the barren stoop and looked up at the large woman in the door. Then she shut the door.

POPULAR MECHANICS

1982

EARLY THAT DAY the weather turned and the snow was melting into dirty water. Streaks of it ran down from the little shoulder-high window that faced the back yard. Cars slushed by on the street outside, where it was getting dark. But it was getting dark on the inside too.

He was in the bedroom pushing clothes into a suitcase when she came to the door.

I'm glad you're leaving! I'm glad you're leaving! she said. Do you hear?

He kept on putting his things into the suitcase.

Son of a bitch! I'm so glad you're leaving! She began to cry. You can't even look at me in the face, can you?

Then she noticed the baby's picture on the bed and picked it up.

He looked at her and she wiped her eyes and stared at him before turning and going back to the living room.

Bring that back, he said.

Just get your things and get out, she said.

He did not answer. He fastened the suitcase, put on his coat, looked around the bedroom before turning off the light. Then he went out to the living room.

She stood in the doorway of the little kitchen, holding the baby.

I want the baby, he said.

Are you crazy?

No, but I want the baby. I'll get someone to come by for his things.

You're not touching this baby, she said.

The baby had begun to cry and she uncovered the blanket from around his head.

Oh, oh, she said, looking at the baby.

He moved toward her.

For God's sake! she said. She took a step back into the kitchen.

I want the baby.

Get out of here!

She turned and tried to hold the baby over in a corner behind the stove.

But he came up. He reached across the stove and tightened his hands on the baby.

Let go of him, he said.

Get away, get away! she cried.

The baby was red-faced and screaming. In the scuffle they knocked down a flowerpot that hung behind the stove.

He crowded her into the wall then, trying to break her grip. He held on to the baby and pushed with all his weight.

Let go of him, he said.

Don't, she said. You're hurting the baby, she said.

I'm not hurting the baby, he said.

The kitchen window gave no light. In the near-dark he worked on her fisted fingers with one hand and with the other hand he gripped the screaming baby up under an arm near the shoulder.

She felt her fingers being forced open. She felt the baby going from her.

No! she screamed just as her hands came loose.

She would have it, this baby. She grabbed for the baby's other arm. She caught the baby around the wrist and leaned back.

But he would not let go. He felt the baby slipping out of his hands and he pulled back very hard.

In this manner, the issue was decided.

TURNING

THREE ELDERLY LADIES, elegantly turned with jewels on their elongated necks, helped one another to hobble from the taxi to the walk. They came toward the house, their white curled heads nodding, anticipated by the little boy watching from behind the curtain. They looked like a motion picture of three swans gliding and bobbing on a pale lake, but caught in a faulty, halting projector that was chewing up the frames of their finale. It was as though these fine creatures could not be crippled; it was merely the illusion of a flawed presentation of them.

Inside the house they settled into Queen Anne chairs; prim but for their knees which would no longer stick together, they looked like great water birds, forced not only onto dry land but into human forms that did not suit them. The little boy pushed his trucks on the carpet near them, making highway sound effects for their entertainment. He peeked into the darkness under their skirts, which was like looking into his View Master without the reels. They turned their heads from side to side examining the boy, like birds who have an eye to each hemisphere.

The boy's mother brought out a decorated cake with four candles, bone china cups for the tea, and a glass of milk with a strawberry in it.

"Why, this cake says 'Robert'; the cake has the same name as you," said the first old lady to the boy.

He giggled and fell back on the carpet. "No," he shrieked, "it's my birthday, Louise Dear." He followed religiously their pet names for one another, pronouncing them with formality and deference. They were Louise Dear, Olivia Sweet, and Ruth Love. Every time he said those names it gave them rare little reverberations of pleasure in their old flesh, like spreading circles on the surface of water.

"Why then," said Ruth, "this pretty box must be for you. It says, 'Happy Birthday.' " Robert shredded the wrapping paper and found a shirt bearing an appliqued lion's face with a yarn mane on the front and a cloth tail attached to the back. Robert put it on over his other shirt. He got the buttons wrong; he watched Ruth's fingers work to correct his carelessness. Her knobby fingers looked like bleached, brittle twigs. Robert wondered if they could push the buttons through, not realizing that the lion had been crafted by those same fingers.

His mother lit the candles, the ladies sang, "Happy Birthday, Dear Robert" like the air rushing from leaky organs. Olivia gave him a package of crayons that willfully changed colors as they were used. Robert drew a picture of them on the large drawing paper that accompanied the crayons. The ladies smiled to see themselves emerge as armless, floating shapes, with stick fingers at the sides of ruffled heads, each finished with a distinct and careful navel. He gave the drawing to Olivia.

"We never expected to *receive* a beautiful present on *your* birthday," she thanked him. They passed the drawing around and cooed at it.

Louise gave him a package with so many bows it looked like a little animal. Robert chose to keep it as it was, not to look inside yet. The ladies laughed and winked.

He served them cake which they faced as birds would face seeds and crumbs smeared with sticky frosting. Robert waited until they politely abandoned the cake; he leaned into Olivia Sweet's lap, wadding her silky dress into his moist fists, "Let's have a story now." His mother gathered the dishes and left them to their ceremonies.

"This is the story," she said vaguely, "of 'The Emperor Who Had No Skin.' "

"No clothes," corrected Louise.

"No flesh," agreed Ruth.

Olivia's way with stories was to take a great solid wall of a story and knock a chink in it with one word, making it possible and necessary to peer through the chink to the other side. Her story, then, was already told; the chink in the old story was itself the new one. They had only now to find it out by playing it out.

"Once upon a time," she said, "there was an Emperor who had no skin. He looked like ivory carvings and cream-colored satin cushions all laced together with fine red and blue threads. The Emperor would have been happy but for two things: he wondered why he, alone, had no skin, and he longed for a wife. As he was very rich, very wise, and extremely handsome (the other ladies arched their eyebrows), he came to realize that he himself was a riddle. So he said, whatever princess should answer his riddle should become his wife. At last, a beautiful princess with golden hair and a blue brocaded gown came to his palace . . ."

"And," Louise took up, "she said to the King, 'I have woven a skin for you from my own golden hair; just pull it tightly at the top, once you're in, by this green cord I plaited from the vines that cling to the church walls. For the riddle of your skin is that it must embrace you like a loving wife and find you like a vine finding its way to a tower'. . . ."

Olivia, who knew that stories if not tended could trickle away, broke in harshly, "But the Emperor tried on the skin and knotted the cord and looked in the mirror. He said, 'I look like a mesh bag of nuts and oranges tied with a shoestring in this skin.' He tore it from himself and the princess left weeping."

Louise blinked several times in the silence until Ruth said excitedly, discreetly dabbing at the bit of saliva escaping the corner of her painted mouth, "But another beautiful princess came to the Emperor and told him that she understood his riddle. To be without his skin, she explained, was to be closer to the world and yet without skin was to never feel its petty pricks and pains. And this princess," said Ruth triumphantly, "rolled off her skin like removing a silk stocking, so that she could be like the Emperor and become his bride . . ."

"Yes," Olivia intervened, "and spilled herself out onto the Emperor's royal carpet. It took twenty royal maids twenty days, picking her up and removing her by the thimblesfull."

Louise and Ruth looked at Olivia. Robert, hearing only the story told but not noticing the story between the tellers, said, "Another princess came."

"Yes," Olivia said, "tell us, Robert, about this princess."

"This princess," said Robert, "was red and blue and green and beautiful, and said to the King, 'I'm going to give you a good skin to wear.' And she took off the skin of her best and favorite and big dog and gave it to the King. The dog died but the King said, 'I like this skin because it is fluffy and because it gives me a tail to wag.' And he did."

"But Robert," said Louise, "that doesn't answer the riddle."

"Oh, but it does," said Olivia, to Robert's relief. They all waited for her to continue. At last she said, "You tell us, Robert." The other ladies knew then that the story had turned to one that Olivia could not swim.

"Well," said Robert, "you know, Olivia Sweet, the riddle is that animals have good skins and people would like tails."

"There you have it," said Olivia.

"But," complained Ruth, "*why* was the Emperor without a skin in the first place? That's part of the riddle."

"So we could find him one," said Robert confidently.

"Insufficient, Robert," said Olivia, and he sensed that she meant for him to say more.

"So he could look at the inside of himself before he got married to a princess?" he asked.

"Excellent!" exclaimed Olivia, and seemed about to soar into the air. "I didn't know the answer to that riddle myself," she confided, and the other two applauded the boy.

"Don't ever forget," said Louise, "to look at the inside of yourself before you marry a princess."

"And," said Robert, unable to stop the momentum of his success, "if you wait a long time for a skin you get one with a tail." They laughed and petted him, but he perceived that his last answer was not as good as his former one. He wondered why, as he himself would trade off a dozen princesses for one tail.

The ladies rose to leave. He kissed them on their thin, powdered cheeks and felt how their skins didn't quite fit them and wondered. As Olivia kissed him she said, "Don't ever, Robert, look for morals after you find out riddles."

Squeezed into their taxi, they looked like large fowl stuffed into a crate for market. They waved their white gloves at the house toward the space pulled in the curtain.

SAY YES

1985

THEY WERE DOING the dishes, his wife washing while he dried. He'd washed the night before. Unlike most men he knew, he really pitched in on the housework. A few months earlier he'd overheard a friend of his wife's congratulate her on having such a considerate husband, and he thought, *I try*. Helping out with the dishes was a way he had of showing how considerate he was.

They talked about different things and somehow got on the subject of whether white people should marry black people. He said that all things considered, he thought it was a bad idea.

"Why?" she asked.

Sometimes his wife got this look where she pinched her brows together and bit her lower lip and stared down at something. When he saw her like this he knew he should keep his mouth shut, but he never did. Actually it made him talk more. She had that look now.

"Why?" she asked again, and stood there with her hand inside a bowl, not washing it but just holding it above the water.

"Listen," he said, "I went to school with blacks, and I've worked with blacks and lived on the same street with blacks, and we've always gotten along just fine. I don't need you coming along now and implying that I'm a racist."

"I didn't imply anything," she said, and began washing the bowl again, turning it around in her hand as though she were shaping it. "I just don't see what's wrong with a white person marrying a black person, that's all."

"They don't come from the same culture as we do. Listen to them sometime—they even have their own language. That's okay with me, I *like* hearing them talk"—he did; for some reason it always made him feel happy—"but it's different. A person from their culture and a person from our culture could never really *know* each other."

"Like you know me?" his wife asked.

"Yes. Like I know you."

"But if they love each other," she said. She was washing faster now, not looking at him.

Oh boy, he thought. He said, "Don't take my word for it. Look at the statistics. Most of those marriages break up."

"Statistics." She was piling dishes on the drainboard at a terrific rate, just swiping at them with the cloth. Many of them were greasy, and there were flecks of food between the tines of the forks. "All right," she said, "what about foreigners? I suppose you think the same thing about two foreigners getting married."

"Yes," he said, "as a matter of fact I do. How can you understand someone who comes from a completely different background?"

"Different," said his wife. "Not the same, like us."

"Yes, different," he snapped, angry with her for resorting to this trick of repeating his words so that they sounded crass, or hypocritical. "These are dirty," he said, and dumped all the silverware back into the sink.

The water had gone flat and gray. She stared down at it, her lips pressed tight together, then plunged her hands under the surface. "Oh!" she cried, and jumped back. She took her right hand by the wrist and held it up. Her thumb was bleeding.

"Ann, don't move," he said. "Stay right there." He ran upstairs to the bathroom and rummaged in the medicine chest for alcohol, cotton, and a Band-Aid. When he came back down she was leaning against the refrigerator with her eyes closed, still holding her hand. He took the hand and dabbed at her thumb with the cotton. The bleeding had stopped. He squeezed it to see how deep the wound was and a single drop of blood welled up, trembling and bright, and fell to the floor. Over the thumb she stared at him accusingly. "It's shallow," he said. "Tomorrow you won't even know it's there." He hoped that she appreciated how quickly he had come to her aid. He'd acted out of concern for her, with no thought of getting anything in return, but now the thought occurred to him that it would be a nice gesture on her part not to start up that conversation again, as he was tired of it. "I'll finish up here," he said. "You go and relax."

"That's okay," she said. "I'll dry."

He began to wash the silverware again, giving a lot of attention to the forks.

"So," she said, "you wouldn't have married me if I'd been black."

"For Christ's sake, Ann!"

"Well, that's what you said, didn't you?"

"No, I did not. The whole question is ridiculous. If you had been black we probably wouldn't even have met. You would have had your friends and I would have had mine. The only black girl I ever really knew was my partner in the debating club, and I was already going out with you by then."

"But if we had met, and I'd been black?"

"Then you probably would have been going out with a black guy." He picked up the rinsing nozzle and sprayed the silverware. The water was so hot that the metal darkened to pale blue, then turned silver again.

"Let's say I wasn't," she said. "Let's say I am black and unattached and we meet and fall in love."

He glanced over at her. She was watching him and her eyes were bright. "Look," he said, taking a reasonable tone, "this is stupid. If you were black you wouldn't be you." As he said this he realized it was absolutely true. There was no possible way of arguing with the fact that she would not be herself if she were black. So he said it again: "If you were black you wouldn't be you."

"I know," she said, "but let's just say."

He took a deep breath. He had won the argument but he still felt cornered. "Say what?" he asked.

"That I'm black, but still me, and we fall in love. Will you marry me?"

He thought about it.

"Well?" she said, and stepped close to him. Her eyes were even brighter. "Will you marry me?"

"I'm thinking," he said.

"You won't, I can tell. You're going to say no."

"Let's not move too fast on this," he said. "There are lots of things to consider. We don't want to do something we would regret for the rest of our lives."

"No more considering. Yes or no."

"Since you put it that way—"

"Yes or no."

"Jesus, Ann. All right. No."

She said. "Thank you," and walked from the kitchen into the living room. A moment later he heard her turning the pages of a magazine. He knew that she was too angry to be actually reading it, but she didn't snap through the pages the way he would have done. She turned them slowly, as if she were studying every word. She was demonstrating her indifference to him, and it had the effect he knew she wanted it to have. It hurt him.

He had no choice but to demonstrate his indifference to her. Quietly, thoroughly, he washed the rest of the dishes. Then he dried them and put them away. He wiped the counters and the stove and scoured the linoleum where the drop of blood had fallen. While he was at it, he decided, he might as well mop the whole floor. When he was done the kitchen looked new, the way it looked when they were first shown the house, before they had ever lived here.

He picked up the garbage pail and went outside. The night was clear and he could see a few stars to the west, where the lights of the town didn't blur them out. On El Camino the traffic was steady and light, peaceful as a river. He felt ashamed that he had let his wife get him into a fight. In another thirty years or so they would both be dead. What would all that stuff matter then? He thought of the years they had spent together, and how close they were, and how well they knew each other, and his throat tightened so that he could hardly breathe. His face and neck began to tingle. Warmth flooded his chest. He stood there for a while, enjoying these sensations, then picked up the pail and went out the back gate.

The two mutts from down the street had pulled over the garbage can again. One of them was rolling around on his back and the other had something in her mouth. Growling, she tossed it into the air, leaped up and caught it, growled again and whipped her head from side to side. When they saw him coming they trotted away with short, mincing steps. Normally he would heave rocks at them, but this time he let them go.

The house was dark when he came back inside. She was in the bathroom. He stood outside the door and called her name. He heard bottles clinking, but she didn't answer him. "Ann, I'm really sorry," he said. "I'll make it up to you, I promise."

"How?" she asked.

He wasn't expecting this. But from a sound in her voice, a level and definite note that was strange to him, he knew that he had to come up with the right answer. He leaned against the door. "I'll marry you," he whispered.

"We'll see," she said. "Go on to bed. I'll be out in a minute."

He undressed and got under the covers. Finally he heard the bathroom door open and close.

"Turn off the light," she said from the hallway.

"What?"

"Turn off the light."

He reached over and pulled the chain on the bedside lamp. The room went dark. "All right," he said. He lay there, but nothing happened. "All right," he said again. Then he heard a movement across the room. He sat up, but he couldn't see a thing. The room was silent. His heart pounded the way it had on their first night together, the way it still did when he woke at a noise in the darkness and waited to hear it again — the sound of someone moving through the house, a stranger.

THE HIT MAN

1980

Early Years

THE HIT MAN'S EARLY YEARS are complicated by the black bag that he wears over his head. Teachers correct his pronunciation, the coach criticizes his attitude, the principal dresses him down for branding preschoolers with a lit cigarette. He is a poor student. At lunch he sits alone, feeding bell peppers and salami into the dark slot of his mouth. In the hallways, wiry young athletes snatch at the black hood and slap the back of his head. When he is thirteen he is approached by the captain of the football team, who pins him down and attempts to remove the hood. The Hit Man wastes him. Five years, says the judge.

Back on the Street

The Hit Man is back on the street in two months.

First Date

The girl's name is Cynthia. The Hit Man pulls up in front of her apartment in his father's hearse. (The Hit Man's father, whom he loathes and abominates, is a mortician. At breakfast the Hit Man's father had slapped the cornflakes from his son's bowl. The son threatened to waste his father. He did not, restrained no doubt by considerations of filial loyalty and the deep-seated taboos against patricide that permeate the universal unconscious.)

Cynthia's father has silver sideburns and plays tennis. He responds to the Hit Man's knock, expresses surprise at the Hit Man's appearance. The Hit Man takes Cynthia by the elbow, presses a twenty into her father's palm, and disappears into the night.

Father's Death

At breakfast the Hit Man slaps the cornflakes from his father's bowl. Then wastes him.

Mother's Death

The Hit Man is in his early twenties. He shoots pool, lifts weights and drinks milk from the carton. His mother is in the hospital, dying of cancer or heart disease. The priest wears black. So does the Hit Man.

First Job

Porfirio Buñoz, a Cuban financier, invites the Hit Man to lunch. I hear you're looking for work, says Buñoz.

That's right, says the Hit Man.

Peas

The Hit Man does not like peas. They are too difficult to balance on the fork.

Talk Show

The Hit Man waits in the wings, the white slash of a cigarette scarring the midnight black of his head and upper torso. The makeup girl has done his mouth and eyes, brushed the nap of his hood. He has been briefed. The guest who precedes him is a pediatrician. A planetary glow washes the stage where the host and the pediatrician, separated by a potted palm, cross their legs and discuss the little disturbances of infants and toddlers.

After the station break the Hit Man finds himself squeezed into a director's chair, white lights in his eyes. The talk-show host is a baby-faced man in his early forties. He smiles like God and all His Angels. Well, he says. So you're a hit man. Tell me — I've always wanted to know — what does it feel like to hit someone?

Death of Mateo Maria Buñoz

The body of Mateo María Buñoz, the cousin and business associate of a prominent financier, is discovered down by the docks on a hot summer morning. Mist rises from the water like steam, there is the smell of fish. A large black bird perches on the dead man's forehead.

Marriage

Cynthia and the Hit Man stand at the altar, side by side. She is wearing a white satin gown and lace veil. The Hit Man has rented a tuxedo, extra-large, and a silk-lined black-velvet hood.

. . . Till death do you part, says the priest.

Moods

The Hit Man is moody, unpredictable. Once, in a luncheonette, the waitress brought him the meatloaf special but forgot to eliminate the peas. There was a spot of gravy on the Hit Man's hood, about where his chin should be. He looked up at the waitress, his eyes like pins behind the triangular slots, and wasted her.

Another time he went to the track with $25, came back with $1800. He stopped at a cigar shop. As he stepped out of the shop a wino tugged at his sleeve and solicited a quarter. The Hit Man reached into his pocket, extracted the $1800 and handed it to the wino. Then wasted him.

First Child

A boy. The Hit Man is delighted. He leans over the edge of the playpen and molds the tiny fingers around the grip of a nickel-plated derringer. The gun is loaded with blanks — the Hit Man wants the boy to get used to the noise. By the time he is four the boy has mastered the rudiments of Tae Kwon Do, can stick a knife in the wall from a distance of ten feet and shoot a moving target with either hand. The Hit Man rests his broad palm on the boy's head. You're going to make the Big Leagues, Tiger, he says.

Work

He flies to Cincinnati. To L.A. To Boston. To London. The stewardesses get to know him.

Half an Acre and a Garage

The Hit Man is raking leaves, amassing great brittle piles of them. He is wearing a black T-shirt, cut off at the shoulders, and a cotton work hood, also black. Cynthia is edging the flowerbed, his son playing in the grass. The Hit Man waves to his neighbors as they drive by. The neighbors wave back.

When he has scoured the lawn to his satisfaction, the Hit Man draws the smaller leaf-hummocks together in a single mound the size of a pickup truck. Then he bends to ignite it with his lighter. Immediately, flames leap back from the leaves, cut channels through the pile, engulf it in a ball of fire. The Hit Man stands back, hands folded beneath the great meaty biceps. At his side is the three-headed dog. He bends to pat each of the heads, smoke and sparks raging against the sky.

Stalking the Streets of the City

He is stalking the streets of the city, collar up, brim down. It is late at night. He stalks past department stores, small businesses, parks, and gas stations. Past apartments, picket fences, picture windows. Dogs growl in the shadows, then slink away. He could hit any of us.

Retirement

A group of businessman-types — sixtyish, seventyish, portly, diamond rings, cigars, liver spots — throws him a party. Porfirio Buñoz, now in his eighties, makes a speech and presents the Hit Man with a gilded scythe. The Hit Man thanks him, then retires to the lake, where he can be seen in his speedboat, skating out over the blue, hood rippling in the breeze.

Death

He is stricken, shrunken, half his former self. He lies propped against the pillows at Mercy Hospital, a bank of gentians drooping round the bed. Tubes run into the hood at the nostril openings, his eyes are clouded and red, sunk deep behind the triangular slots. The priest wears black. So does the Hit Man.

On the other side of town the Hit Man's son is standing before the mirror of a shop that specializes in Hit Man attire. Trying on his first hood.

A QUESTIONNAIRE
FOR RUDOLPH GORDON

1) HOW MANY TIMES was this questionnaire forwarded through the mail before it caught up with you?

2) List the various things that had occupied your mind during the morning before it arrived.

3) How many of your father's paintings have you now sold?

4) Do you sense that you are nearing the end of your "resources"?

5) Do you still dream of that little boat, nosing at the dock as if it were alive and waiting for you?

6) Did you sell the painting in which your father had put the boat?

7) This painting also showed a woman, leaning over and scooping up sand; who was the little boy she was facing?

8) Do you remember that heavy cloth bathing suit, with its straps and the heavy, scratchy wool against your skin?

9) What was your mother saying as your father painted the picture?

10) Why had you been crying?

11) Were you aware of his sitting back there, farther up the bank, painting as your mother talked to you?

12) The woman had been singing a song to calm you down; what was this song?

13) Was the woman truly your mother?

14) What if she lied to you; what if all your life she merely *pretended* to be your mother?

15) What if the man painting the picture with both of you in it (not to mention the little rowboat) was also a Pretender?

16) Why would they want to deceive you like that?

17) Why were you crying before your "mother" sang the little song to calm you down and amuse you?

18) Can you remember times when they talked to you lovingly, and you felt totally secure with them . . . only to see her eyes slip nervously to the side, to look at *him* . . . and only for him to look troubled, worried, as if they had both gotten beyond their depth?

19) Can you remember the woman saying, "No, we shouldn't have done it," and the man answering, "Anyway, it's too late now to change"?

20) The little beach cottage you stayed in was painted blood red; its porch and shutters were painted white; what was behind the little cottage?

21) Do you remember climbing this steep hill one day, and having the woman cry out in fear that you would fall and hurt yourself?

22) Can you remember the smell of the pine needles and the rough warmth of the stones as you climbed steadily upward, and then turned to look into the wind, at the bay?

23) She was smaller than you, down below; and the man was smaller, too, because they existed far beneath your feet; what did you say when they begged for you to come down?

24) Why did you say "never," instead of "no"?

25) Why were you not afraid?

26) What did you see in the bay?

27) What was the name of the great ship that lay like a shadow in the haze of water?

28) Are you certain you cannot remember the shapes of the letters of her name, so that *now* you can read what was then only the mystery of print?

29) Why is the name of this ship unimportant?

30) Were you surprised when you looked down and saw that he had climbed so near, without your being aware?

31) Can you remember the dark expression of anger on his face as he reached out to clasp your ankle?

32) Did he hurt you, carrying you so roughly down through the rocks and pine trees to the back of the cottage?

33) What was the song you could hear so faintly from the cabin next door?

34) Was this the first phonograph you can remember ever hearing?

35) Was this the song the woman sang to you later, after you were taken down to the shore?

36) Were you crying because of the scolding you received for climbing the steep hill in back?

37) Do you remember the old smell of salt and dead fish that drifted in the air?

38) Where were your real parents?

39) Had you been kidnapped?

40) Has this thought ever occurred to you before?

41) Do you remember the toy revolver and holster you wore?

42) Do you remember the little suitcase they let you carry?

43) Do you remember the photograph of a man and woman smiling out at you in your bedroom?

44) What was written on the photograph?

45) Did the man and woman read it to you, so that you are certain it said, "From Mom and Dad with Love"?

46) Why can't you remember the faces in the photograph?

47) Was your *real* father a painter?

48) Was this man . . . *could* this man have been your real father?

49) Could the woman have been your real mother?

50) But how can you be certain they lied to you in other matters?

51) Don't we all lie to one another?

52) Isn't the lie we tell our children one expression of love?

53) Isn't it also an expression of our fear?

54) Can there be love without fear?

55) Is it possible that this man and this woman, even though they remember the specific moment you came out of *her* body, are still not certain that you are *their son*?

56) What is a father?

57) What is a mother?

58) What is a son?

59) Why have you refused to answer these questions?

60) Why have you sold so many of your father's paintings?

61) Why do you need so much money to live?

62) Why can't you find a job?

63) When did the woman die?

64) Were you there when her eyes clouded over?

65) Were you present when your father was run down by the trolley car in the city?

66) Did you know that his legs and back were terribly mutilated in the accident, and he was dead before the ambulance arrived, hemorrhaging brilliant red streams against the black asphalt of the street?

67) In your opinion, did he think of you as he was dying?

68) Did your mother think of you as she was dying?

69) Why do you think you cannot answer such questions?

70) Do you see yourself in the painting with the little boy, and the mother scooping sand up in her hand, and the rowboat nudging at the dock, like a small hungry animal desiring suck?

71) What color is the sky in the painting?

72) Why is it darker than the land?

73) Why is it darker than the water?

74) Have you sold this painting yet?

75) Is it the last of your father's paintings in your possession?

76) When you do sell it, will something break loose and drift away?

77) Will the hand be seized by a spasm, and will sand spill from it?

78) Will the child cry again, staring out upon an empty scene, while the ship fades into pale gray, leaking color out of the letters of its name?

79) Who is in the red cottage now?

80) Why do you think it is empty or torn down?

81) If your father were alive, could he reach you now and carry you back to safety?

82) Could the blood on the asphalt be thought of as your father's last and most original composition?

83) Were your father and mother as lonely as children in those last moments?

84) Would you have helped them in some way *if you could have been sure*?

85) Why do you pretend you don't know *sure of what*?

86) Have you never doubted their authenticity before?

87) Aren't there other reasons than kidnapping for stealing a child?

88) Perhaps they didn't know how you came about, and felt guilty?

89) Who can say where these things all begin?

90) Don't you understand that "these things" are the cabin, the steep hill, the boat, the sand, the man, the woman, the child?

91) Were you aware that the painting was omitted in 90?

92) If you sell it, finally, will you have enough money?

93) Don't you have the pride and the skill to make your own way in life?

94) Why does that expression remind you of him?

95) If you sell it finally, will you ever sleep again?

96) Why do you think there is no one now to sing a song to you and dry your tears and pretend to be your mother?

97) When will you stop lying in your answers?

98) Do you think even *this* would turn us away, if our hands and hearts and mouths were not packed with earth?

99) Do you truly believe that some things do not abide, beyond the habit and the way of the world?

100) Truly, this is enough for now, and somehow you must rest content with this personal questionnaire.

Love always,
Mom and Dad

I SEE YOU NEVER

THE SOFT KNOCK CAME at the kitchen door, and when Mrs. O'Brian opened it, there on the back porch were her best tenant, Mr. Ramirez, and two police officers, one on each side of him. Mr. Ramirez just stood there, walled in and small.

"Why, Mr. Ramirez!" said Mrs. O'Brian.

Mr. Ramirez was overcome. He did not seem to have words to explain.

He had arrived at Mrs. O'Brian's rooming house more than two years earlier and had lived there ever since. He had come by bus from Mexico City to San Diego and had then gone up to Los Angeles. There he had found the clean little room, with glossy blue linoleum, and pictures and calendars on the flowered walls, and Mrs. O'Brian as the strict but kindly landlady. During the war he had worked at the airplane factory and made parts for the planes that flew off somewhere, and even now, after the war, he still held his job. From the first he had made big money. He saved some of it, and he got drunk only once a week — a privilege that, to Mrs. O'Brian's way of thinking, every good workingman deserved, unquestioned and unreprimanded.

Inside Mrs. O'Brian's kitchen, pies were baking in the oven. Soon the pies would come out with complexions like Mr. Ramirez' — brown and shiny and crisp, with slits in them for the air almost like the slits of Mr. Ramirez' dark eyes. The kitchen smelled good. The policemen leaned forward, lured by the odor. Mr. Ramirez gazed at his feet, as if they had carried him into all this trouble.

"What happened, Mr. Ramirez?" asked Mrs. O'Brian.

Behind Mrs. O'Brian, as he lifted his eyes, Mr. Ramirez saw the long table laid with clean white linen and set with a platter, cool, shining glasses, a water pitcher with ice cubes floating inside it, a bowl of fresh potato salad and one of bananas and oranges, cubed and sugared. At this table sat Mrs. O'Brian's children — her three grown sons, eating and conversing, and her two younger daughters, who were staring at the policemen as they ate.

"I have been here thirty months," said Mr. Ramirez quietly, looking at Mrs. O'Brian's plump hands.

"That's six months too long," said one policeman. "He only had a temporary visa. We've just got around to looking for him."

Soon after Mr. Ramirez had arrived he bought a radio for his little room; evenings, he turned it up very loud and enjoyed it. And he bought a wrist watch and enjoyed that too. And on many nights he had walked silent streets and seen the bright clothes in the windows and bought some of them, and he had seen the jewels and bought some of them for his few lady friends. And he had gone to picture shows five nights a week for a while. Then, also, he had ridden the streetcars — all night some nights — smelling the electricity, his dark eyes moving over the advertisements, feeling the wheels rumble under him, watching the little sleeping houses and big hotels slip by. Besides that, he had gone to large restaurants, where he had eaten many-course dinners, and to the opera and the theater. And he had bought a car, which later, when he forgot to pay for it, the dealer had driven off angrily from in front of the rooming house.

"So here I am," said Mr. Ramirez now, "to tell you I must give up my room, Mrs. O'Brian. I come to get my baggage and clothes and go with these men."

"Back to Mexico?"

"Yes. To Lagos. That is a little town north of Mexico City."

"I'm sorry, Mr. Ramirez."

"I'm packed," said Mr. Ramirez hoarsely, blinking his dark eyes rapidly and moving his hands helplessly before him. The policemen did not touch him. There was no necessity for that.

"Here is the key, Mrs. O'Brian," Mr. Ramirez said. "I have my bag already."

Mrs. O'Brian, for the first time, noticed a suitcase standing behind him on the porch.

Mr. Ramirez looked in again at the huge kitchen, at the bright silver cutlery and the young people eating and the shining waxed floor. He turned and looked for a long moment at the apartment house next door, rising up three stories, high and beautiful. He looked at the balconies and fire escapes and back-porch stairs, at the lines of laundry snapping in the wind.

"You've been a good tenant," said Mrs. O'Brian.

"Thank you, thank you, Mrs. O'Brian," he said softly. He closed his eyes.

Mrs. O'Brian stood holding the door half open. One of her sons, behind her, said that her dinner was getting cold, but she shook her head at him and turned back to Mr. Ramirez. She remembered a visit she had once made to some Mexican border towns — the hot days, the endless crickets leaping and falling or lying dead and brittle like the small cigars in the shopwindows, and the canals taking river water out to the farms, the dirt roads, the scorched landscape. She remembered the silent towns, the warm beer, the hot, thick foods each day. She remembered the slow, dragging horses and the parched jack rabbits on the road. She remembered the iron mountains and the dusty valleys and the ocean beaches that spread hundreds of miles with no sound but the waves — no cars, no buildings, nothing.

"I'm sure sorry, Mr. Ramirez," she said.

"I don't want to go back, Mrs. O'Brian," he said weakly. "I like it here, I want to stay here. I've worked, I've got money. I look all right, don't I? And I don't want to go back!"

"I'm sorry, Mr. Ramirez," she said. "I wish there was something I could do."

"Mrs. O'Brian!" he cried suddenly, tears rolling out from under his eyelids. He reached out his hands and took her hand fervently, shaking it, wringing it, holding to it. "Mrs. O'Brian, I see you never, I see you never!"

The policemen smiled at this, but Mr. Ramirez did not notice it, and they stopped smiling very soon.

"Goodbye, Mrs. O'Brian. You have been good to me. Oh, goodbye Mrs. O'Brian. I see you never!"

The policemen waited for Mr. Ramirez to turn, pick up his suitcase, and walk away. Then they followed him, tipping their caps to Mrs. O'Brian. She watched them go down the porch steps. Then she shut the door quietly and went slowly back to her chair at the table. She pulled the chair out and sat down. She picked up the shining knife and fork and started once more upon her steak.

"Hurry up, Mom," said one of the sons. "It'll be cold."

Mrs. O'Brian took one bite and chewed on it for a long, slow time; then she stared at the closed door. She laid down her knife and fork.

"What's wrong, Ma?" asked her son.

"I just realized," said Mrs. O'Brian — she put her hand to her face — "I'll never see Mr. Ramirez again."

CHILDREN OF STRIKERS

THEY WERE WALKING, the twelve-year-old girl and the younger bleached-looking boy, by the edge of the black chemical river. A dreadful stink rose off the waters but they scarcely noticed it, scuffling along in the hard sawgrass among the stones. It was a dim day, rain-threatening, and the girl's dun face and dark eyes looked even darker than usual. The boy trailed some little distance behind her and would stop now and again and shade his eyes and look upstream and down. But there was no more reason for him to look about than there was for him to shade his eyes.

Occasionally the girl would bend down and look at something that caught her eye. A scrap of tin, a bit of drowned dirty cloth, jetsam thrown up from the river that poured through the paper factory above and then by the mill settlement behind them. This, "Fiberville," was a quadruple row of dingy little bungalows, and it was where the two of them lived. In the girl's dark face was something harsh and tired, as if she had foretold all her life and found it joyless.

Now she reached down and plucked something off a blackened wale of sand. She glanced at it briefly and thrust it into the pocket of her thin green sweater.

The boy had seen. He caught up with her and demanded to have a look.

"Look at what?" she asked.

"What you found, let me see it."

"It ain't nothing you'd care about."

"How do you know what I care? Let me have a look."

She turned to face him, gazed directly into his sallow annoying face, those milky blue eyes. "I ain't going to let you," she said.

He gave her a stare, then turned aside and spat. "Well, hell then, it ain't nothing."

"That's right." She walked on and he kept behind. But she knew he was gauging his chances, considering when to run and snatch it out of her pocket. When she heard his footsteps coming sneaky-fast, she wheeled and, without taking aim, delivered such a ringing slap that his eyes watered and his face flushed.

"God damn you," he said, but he didn't cry.

"I've told you to keep your hands away from me. I told you I wouldn't say it again."

"You ain't so much," he said. "I seen better." But his voice, though resentful, was not bitter.

They walked on a space and she began to relent. "It's a foot," she said.

"What you mean? What kind of foot?"

"It's a baby's foot."

"No!" He glared at her. "I ain't believing that."

"You can believe just whatever little thing you want to."

"I ain't believing you found no baby's foot. Let me see it."

"No."

"Well then, you ain't got nothing. . . . How big is it?"

"It's real tiny."

"Gaw," he said. It had seized his imagination. "Somebody probably kilt it."

"Might be."

"They must of kilt it and cut it up in little bits and throwed it in the river." He was wild with the thought of it. "It was some girl got knocked up and her boy friend made her do it."

She shrugged.

"Ain't that awful to think about? A poor little baby. . . . Come on and show it to me. I got to see that baby foot."

"What'll you give me?"

They marched along, and he struck a mournful air. "Nothing," he said at last. "I ain't got nothing to give."

She stopped and looked at him, surveyed him head to toe with a weary satisfaction. "No, I guess you ain't," she said. "You ain't got a thing."

"Well then, what you got? Nothing but a poor little dead baby's foot that I don't believe you've got anyhow."

Slowly she reached into her pocket and produced it, held it toward him in her open palm, and he leaned forward, breathless, peering. He shivered, almost imperceptibly. Then his face darkened and his eyes grew brighter and he slapped her hand. The foot jumped out of her hand and fell among the grasses.

"That ain't nothing. It's a doll, it's just a doll-baby's foot."

She could tell that he was disappointed but feeling smug too because, after all, he had caught her in the expectable lie. "I never told you it was real." She stopped and retrieved it. It lay pink and soiled in her soiled palm. Bulbous foot and ankle, little toes like beads of water. It looked too small and too separate from the rest of the world to be anything at all.

He took it from her. "I knowed it wasn't no real baby." He became thoughtful, turning it in his fingers. "Hey, look at this."

"I don't see nothing."

He held the tubular stub of it toward her. "Look how smooth it's cut off. It's been cut with a knife."

She touched it and the amputation was as smooth as the mouth of a soft drink bottle. "What's that got to do with anything?"

It had got darker now, drawing on toward the supper hour. Fiberville grew gloomier behind them, though most of the lights were on in the kitchens of the houses.

"Means that somebody went and cut it on purpose. . . ." Another flushed fantasy overcame him. "Say, what if it was a Crazy Man? What if it was a man practicing up before he went and kilt a real baby?"

"It's just some little kid messing around," she said.

"Ain't no kid would have a knife like that." He ran his thumb over the edge of the cut. "Had to be a real *sharp* knife. Or an axe. Maybe it was a meat chopper!"

"Kid might get a knife anywhere."

He shook his head firmly. "No. Look how even it is and ain't hacked up. Kid would rag it up. A man went and done it, being real careful."

At last she nodded assent. Now at the same moment they turned and looked up the river bank into Fiberville, the squat darkening houses where the fathers and mothers and older sons now wore strained strange faces. The men didn't shave everyday now and the women cried sometimes. They had all turned into strangers, and among them at night in the houses were real strangers from far-off places saying hard wild sentences and often shouting and banging tabletops. In the overheated rooms both the light and the shadows loomed with an unguessable violence.

THE BANK ROBBERY

THE BANK ROBBER TOLD his story in little notes to the bank teller. He held the pistol in one hand and gave her the notes with the other. The first note said:

> *This is a bank holdup because money is just like time and I need more to keep on going, so keep your hands where I can see them and don't go pressing any alarm buttons or I'll blow your head off.*

The teller, a young woman of about twenty-five, felt the lights that lined her streets go on for the first time in years. She kept her hands where he could see them and didn't press any alarm buttons. Ah danger, she said to herself, you are just like love. After she read the note, she gave it back to the gunman and said:

"This note is far too abstract. I really can't respond to it."

The robber, a young man of about twenty-five, felt the electricity of his thoughts in his hand as he wrote the next note. Ah money, he said to himself, you are just like love. His next note said:

> *This is a bank holdup because there is only one clear rule around here and that is* WHEN YOU RUN OUT OF MONEY YOU SUFFER, *so keep your hands where I can see them and don't go pressing any alarm buttons or I'll blow your head off.*

The young woman took the note, touching lightly the gunless hand that had written it. The touch of the gunman's hand went immediately to her memory, growing its own life there. It became a constant light toward which she could move when she was lost. She felt that she could see everything clearly as if an unknown veil had just been lifted.

"I think I understand better now," she said to the thief, looking first in his eyes and then at the gun. "But all this money will not get you what you want." She looked at him deeply, hoping that she was becoming rich before his eyes.

Ah danger, she said to herself, you are the gold that wants to spend my life.

The robber was becoming sleepy. In the gun was the weight of his dreams about this moment when it was yet to come. The gun was like the heavy eyelids of someone who wants to sleep but is not allowed.

Ah money, he said to himself, I find little bits of you leading to more of you in greater little bits. You are promising endless amounts of yourself but others are coming. They are threatening our treasure together. I cannot pick you up fast enough as you lead into the great, huge quiet that you are. Oh money, please save me, for you are desire, pure desire, that wants only itself.

The gunman could feel his intervals, the spaces in himself, piling up so that he could not be sure of what he would do next. He began to write. His next note said:

> *Now is the film of my life, the film of my insomnia: an eerie bus ride, a trance in the night, from which I want to step down, whose light keeps me from sleeping. In the streets I will chase the wind-blown letter of love that will change my life. Give me the money, my Sister, so that I can run my hands through its hair. This is the unfired gun of time, so keep your hands where I can see them and don't go presing any alarm buttons or I'll blow your head off with it.*

Reading, the young woman felt her inner hands grabbing and holding onto this moment of her life.

Ah danger, she said to herself, you are yourself with perfect clarity. Under your lens I know what I want.

The young man and woman stared into each other's eyes forming two paths between them. On one path his life, like little people, walked into her, and on the other hers walked into him.

"This money is love," she said to him. "I'll do what you want." She began to put money into the huge satchel he had provided.

As she emptied it of money, the bank filled with sleep. Everyone else in the bank slept the untroubled sleep of trees that would never be money. Finally she placed all the money in the bag.

The bank robber and the bank teller left together like hostages of each other. Though it was no longer necessary, he kept the gun on her, for it was becoming like a child between them.

TENT WORMS

Billy Foxworth had been grumbling for days about the tent worms that were building great, sagging canopies of transparent gray tissue among the thickly grown berry trees that surrounded their summer cottage on the cape. His wife, Clara, had dreams and preoccupations of her own, and had listened without attention to these grumblings. Once in a while she had looked at him darkly and thought, If he but knew! He has more to worry about than those tent worms! "Tent worms? What are tent worms?" she once murmured dreamily, but her mind wandered off while he defined them to her. He must have gone on talking about them for quite a while, for her mind described a wide orbit among her private reflections before he brought her back to momentary attention by slamming his coffee cup down on the saucer and exclaiming irritably, "Stop saying 'Yes, yes, yes' when you're not listening to a goddamn word I say!"

"I heard you," she protested crossly. "You were maundering like an old woman about those worms! Am I supposed to sit here starry-eyed with excitement while you—"

"All right," he said. "You asked me what they were, and I was trying to tell you."

"I don't care what they are," she said. "Maybe they bother you, but they don't bother me."

"Stop being childish!" he snapped.

They had a sun terrace on the back of their cottage where Clara reclined in a deck chair all afternoon, enjoying her private reflections while Billy worked at his typewriter on the screened porch just within. For five years Clara had not thought about the future. She was thinking about it now. It had become a tangible thing once more, owing to the information she had, to which Billy did not have access, in spite of the fact that it concerned Billy even more than herself, because it concerned what was happening to Billy that Billy did not or was not supposed to know about. No, he did not know about it, she was practically sure that he didn't, or if he did, it was only in his unconscious, kept back there because he refused to accept it or didn't even dare to suspect it. That was why he had become so childish this summer, maundering like an idiot about those worms when it was August and they would be leaving here soon, going back to New York, and certainly Billy would never come back here again and she, God knows—let the worms eat the whole place up, let them eat the trees and the house and the beach and the ocean itself as far as she was concerned!

But about three o'clock one afternoon she smelled smoke. She looked around and there was Billy with a torch of old newspapers, setting fire to the tent worms' canopies of webby gray stuff. There he was in his khaki shorts holding up a flaming torch of newspapers to the topmost branches of the little stunted trees where the tent worms had built their houses.

He was burning them out, childishly, senselessly, in spite of the fact that there were thousands of them. Yes, looking over the trees from the sun terrace she could see that the tent worms had spread their dominion from tree to tree till now, finally, near the end of the summer, there was hardly a tree that did not support one or more of the gray tissue canopies that devoured their leaves. Still Billy was attempting to combat them single-handed with his silly torches of paper.

Clara got up and let out a loud cry of derision.

"What in hell do you think you are doing!"

"I am burning out the tent worms," he answered gravely.

"Are you out of your mind? There are millions of them!"

"That's all right. I'm going to burn them all out before we leave here!"

She gave up. Turned away and sank back in her deck chair.

All that afternoon the burning continued. It was no good protesting, although the smoke and odor were quite irritating. The best that Clara could do was drink, and so she did. She made herself a thermos of Tom Collinses, and she drank them all afternoon while her husband attacked the insects with his paper torches. Along about five o'clock Clara Foxworth began to feel happy and carefree. Her dreams took a sanguine turn. She saw herself that winter in expensive mourning, in handsomely tailored black suits with a little severe jewelry and a cape of black furs, and she saw herself with various escorts, whose features were still indistinguishable, in limousines that purred comfortably through icy streets from a restaurant to a theater, from a theater to an apartment, not yet going to nightclubs so soon after—

Ah! Her attitude was healthy, she was not being insincere and pretending to feel what she didn't. Pity? Yes, she felt sorry for him but when love had ceased being five or six years ago, why make an effort to think it would be a loss?

Toward sundown the phone rang.

It rang so rarely now that the sound surprised her. Not only she but their whole intimate circle—of friends?—had drawn back from them into their own concerns, as actors disperse to their offstage lives when a curtain has fallen and they're released from performance.

She took her time about answering, having already surmised that the caller would be their doctor, and it was.

Professional cheer is uncheering.

"How's it going, sweetie?"

"How's what going?"

"Your escape from the poisonous vapors of the metropolis?"

"If that's a serious question, Doc, I'll give you a serious answer. Your patient is nostalgic for the poisonous vapors and so is creating some here."

"What, what?"

"Is the connection bad?"

"No, just wondered what you meant."

"I will enlighten you gladly. Billy, your patient, is polluting the air of our summer retreat by burning out something called tent worms. The smoke is suffocating, worse than carbon monoxide in a traffic jam in a tunnel. I'm coughing and choking and still he keeps at it."

"Well, at least he's still active."

"Oh, that he is. Would you like me to call him to the phone?"

"No, just tell him I—no, don't tell him I called, he might wonder why."

"Why in hell didn't you tell him so he'd know and—"

She didn't know how to complete her protestation so she cried into the phone: "I can't bear it, it's more than I can bear. My mind is full of awful, awful thoughts, speculations about how long I'll have to endure it, when will it be finished."

"Easy, sweetie."

"Easy for you, not me. And don't call me sweetie. I'm not a sweetie, there's nothing sweet about me. I've turned savage. Unless he stops burning those tent worms, I'm going to go, alone, back to the city, at least no diseased vegetation and paper torches, and him staggering out there. Got to hang up. He's coming toward the house."

"Clara, it's hard to be human, but for God's sake try."

"Can you tell me how to? Write me a prescription so that I can?"

She glanced out the picture window between the phone and the slow, exhausted return of Billy toward the sun deck, which the sun was deserting.

"Clara, love takes disguises. Your mind is probably full of fantasies that you'll dismiss with shame when this ordeal is over."

"You scored a point there. I'm full of fantasies of a bit of a future."

"You mentioned a prescription."

"Yes. What?"

"Recollection of how it was before."

"Seems totally unreal."

"Right now, yes, but try to."

"Thanks. I'll try to breathe. If only the sea wind would blow the smoke away. . . ."

When she returned to the sun deck he had completed his exhausted return. He had a defeated look and he had burned himself in several places and applied poultices of wet baking soda, which smelled disagreeably. He took the other sun chair and pulled it a little away from where his wife was reclining and turned it so that she wouldn't look at his face.

"Giving it up?" she murmured.

"Ran out of paper and matches," he answered faintly.

There was no more talk between them. The tide was returning shoreward, and now the smooth water was lapping quietly near them.

Tent worms, she said to herself.

Then she said it out loud: "Tent worms!"

"Why are you shouting about it, it's nothing to shout about. A blight on vegetation is like a blight on your body."

"This is just a place rented for summer and we'll never come back."

"A man in his youth is like a summer place," he said in such a soft, exhausted voice that she didn't catch it.

"What was that?"

He repeated it to her a little louder.

Then she knew that he knew. Their chairs remained apart on the sun deck as the sun disappeared altogether.

As dark falls, a pair of long companions respond to the instinct of drawing closer together.

Unsteadily she rose from her deck chair and hauled it closer to his. His scorched hand rested on his chair arm. After a while, the sentimental moon risen from the horizon to replace the sun's vigil, she placed her hand over his.

A chill wind of shared apprehension swept over the moonlit sun deck and their fingers wound together. She thought of their early passion for each other and how time had burned it down as he attempted to burn the tent worms away from their summer place to which they, no, would never return, separately or together.

SITTING

IN THE MORNING the man and woman were sitting on his front steps. They sat all day. They would not move.

With metronomic regularity he peered at them through the pane in the front door.

They did not leave at dark. He wondered when they ate or slept or did their duties.

At dawn they were still sitting there. They sat through sun and rain.

At first only the immediate neighbors called: Who are they? What are they doing there?

He did not know.

Then neighbors from farther down the street called. People who passed and saw the couple called.

He never heard the man and woman talk.

When he started getting calls from all over the city, from strangers and city fathers, professionals and clerks, garbage and utilities men, and the postman, who had to walk around them to deliver letters, he had to do something.

He asked them to leave.

They said nothing. They sat. They stared, indifferent.

He said he would call the police.

The police gave them a talking to, explained the limits of their rights, and took them away in the police car.

In the morning they were back.

The next time the police said they would put them in jail if the jails were not so full, though they would have to find a place for them somewhere, if he insisted.

That is your problem, he said.

No, it is really yours, the police told him, but they removed the pair.

When he looked out the next morning, the man and woman were sitting on the steps.

They sat there every day for years.

Winters he expected them to die from the cold.

But he died.

He had no relatives, so the house went to the city.

The man and woman went on sitting there.

When the city threatened to remove the man and woman, neighbors and citizens brought a suit against the city: after sitting so long, the man and woman deserved the house.

The petitioners won. The man and woman took over the house.

In the morning strange men and women were sitting on front steps all over the city.

THE BRIDGE

A BICYCLE WHIZZES past her from behind just as she steps onto the pedestrian walkway of the bridge. It startles her. It also startles a young woman who is walking slowly fifty feet ahead of her, cradling a bundle of something — a potted plant, flowers, a baby — she can't tell what. She has the impulse belatedly to call something nasty to the young man on the bicycle, but he is moving away too fast, his legs pumping hard. Anyway the young woman must have said something to him because he turns his head around to her, slowing down just slightly. He could have injured them both. The mother and the baby. Or crushed the flowers.

She carries her purse slung over her shoulder on a long strap and in her left hand a bag of groceries — no jars or cans to make it heavy. English muffins, tea, two lamb chops, a bottle of white wine, and a ripe cantaloupe. The wind from the bay is brisk, cool. She stops to button her jacket, wrap her scarf smartly around her neck. The scarf matches her skirt, which pleases her. The young woman ahead of her has also stopped. She doesn't know why she says "young woman" because indeed she might have been a grandmother out for a stroll or a volunteer for the elderly on her way with bright flowers and a lot to say. Squinting the young woman into sharper focus brings no more illuminating details than a scarf that matches nothing else she wears. She has changed the bundle from her left to right arm.

If she catches up to the young woman, and if there is a child bundled into a blanket, perhaps they might talk for part of their trip across the bridge. About the rudeness of the boy on the bicycle. She will smile at the baby, admire its hair or eyes or nose, or if nothing warrants, the charm of children. "How old?" she might ask. "Is it a boy or girl?" "The name?" Or perhaps "What lovely flowers," although she can imagine that people might not respond to this beyond a polite murmur of agreement. Perhaps because they have nothing to do with making them.

Ahead of her the young woman stops again and is leaning over the heavy iron railing of the bridge. She is looking down into the water as if something has caught her eye, something worth the pause. She too stops, torn between catching up to the young woman and wanting to see what holds her interest in the water. She sets her grocery bag down between her feet and peers over the shoulder-high railing down into the river below the young woman. There are no barges or colorful sailing boats, no sightseeing cruises with loudspeakers blaring a bored voice. Just as she looks back up again, in a graceful curve as of a ballet gesture, the young woman throws her bundle over the side of the bridge.

She tries to guess the weight of it, the drift of flowers or the downward spiral of a helpless infant, but she cannot. It lands with a soft plop (like a tire puncture?), floats an instant then disappears with tiny bubbles. Paper of the kind from a florist's long roll or a small square of blanket drifts past the original spot until it too has gathered enough water to sink. There has been no color at all, white paper around flowers, or a white baby's blanket.

She tries to scream, whirling around to the passing cars, turning back to the railing, toward the young woman whose coat is blowing open in the breeze. She realizes immediately that if it was or rather is a baby — what would be the difference? Would she throw down the groceries, tear off her jacket and scarf leaving them draped over the railing, kick off her shoes, call to anyone to witness her leap, even the young mother who now stands motionless, her arms withdrawn from the graceful arc of her throw? And then after the climb onto the iron railing higher than it looks, the leap into the water? The cold high shock of the water. Even now, half-believing, something has died for her. She does not jump.

She hurries toward the young woman, her heels clicking like a mugger sure of his prey and silence no longer necessary. She half expects the young woman to turn toward her and then run. Another bicycle passes and she wants to send for help, but she can't find the words to convince. What can she tell even her husband? She glances below again to the darkening river, scraping her elbow as she continues to run. A large camellia floats on the water where the bundle has dropped, or a small baby's bonnet, white and scalloped. She runs on, the grocery bag banging against her legs, bruising the cantaloupe. "I was watching!" she calls to the young woman, breathless. She points from where she has just come. "I was stand-ing over there." She tries to determine just how far away she was but can't find a point to identify her place along the stark railing of the bridge.

The young woman turns but doesn't run. Together they stare at the place where she stood. The young woman's face is smooth and shiny like a plate and, yes, young. She might have been look-ing for signs of changing weather. Her hands fill in her pockets, her arms tight against her sides where a bundle was. Is she used to strangers talking to her, calling to her breathless from fifteen, ten feet away? She herself isn't used to watching babies being thrown from a bridge, or even flowers. There is a story in flowers too although a far different tale, probably romantic and full of empty gestures, predictable details. But what happened? There is a new emptiness inside her. What must there be in this young woman whose life has changed, perhaps by the crossing of a bridge in fall. "I saw you throw something into the river," she tells her.

The young woman seems to consider everything, then says, "You called. Are you all right?" as she pulls her coat closer about her. The young woman continues, "I think it is going to rain again. It's ruined everything I planned." The grocery bag feels heavy and she sets it down as if it contains bottles, quarts of heavy rich milk. "What was it?" she asks the young woman. "*What?*" The young woman seems to think the question does not refer to anything specific like flowers or babies as she glances at the bag of groceries — perhaps wondering if she should offer to carry them, or making a list of what she needs from the store. "I have to go," she says, shak-ing her head, and she goes.

And so. She watched the young woman once again recede into the distance. In her wake, Cambridge neon begins to breathe above the water. The subway thunders past her on its short sojourn out-side the tunnel. How much does a baby weigh? She stoops down and moves the English muffins aside. She hefts the cantaloupe before lifting it out with both hands. She palms it like a basketball, but can't suspend it in one hand and so pulls her arm back over her shoul-der, her hand under the fruit. Like a catapult she heaves it out into the river, lacking the grace of the young woman's motion. She tries to remember the soft plop of entry, and failing that, listens for a cry.

DOG LIFE

Glover barlett and his wife Tracy lay in their king-size bed under a light blue cambric comforter stuffed with down. They stared into the velvety, perfumed dark. Then Glover turned on his side to look at his wife. Her golden hair surrounded her face, making it seem smaller. Her lips were slightly parted. He wanted to tell her something. But what he had to say was so charged that he hesitated. He had mulled it over in private; now he felt he must bring it into the open, regardless of the risks. "Darling," he said, "there's something I've been meaning to tell you."

Tracy's eyes widened with apprehension. "Glover, please, if it's going to upset me, I'd rather not hear. . . ."

"It's just that I was different before I met you."

"What do you mean 'different'?" Tracy asked, looking at him.

"I mean, darling, that I used to be a dog."

"You're putting me on," said Tracy.

"No, I'm not," said Glover.

Tracy stared at her husband with mute astonishment. A silence weighted with solitude filled the room. The time was ripe for intimacy; Tracy's gaze softened into a look of concern.

"A dog?"

"Yes, a collie," said Glover reassuringly. "The people who owned me lived in Connecticut in a big house with lots of lawn, and there were woods out back. All the neighbors had dogs, too. It was a happy time."

Tracy's eyes narrowed. "What do you mean 'a happy time'? How could it have been 'a happy time'?"

"It was. Especially in autumn. We bounded about in the yellow twilight, excited by the clicking of branches and the parade of odors making each circuit of air an occasion for reverie. Burning leaves, chestnuts roasting, pies baking, the last exhalations of earth before freezing, drove us practically mad. But the autumn nights were even better: the blue lustre of stones under the moon, the spectral bushes, the gleaming grass. Our eyes shone with a new depth. We barked, bayed, and babbled, trying again and again to find the right note, a note that would reach back thousands of years into our origins. It was a note that if properly sustained would be the distilled wail of our species and would carry within it the triumph of our collective destiny. With our tails poised in the stunned atmosphere, we sang for our lost ancestors, our wild selves. Darling, there was something about those nights that I miss."

"Are you telling me that something is wrong with our marriage?"

"Not at all. I'm only saying that there was a tragic dimension to my life in those days. You have to imagine me with a friend or two on the top of a windswept knoll, crying for the buried fragments of our cunning, for the pride we lost during the period of our captivity, our exile in civilization, our fateful domestication. There were times when I could detect within the coarsest bark a futility I have not known since. I think of my friend Spot; her head high, her neck extended. Her voice was operatic and filled with a sadness that was thrilling as she released, howl by howl, the darkness of her being into the night."

"Did you love her?" Tracy asked.

"No, not really. I admired her more than anything."

"But there were dogs you did love?"

"It's hard to say that dogs actually love," said Glover.

"You know what I mean," said Tracy.

Glover turned on his back and stared at the ceiling. "Well, there was Flora, who had a lovely puff of hair on her head, inherited from her Dandie Dinmont mother. She was teeny, of course, and I felt foolish, but still. . . . And there was Muriel, a melancholic Irish setter. And Cheryl, whose mother was a long-coated Chihuahua and whose father was a cross between a fox terrier and a shelty. She was intelligent, but her owners made her wear a little tartan jacket that humiliated her. She ran off with a clever mutt — part puli, part dachshund. After that I saw her with a black and white Papillon. Then she moved, and I never saw her again."

"Were there others?" said Tracy.

"There was Peggy Sue, a German short-haired pointer whose owners would play Buddy Holly on their stereo. The excitement we experienced when we heard her name is indescribable. We would immediately go to the door and whimper to be let out. How proudly we trotted under the gaudy scattering of stars! How immodest we were under the moon's opalescence! We pranced and pranced in the exuberant light."

"You make it sound so hunky-dory. There must've been bad times."

"The worst times were when my owners laughed. Suddenly they became strangers. The soft cadences of their conversation, the sharpness of their commands, gave way to howls, gurgles, and yelps. It was as if something were released in them, something absolute and demonic. Once they started it was hard for them to stop. You can't imagine how frightening and confusing it was to see my protectors out of control. The sounds they made seemed neither expressive or communicative, nor did they indicate pleasure or pain, but rather a weird mixture of both. It was a limbo of utterance from which I felt completely excluded. Buy why go on, those days are past."

"How do you know?"

"I just do. I feel it."

"But if you were a dog once, why not a dog twice?"

"Because there are no signs of that happening again. When I was a dog, there were indications that I would end up as I am now. I never liked exposing myself and was pained by having to perform private acts in public. I was embarrassed by the pomp of bitches in heat—their preening and wagging, by the panting lust of my brothers. I became withdrawn; I brooded; I actually suffered a kind of canine *terribilità*. It all pointed to one thing."

When Glover had finished, he waited for Tracy to speak. He was sorry he had told her so much. He felt ashamed. He hoped she would understand his having been a dog was not his choice, that such aberrations are born of necessity and are not lamentable. At times, the fury of a man's humanity will find its finest manifestation in amazing alterations of expectedness. For people are only marginally themselves. Glover, who earlier in the night had begun to slide into an agony of contrition, now felt righteous pride. He saw that Tracy's eyes were closed. She had fallen asleep. The truth had been endurable, had been overshadowed by a need that led her safely into the doom of another night. They would wake in the early morning and look at each other as always. What he had told her would be something they would never mention again, not out of politeness, or sensitivity for the other, but because such achievements of frailty, such lyrical lapses, are unavoidable in every life.

THE HATCHET MAN
IN THE LIGHTHOUSE

WE ARE SITTING ON the trunk of a fallen palmetto pine, Miss Peaches and I, waiting for the sun to set. Far down the beach, where curving strand and sky merge, we can glimpse the pale blue-pink smudge that is Savannah. Below us a few vacationers still linger on the sand, but to the east the shore is deserted; it is almost time to go home to dinner. The moon has not yet risen; the tide is coming in. Out of nowhere a boy jogs toward us, he is neither city-pale nor tidewater-tan; he looks to be between six and seven years old. A few yards from us he slows down, hesitates, finally stops in front of Miss Peaches.

"Hi," she says, and smiles; so do I.

"Hello," he replies, somewhat formally, a city boy, from Savannah perhaps, maybe Beaufort. He is a fine-looking youngster, well formed and with clear blue eyes.

"Been swimming?" I ask, a foolish question, his hair is wet, soaking wet. "How was the water?"

"Yes," he says, and scratches in the sand with his toes. "It was good."

Miss Peaches nods agreement. "We've been in twice today. The surf was wonderful. Just right."

The boy starts to say something, hesitates, and points across the shining sea toward the mainland. "I've been *there*, too," he announces. "Have you?"

We nod, the boy squints, and points again. "Do you see *it*?"

"See what?" I ask, squinting in turn.

"The Lighthouse." His voice is mildly patronizing. "Way down there. The Lighthouse."

"There's no lighthouse there," I start to say, but Miss Peaches interrupts.

"Yes," she tells the boy. "We see it."

"Have you ever *been* there?"

"No," I say, "no, we've never been there."

"I have." His voice is firm, it brooks no disagreement. "My Mom and Dad took me there."

"Did they?" Miss Peaches asks. "What fun that must have been. What's the lighthouse like?"

He hesitates. "It's big," he says, after a pause. "It's very big."

"Is it," I say. "How big?"

He looks through me and beyond me, eyes narrowed, scanning the horizon. "It's big enough for *him*."

"For him?" Miss Peaches and I speak in unison, as though the scene had been rehearsed.

"The hatchet man." His voice is very serious, very earnest. "A giant hatchet man."

"The hatchet man?" I say. "I never knew . . . I mean, what's he like, this hatchet man?"

The boy's clear blue eyes travel from mine, he is seeing something I cannot see.

"He's huge." He gestures with both hands. "He's . . . he's *gargantuan*."

"Is he!" I suppress a smile, shake my head and glance toward Miss Peaches.

The boy nods emphatically. "There are seahorses out there, too." He extends his arms, embracing the entire expanse of land and slowly-darkening sea. "Man-sized seahorses."

"Yes," Miss Peaches says. "We've seen *them*. But we've never seen the hatchet man. What does he *do* there? What's he *like*?"

Again the boy scratches the sand with his toes. "He's very ugly," he says after a long, thoughtful pause. "He's as ugly as *sin*." He hesitates, while I bite my lip to suppress a smile. "But he's very . . . very kind."

"Kind?" I say. "That's good to know. I'm glad to know that he's kind. But why . . . why do you call him the hatchet man?"

He looks at me with diminishing patience. "Because that's who he *is*. Everybody . . . ." He slowly shakes his head as if in disbelief. "*Almost* everybody knows that."

Toward Savannah the blue-pink smudge has turned the color of smoke, but in the east a faint glimmer illuminates the water; soon the moon will be rising, there is a slight offshore breeze but there may be some mosquitoes, it is time for us to go back to the house. I extend my hand toward the boy.

"It's very interesting, all these things. Perhaps we'll see you again tomorrow, and you can tell us more about him. We'd like to hear more about the hatchet man . . . and the seahorses, too."

He shakes my hand, he no longer seems irritated at my stupidity. "I'll come back," he says. "I'll come back tomorrow morning."

"Be sure to," Miss Peaches says. "We want to hear more about them."

She leans over and runs her hand lightly through his damp hair. He smiles, heads toward the hard-packed sand at the edge of the sea, and turns and waves to us; we wave back.

"My Mom," he calls, his voice clear and distinct. "My Mom's dead. . . . She died yesterday."

We say nothing as he turns again and jogs off, well-coordinated, light on his feet. He will become a good middle-distance runner. Miss Peaches and I watch him, without speaking, until he is only a speck in the distance. I think he stops once to wave, but at that distance and without my glasses I cannot be sure.

HAPPY

SHE FLEW HOME at Christmas, her mother and her mother's new husband met her at the airport. Her mother hugged her hard and told her she looked pretty, and her mother's new husband shook hands with her and told her, Yes she sure did look pretty, and welcome home. His sideburns grew razor sharp into his plump cheeks and changed color, graying, in the lower part of his face. In his handshake her hand felt small and moist, the bones close to cracking. Her mother hugged her again, God I'm so happy to see you, veins in her arms ropier than the girl remembered, the arms themselves thinner, but her mother was happy, you could feel it all about her. The pancake makeup on her face was a fragrant peach shade that had been blended skillfully into her throat. On her left hand she wore her new ring: a small glittering diamond set high in spiky white-gold prongs.

They stopped for a drink at Easy Sal's off the expressway, the girl had a club soda with a twist of lime (*That's* fancy, her mother said), her mother and her mother's new husband had martinis on the rocks, which were their "celebration" drinks. For a while they talked about what the girl was studying and what her plans were and when that subject trailed off they talked about their own plans, getting rid of the old house, that was one of the first chores, buying something smaller, newer, or maybe just renting temporarily. There's a new condominium village by the river, the girl's mother said, we'll show you when we drive past; then she smiled at something, took a swallow of her martini, squeezed the girl's arm, and leaned her head toward hers, giggling. Jesus, she said, it just makes me so happy, having the two people I love most in the world right here with me. Right here right now. A waitress in a tight-fitting black satin outfit brought two more martinis and a tiny glass bowl of beer nuts. Thanks sweetheart! her mother's new husband said.

The girl had spoken with her mother no more than two or three times about her plans to be remarried, always long distance, her mother kept saying Yes it's sudden in your eyes but this kind of thing always is, you know right away or you don't know at all. Wait and see. The girl said very little, murmuring Yes or I don't know or I suppose so. Her mother said in a husky voice He makes me feel like living again. I feel, you know, like a woman again, and the girl was too embarrassed to reply. As long as you're happy, she said.

Now it was nearly eight-thirty, and the girl was light-headed with hunger, but her mother and her mother's new husband were on their third round of drinks. Easy Sal's had entertainment, first a pianist who'd been playing background music, old Hoagy Carmichael favorites, then a singer, female, black, V-necked red spangled dress, then a comedian, a young woman of about twenty-six, small bony angular face, no makeup, punk hairdo, dark brown, waxed, black fake-leather jumpsuit, pelvis thrust forward in mock-Vogue-model stance, her delivery fast brash deadpan in the nature of mumbled asides, thinking aloud, as if the patrons just happened to overhear, The great thing about havin your abortion early in the day is, uh like y'know the rest of the day's uh gonna be fuckin uphill, right? There's these half-dozen people in a uh Jacuzzi, uh lesbians in a hot tub, hot new game called "musical holes," uh maybe it just ain't caught on yet in New Jersey's why nobody's laughin, huh? the words too quick and muttered for the girl to catch but her mother and her mother's new husband seemed to hear, in any case they were laughing, though afterward her mother's new husband confided he did not approve of dirty language issuing from women's lips, whether they were dykes or not.

They stopped for dinner at a Polynesian restaurant ten miles up the Turnpike, her mother explaining that there wasn't anything decent to eat at home, also it was getting late wasn't it, tomorrow she'd be making a big dinner, That's okay honey isn't it? She and her new husband quarreled about getting on the Turnpike then exiting right away, but at dinner they were in high spirits again, laughing a good deal, holding hands between courses, sipping from each other's tall frosted bright-colored tropical drinks. Jesus I'm crazy about that woman, her mother's new husband told the girl when her mother was in the powder room, Your mother is a high-class lady, he said. He shifted his cane chair closer, leaned moist and warm, meaty, against her, an arm across her shoulders. There's nobody in the world precious to me as that lady, I want you to know that, he said, and the girl said Yes I know it, and her mother's new husband said in a fierce voice close to tears, Damn right, sweetheart: you know it.

DINNER TIME

AN OLD MAN SITTING at a table was waiting for his wife to serve dinner. He heard her beating a pot that had burned her. He hated the sound of a pot when it was beaten, for it advertised its pain in such a way that made him wish to inflict more of the same. And he began to punch at his own face, and his knuckles were red. How he hated red knuckles, that blaring color, more self-important than the wound.

He heard his wife drop the entire dinner on the kitchen floor with a curse. For as she was carrying it in it had burned her thumb. He heard the forks and spoons, the cups and platters all cry at once as they landed on the kitchen floor. How he hated a dinner that, once prepared, begins to burn one to death, and as if that weren't enough, screeches and roars as it lands on the floor, where it belongs anyway.

He punched himself again and fell on the floor.

When he came awake again he was quite angry, and so he punched himself again and felt dizzy. Dizziness made him angry, and so he began to hit his head against the wall, saying, now get real dizzy if you want to get dizzy. He slumped to the floor.

Oh, the legs won't work, eh? . . . He began to punch his legs. He had taught his head a lesson and now he would teach his legs a lesson.

Meanwhile he heard his wife smashing the remaining dinnerware and the dinnerware roaring and shrieking.

He saw himself in the mirror on the wall. Oh, mock me, will you. And so he smashed the mirror with a chair, which broke. Oh, don't want to be a chair no more; too good to be sat on, eh? He began to beat the pieces of the chair.

He heard his wife beating the stove with an ax. He called, when're we going to eat? as he stuffed a candle into his mouth.

When I'm good and ready, she screamed.

Want me to punch your bun? he screamed.

Come near me and I'll kick an eye out of your head.

I'll cut your ears off.

I'll give you a slap right in the face.

I'll kick you right in the breadbasket.

I'll break you in half.

The old man finally ate one of his hands. The old woman said, damn fool, whyn't you cook it first? you go on like a beast — You know I have to subdue the kitchen every night, otherwise it'll cook me and serve me to the mice on my best china. And you know what small eaters they are; next would come the flies, and how I hate flies in my kitchen.

The old man swallowed a spoon. Okay, said the old woman, now we're short one spoon.

The old man, growing angry, swallowed himself.

Okay, said the woman, now you've done it.

THE ANATOMY OF DESIRE

BECAUSE HANLEY'S SKIN had been stripped off by the enemy, he could find no one who was willing to be with him for long. The nurses were obligated, of course, to see him now and then, and sometimes the doctor, but certainly not the other patients and certainly not his wife and children. He was raw, he was meat, and he would never be any better. He had a great and natural desire, therefore, to be possessed by someone.

He would walk around on his skinned feet, leaving bloody footprints up and down the corridors, looking for someone to love him.

"You're not supposed to be out here," the nurse said. And she added, somehow making it sound kind, "You untidy the floor, Hanley."

"I want to be loved by someone," he said. "I'm human too. I'm like you."

But he knew he was not like her. Everybody called her the saint.

"Why couldn't it be you?" he said.

She was swabbing his legs with blood retardant, a new discovery that kept Hanley going. It was one of those miracle medications that just grew out of the war.

"I wasn't chosen," she said. "I have my skin."

"No," he said. "I mean why couldn't it be you who will love me, possess me? I have desires too," he said.

She considered this as she swabbed his shins and the soles of his feet.

"I have no desires," she said. "Or only one. It's the same thing."

He looked at her loving face. It was not a pretty face, but it was saintly.

"Then you will?" he said.

"If I come to know sometime that I must," she said.

.   .   .

The enemy had not chosen Hanley, they had just lucked upon him sleeping in his trench. They were a raid party of four, terrified and obedient, and they had been told to bring back an enemy to serve as an example of what is done to infiltrators.

They dragged Hanley back across the line and ran him, with his hands tied behind his back, the two kilometers to the general's tent.

The general dismissed the guards because he was very taken with Hanley. He untied the cords that bound his wrists and let his arms hang free. Then slowly, ritually, he tipped Hanley's face toward the light and examined it carefully. He kissed him on the brow and on the cheek and finally on the mouth. He gazed deep and long into Hanley's eyes until he saw his own reflection there looking back. He traced the lines of Hanley's eyebrows, gently, with the tip of his index finger. "Such a beautiful face," he said in his own language. He pressed his palms lightly against Hanley's forehead, against his cheekbones, his jaw. With his little finger he memorized the shape of Hanley's lips, the laugh lines at his eyes, the chin. The general did Hanley's face very thoroughly. Afterward he did some things down below, and so just before sunrise when the time came to lead Hanley out to the stripping post, he told the soldiers with the knives: "This young man could be my own son; so spare him here and here."

The stripping post stood dead-center in the line of barbed wire only a few meters beyond the range of gunfire. A loudspeaker was set up and began to blare the day's message. "This is what happens to infiltrators. No infiltrators will be spared." And then as troops from both sides watched through binoculars, the enemy cut the skin from Hanley's body, sparing — as the general had insisted — his face and his genitals. They were skilled men and the skin was stripped off expeditiously and they hung it, headless, on the barbed wire as an example. They lay Hanley himself on the ground where he could die.

He was rescued a little after noon when the enemy, for no good reason, went into sudden retreat.

Hanley was given emergency treatment at the field unit, and when they had done what they could for him, they sent him on to the vets' hospital. At least there, they told each other, he will be attended by the saint.

It was quite some time before the saint said yes, she would love him.

"Not just love me. Possess me."

"There are natural reluctancies," she said. "There are personal peculiarities," she said. "You will have to have patience with me."

"You're supposed to be a saint," he said.

So she lay down with him in his bloody bed and he found great satisfaction in holding this small woman in his arms. He kissed her and caressed her and felt young and whole again. He did not miss his wife and children. He did not miss his skin.

The saint did everything she must. She told him how handsome he was and what pleasure he gave her. She touched him in the way he liked best. She said he was her whole life, her fate. And at night when he woke her to staunch the blood, she whispered how she needed him, how she could not live without him.

This went on for some time.

The war was over and the occupying forces had made the general mayor of the capital city. He was about to run for senator and wanted his past to be beyond the reproach of any investigative committee. He wrote Hanley a letter which he sent through the International Red Cross.

"You could have been my own son," he said. "What we do in war is what we have to do. We do not choose cruelty or violence. I did only what was my duty."

"I am in love and I am loved," Hanley said. "Why isn't this enough?"

The saint was swabbing his chest and belly with blood retardant.

"Nothing is ever enough," she said.

"I love, but I am not possessed by love," he said, "I want to be surrounded by you. I want to be enclosed. I want to be enveloped. I don't have the words for it. But do you understand?"

"You want to be possessed," she said.

"I want to be inside you."

And so they made love, but afterward he said, "That was not enough. That is only a metaphor for what I want."

The general was elected senator and was made a trustee of three nuclear-arms conglomerates. But he was not well. And he was not sleeping well.

He wrote to Hanley, "I wake in the night and see your face before mine. I feel your forehead pressing against my palms. I taste your breath. I did only what I had to do. You could have been my son."

"I know what I want," Hanley said.
"If I can do it, I will," the saint said.
"I want your skin."

And so she lay down on the long white table, shuddering, while Hanley made his first incision. He cut along the shoulders and then down the arms and back up, then down the sides and the legs to the feet. It took him longer than he had expected. The saint shivered at the cold touch of the knife and she sobbed once at the sight of the blood, but by the time Hanley lifted the shroud of skin from her crimson body, she was resigned, satisfied even.

Hanley had spared her face and her genitals.

He spread the skin out to dry and, while he waited, he swabbed her raw body carefully with blood retardant. He whispered little words of love and thanks and desire to her. A smile played about her lips, but she said nothing.

It would be a week before he could put on her skin.

The general wrote to Hanley one last letter. "I can endure no more. I am possessed by you."

Hanley put on the skin of the saint. His genitals fitted nicely through the gap he had left and the skin at his neck matched hers exactly. He walked the corridors and for once left no bloody tracks behind. He stood before mirrors and admired himself. He touched his breasts and his belly and his thighs and there was no blood on his hands.

"Thank you," he said to her. "It is my heart's desire fulfilled. I am inside you. I am possessed by you."

And then, in the night, he kissed her on the brow and on the cheek and finally on the mouth. He gazed deep and long into her eyes. He traced the lines of her eyebrows gently, with the tip of his index finger. "Such a beautiful face," he said. He pressed his palms lightly against her forehead, her cheekbones, her jaw. With his little finger he memorized the shape of her lips.

And then it was that Hanley, loved, desperate to possess and be possessed, staring deep into the green and loving eyes of the saint, saw that there can be no possession, there is only desire. He plucked at his empty skin, and wept.

CLASS NOTES

TED MECHAM MAY BE the first member of the Class of '66 to retire. I met him and his beautiful wife Kathy at a Buccaneers game in Tampa Bay in October. His investments in sugar refining and South American cattle have paid off handsomely. Any secret? "Yes," says Ted. "In and out, that's the key." Also in Florida, I saw JIM HASLEK and BILL STEBBINS. They left their families behind in Columbus and Decatur, respectively, to tune up a 1300-h.p. open-class, ocean racing boat, Miss Ohio, for trial runs near Miami. The racing season is set to open there in December, and Jim and Bill (famous for their Indy 500 pilgrimages) are among the favorites. JOHN PESKIN writes to say, sad to relay, that he has been sued by BILL TESKER. Bill, general manager at the Dayton office of TelDyne Industries, claims he gave John the idea for a sit-com episode that John subsequently sold to NBC. It all took place 16 years ago and is more than I can believe. RALPH FENTIL, handling the case for Bill, made it clearer. Ralph is director of Penalty, Inc., a franchised California paralegal service, which helps clients develop lawsuits. "This is a growing and legitimate consumer-interest area. We encourage people to come in, we go over their past. It's a potential source of income for the client. We let the courts decide what's right and wrong." Hmmm. RICHARD ENDERGEL phoned a few weeks ago from Houston, under arrest for possession of cocaine — third time since 1974. Richard thinks this is it. Unless a miracle happens he is looking at 15 years or more for dealing in a controlled substance. STANFORD CRIBBS, mangled practically beyond recognition in an automobile accident in 1979, took his own life on March 19, according to a clipping from the Kansas City *Star*. His former roommate, BRISTOL LANSFORD, has fared no better. Bristol was shot in the head by his wife's lover at the Lansfords' vacation home outside Traverse City. ROBERT DARKO of Palo Alto (where else?) sends word he is moving up very quickly at Mastuchi

Electronics, and to thank DAVID WHITMAN. David, of Shoremann, Polcher & Edders, Los Angeles, specializes in celebrity and personality contracts. Bob Darko is the sixth middle-management executive hired in David's Free Corporate Agent draft. "Corporate loyalty is something from the fifties," says David. "I want to market people on a competitively-bid, short-term contract basis, with incentive and bonus clauses." Tell that to STEVEN PARKMAN. He has been living on unemployment benefits and his wife's income from a hairdressing concern since April of last year — with four kids. FRANK VESTA is certainly glad his job (in aerospace planning with General Dynamics of St. Louis) is holding up — he and wife Shirley had their ninth — a boy — in July. GREG OUTKIRK has grim news — daughter Michelle rode her thoroughbred Arabian, Botell III, off the boat dock in front of their Waukegan home in an effort to make the animal swim. It drowned almost immediately. DENNIS MITFORD, owner of a well-known Nevada wh---house (no class discounts, he jokes), reports an unruly customer was shot on the premises in October by his bodyguard, LAWRENCE ADENSON. Larry, who served in Vietnam, says the publicity is awful. He may go back to New York — after Denny officially fires him for the violence. Violence is no stranger to BILL NAST. His wife turned up in terrible shape at Detroit General Hospital two months ago, the victim of Bill's hot temper. Fifth time in memory. Four hours in surgery? JACK ZIMMERMAN'S second wife and two children by his first wife visited over Easter. Sue ZIMMERMAN was a 1978 Penthouse Pet. Jack is managing her modeling career, his entertainment career, *and* raising the kids. Kudos, Jack. TIM GRAYBULL is dead (of alcohol abuse) in Vermillion, South Dakota, where he taught English at the university. (Please let the editor of *Alumnus* know you want to see Tim's poems in a future issue.) ALEX ROBINSON won't say what films he distributes, but hints broadly that "beauty is in the eye of the beholder," even in *that* area. The profit margin, he claims, is not to be believed. I'm reminded of KEVIN MITCHELL, who embezzled $3.2 million from Sperry Tool in 1971. He periodically calls from I-know-not-where. Kevin was home free in 1982, with the expiration of the case. DONALD OVERBROOK — more bad news — is in trouble with the police again for unrequited interest in young ladies, this time in Seattle. JAMES COLEMAN called to say so. Jim and his wife Nancy are quitting their jobs to sail around the world in their 32' ferroconcrete boat. Nancy's parents died and

left them well-off. "We were smart *not* to have kids," Jim commented.
HAROLD DECKER writes from Arkansas that he is angry about
Alumni Association fund-raising letters that follow him everywhere
he goes. "I haven't got s---, and wouldn't give it if I did." Wow.
NORMAN BELLOWS has been named managing editor of *Attitude*. He says the magazine's 380,000 readers will see a different
magazine under his tutelage—"aimed at aggressive, professional
people. No tedious essays." Norm's erstwhile literary companion in
New York, GEORGE PHILMAN (Betsy BELLOWS and George
are living together, sorely testing that close friendship from *Spectator* days) reports *Pounce* is doing very well. George's "funny but
vicious" anecdotes about celebrities appear bi-weekly in the fledgling, nationally-syndicated column. "At first the humor went right
by everyone," says George, feigning disbelief. "George is an a--h---,"
was GLEN GREEN's observation when I phoned. Glen opens a
five-week show in Reno in January (and *he* will see to it that you
get a free drink *and* best seats in the house). Another class celebrity,
actor BOYD DAVIDSON, has entered Mt. Sinai, Los Angeles, for
treatment of cocaine and Percodan addiction. Dr. CARNEY OLIN,
who broke a morphine habit at Mt. Sinai in 1979, thinks it's the best
program in the country. Carney says he's fully recovered and back
in surgery in the Phoenix area. THOMAS GREENVILLE's business brochure arrived in the mail last week. He has opened his
fifteenth *Total Review* salon. Tom combines a revitalizing physical-
fitness program with various types of modern therapy, like est, to
provide clients with brand-new life-paths. Some sort of survival prize
should go to DEAN FRANCIS. MBA Harvard 1968. Stanford Law
1970. Elected to the California State Assembly in 1974, after managing Sen. Edward Eaton's successful '72 election campaign. In 1978,
elected to Congress from California's 43rd District. It all but collapsed like a house of cards last fall. A jealous brother-in-law, and
heir to the Greer fortune, instigated a series of nasty suits, publicly
denounced Dean as a fraud, and allegedly paid a woman to sexually embarrass him. Dean won re-election, but the word is his marriage is over—and Phyllis Greer FRANCIS will go to court to
recover damages from her brother. A sadder story came to light
when I met DOUGLAS BRAND for drinks after the Oklahoma
game last fall. Doug's wife Linda went berserk in August and killed
their three children. She's in prison. Doug said he used to bait her
to a fury with tales of his adulteries and feels great remorse.
BENJAMIN TROPPE has been named vice-president for

marketing for Temple Industries of Philadelphia. BERNARD HANNAH is new corporate counsel in Conrad Communications, Atlantic City. HENRY CHURCH was killed by police in Newark for unspecified reasons. Well-known painter DAVID WHITCOMB moved to Guatemala and left no forwarding address (Dave?). FREDERICK MANDELL weeps uncontrollably in his crowded apartment in Miami Beach. JOEL REEDE lives in self-destructive hatred in Rye, New York. JAY LOGAN has joined insurgency forces in Angola. ADRIAN BYRD travels to the Netherlands in the spring to cover proceedings against the Federal Government at The Hague for *Dispatch*. GORDON HASKINS has quit the priesthood in Serape, a violent New Mexican border town, to seek political office. ANTHONY CREST succeeds father Luther (Class of '36) as chairman of Fabré. DANIEL REDDLEMAN continues to compose classical music for the cello in Hesterman, Tennessee. ODELL MASTERS cries out in his dreams for love of his wife and children. PAUL GREEN, who never married, farms 1200 acres in eastern Oregon with his father. ROGER BOLTON, who played professional baseball for nine years, lost his family in flooding outside New Orleans and has entered a Benedictine monastery. (Paul Jeffries, 1340 North Michigan, Chicago, IL 60602.)

A VERY SHORT STORY

ONE HOT EVENING in Padua they carried him up onto the roof and he could look out over the top of the town. There were chimney swifts in the sky. After a while it got dark and the searchlights came out. The others went down and took the bottles with them. He and Luz could hear them below on the balcony. Luz sat on the bed. She was cool and fresh in the hot night.

Luz stayed on night duty for three months. They were glad to let her. When they operated on him she prepared him for the operating table; and they had a joke about friend or enema. He went under the anesthetic holding tight on to himself so he would not blab about anything during the silly, talky time. After he got on crutches he used to take the temperatures so Luz would not have to get up from the bed. There were only a few patients, and they all knew about it. They all liked Luz. As he walked back along the halls he thought of Luz in his bed.

Before he went back to the front they went into the Duomo and prayed. It was dim and quiet, and there were other people praying. They wanted to get married, but there was not enough time for the banns, and neither of them had birth certificates. They felt as though they were married, but they wanted everyone to know about it, and to make it so they could not lose it.

Luz wrote him many letters that he never got until after the armistice. Fifteen came in a bunch to the front and he sorted them by the dates and read them all straight through. They were all about the hospital, and how much she loved him, and how it was impossible to get along without him, and how terrible it was missing him at night.

After the armistice they agreed he should go home to get a job so they might be married. Luz would not come home until he had a good job and could come to New York to meet her. It was understood he would not drink, and he did not want to see his friends or anyone in the States. Only to get a job and be married. On the train from Padua to Milan they quarreled about her not being willing to come home at once. When they had to say goodbye, in the station at Milan, they kissed goodbye, but were not finished with the quarrel. He felt sick about saying goodbye like that.

He went to America on a boat from Genoa. Luz went back to Pordenone to open a hospital. It was lonely and rainy there, and there was a battalion of arditi quartered in the town. Living in the muddy, rainy town in the winter, the major of the battalion made love to Luz, and she had never known Italians before, and finally wrote to the States that theirs had been only a boy and girl affair. She was sorry, and she knew he would probably not be able to understand, but might someday forgive her, and be grateful to her, and she expected, absolutely unexpectedly, to be married in the spring. She loved him as always, but she realized now it was only a boy and girl love. She hoped he would have a great career and believed in him absolutely. She knew it was for the best.

The major did not marry her in the spring, or any other time. Luz never got an answer to the letter to Chicago about it. A short time after he contracted gonorrhea from a salesgirl in a loop department store while riding in a taxicab through Lincoln Park.

SUNDAY AT THE ZOO

We DECIDED TO STOP drinking and spend Sunday at the zoo. It was going nicely until she worked herself up over the observation that it was a horrible thing to cage the animals.

"*That's* not very profound," I said, "everybody who goes to the zoo feels that sometime."

"Oh, you cruel bastard," she screamed, "I'm not *everybody!*"

She bellied over the guardrail and flung herself against the bars of the wolves' cage.

Three wolves had been circling and as soon as she touched the bars they froze, fur bristling along their spines.

She had her arms stuck in between the bars up to her shoulders and as much of her face as she could wedge in yelling, "Eat me! Eat me!" to the wolves.

Just that week the newspapers had carried an account of how a small girl had an arm gnawed off—she'd reached in to pet them and one wolf held it while the other ate. It was, in fact, what had led us, along with the crowd, relentlessly to the wolves' cage.

But the wolves held their ground, snarling, stiff-legged.

An attendant came running down the aisle between the fence and cages and grabbed her by the hair and throat, wrestling her back. She locked her arms around the bars and he kept slapping her face with a thick, purplish slab of meat he must have been feeding to one of the animals.

"I'll give you 'Eat me, Eat me,' " he grinned, kicking her down and grabbing his crotch.

At that instant all three wolves rushed against the bars so that they shook, and you could hear their teeth breaking on the metal. Their bloodied snouts jabbed through, snapping at air.

"Stop abusing that woman," I shouted from the crowd.

THINGS I DID
TO MAKE IT POSSIBLE

One. I MADE LOVE to Margaret only in the missionary position. We are not baboons.

Two. I went to the ocean every chance I got. My favorite place was the Santa Monica Pier but I also went to the Malibu Pier, Topanga Beach, Zuma Beach, Newport Harbor. Sometimes I fished. Mackerel scream when they are pulled out of the water, but they probably don't feel much. Certainly they don't know what's happening to them.

Three. One of the hardest things was watching my weight. I'll never be a fat man if I can help it. Ate a lot of celery, tomatoes by the dozen, lettuce. Gobbled cucumbers just so I'd have something in my mouth.

Four. Sometimes talking to Margaret is like pissing in a violin, as my mother used to say. She listens but she doesn't believe. Still I try.

Five. I ran four miles a day around the golf course in Tarzana. Sometimes with Marty, more often alone; he's like an old man— his tits joggle sadly when he runs, and he gets out of breath and asks me to stop and wait for him every few hundred yards. One leg of our course runs along the bank of the Los Angeles River, a terrible place.

Six. The tree in my back yard throws fish-shaped leaf-shadows on the patio bricks. Let a little breeze blow and clouds of shadow-fish wriggle across the bricks.

Seven. Life in a tropical paradise. Lagoon is one of the great words in the language. Listen to the sound of it. *Lagoon.* I don't know why she should be fucking Marty.

Eight. If she is. He's forty like me, and not in nearly as good a condition. What's she getting out of it? I could ask.

Nine. Another thing I did: I quit smoking.

Ten. I went to Tijuana and bought Margaret an armadillo purse with red-glass eyes. The paws curl under the hollow belly, where she can put things.

Eleven. When we were going to the university she was fucking our friend Campbell the playwright. Artsy-craftsy Campbell weighed about ninety pounds and came up to my shoulder, but he had an agile mind. And a way with women.

Twelve. I loved my wife.

Thirteen. Help me, Dr. Eisenberg. You comedian, you.

Fourteen. Margaret has to my knowledge slept with: Campbell, Marty, myself. I think she also went to bed with Norman Haas at least once. He had polio and is even smaller than Campbell. He can only move one arm, and not all of that. The woman is a saint, possibly, in her own view.

Fifteen. I also bought some armadillo boots for myself. Armadillo babies. God but that's sad. I'm wearing their mama on my feet.

Sixteen. We are nature. The smog is nature. I tried to learn to love it. I sucked it in deep when I ran, and made it a part of myself. Listened to the golf balls whizzing in the cottonwood leaves above my head and took deep breaths. Jumped over small snakes. Told myself that by the time I was ready to die it would seem natural to me. Maybe necessary. Conceivably beautiful.

Seventeen. Here are some things I collected during this time and did not use: a French postcard of a woman with bare breasts and one eye closed to indicate sexiness; a 1941 Buick with side-mount spare wheels and burned valves; an Italian coin made out of aluminum; a black pebble from the beach, cut in half by a clear streak of quartz; a dried blowfish from the souvenir shop on Santa Monica Pier; a sterling-silver medal of Benjamin Franklin; the white skull of a small animal with long front teeth.

Eighteen. I went for long walks at night and thought about the world.

Nineteen. We are not baboons or dogs. Something else.

Twenty. Fourteen years? Almost exactly now. It seems like no time at all since we were all innocent in Tucson.

Twenty-one. I picked up a little girl hitchhiking on the corner of Sunset and Doheny, and drove her out to Zuma Beach.

Twenty-two. What's this life all about anyway?

Twenty-three. In general I tried. I think I can say that much. I loved the smog; I loved the yellow grass that looks dead on the hillsides from the middle of May onward; I loved the long loose whips of the freeways that connect this town; I loved the Santa Ana wind that makes the best of us crazy; I loved the rain in winter.

Twenty-four. Try to be an angel — see where it gets you.

Twenty-five. Sweet little girl from somewhere back East. She blew me under one of the lifeguard towers in the middle of the night, and we talked until the sun came up while I smoked her cigarettes and listened to the surf. Boom-boom-boom. Saddest goddamn sound on earth.

Twenty-six. I had trouble with the video portion of my life. I kept fading in and out.

Twenty-seven. I gave money to: the City of Hope; Muscular Dystrophy; United Good Neighbors; the Heart Fund; the Cancer Society; the Boy Scouts of America; two little Mexican girls who came to the front door selling scented candles; my hitchhiker.

Twenty-eight. A dream where my father was a small blue pyramid with a single brown eye, like the picture on the dollar-bill. In my sleep he seemed perfectly natural in that form. We carried on a long conversation about life. I'm not a big-time dreamer; not many of the dreams that I can remember are as strange as that, or as interesting. Usually it's the old naked-in-a-crowd-of-strangers, or flying-over-the-hills sequence. Now and then I dream of a golden girl and love so tender I wake up with tears on my face.

Twenty-nine. Eisenberg said I should expect to feel like this. Then he laughed like a duck.

Thirty. I'm not a big-time *anything*. Not strictly true. I want. I'm a big-time wanter, maybe.

Thirty-one. I told the girl what I had to have if I was to keep going. Love, warmth, not to be alone. She touched me. No, not that, I said. You don't understand. Yes I do, she said. Lie back and listen to the water.

Thirty-two. I drove her all the way to Santa Barbara and left her by the side of the highway, under the big fig tree on Anacapa Street. Where was she going from there? I don't think she knew for sure. Should I have made myself responsible for her? Not left her to work her way up the coast? Not picked her up in the first place, when I knew what was going to happen because I wanted it, because she wanted it? I don't suppose I'll ever know.

Thirty-three. I took Margaret and Marty to dinner at The Yellowfingers on Ventura Boulevard. I got them both drunk, and then I picked a fight with the waitress for no earthly reason at all, and then I got up and went home and left Marty and Margaret to straighten it all out. I don't think either one of them could walk or say a straight sentence after all the Manhattans I made them drink.

Thirty-four. I sat under my tree and watched the fish-shaped leaf-shadows drift across the bricks. I've had no luck in my life.

NOEL

MRS. HATHAWAY BROUGHT the children downstairs single file and seated them on straight-back chairs around the reception room, boy-girl-boy-girl, seventeen in all. In the corner stood a robust Christmas tree bedecked with candy canes and tinsel tresses. The air was thick with the scent of pine and furniture polish as a phantom choir sang "Noel" to the strains of a vinyl disc orchestra. Mrs. Hathaway was still fussing over their appearance, fixing the boys' neckties and correcting the girls' posture, when the first couple arrived. In hushed tones they spoke with Mrs. Overton at the front desk. "We were thinking about a girl," said the woman. Mrs. Overton smiled broadly and made a sweeping motion with her hand. "We have a wonderful selection of girls," she said. At this the girls came to attention in their places, each freckle blooming on rosy cheeks. And as Mrs. Hathaway presented them, each one stood and curtsied on cue. "Christa is a lovely child, age eight . . . Melinda has a beautiful singing voice for carols . . . Stephanie has an exceptionally sweet temperament. . . ."

The clients turned to Mrs. Overton and quietly indicated their choice. She nodded, poker-faced, and prepared the papers. Money changed hands. The girls eyed each other nervously as Mrs. Overton recited the rental stipulations: "You understand that this is only a 48-hour agreement. The girl must be returned by noon on the day after Christmas or late charges will be assessed at ten dollars per hour and you will forfeit the insurance deposit." When everything was in order she looked over at Mrs. Hathaway and said, "Melinda, please." A little squeak of joy escaped into the room as Melinda jumped up and rushed to join her hosts for the holiday. The other girls watched her go, their hope renewing as another pair of patrons entered the room from the foyer.

Throughout the afternoon they came two by two, childless on Christmas Eve. They were high-rise dwellers and they were pensioners from South Side bungalows. A few were first-timers, uneasy, unable to meet the children's eyes. (The repeat customers, who each year made up a majority of the business, had reserved their "Kristmas Kid" by name, weeks in advance, and had come by in the morning for express pick-up.) Most of those now arriving to browse among the leftovers were last minute shoppers.

The girls were in great demand, especially the youngest candidates in curls. Dimples and bangs, once again, were very popular. And for the boys, missing teeth and cowlicks were favorite features. Considering the irregular inventory, business was good. Of the original lot, only two rather plain-looking lads remained at six o'clock, closing time. Both bore the stigma of a pubescent mustache.

Mrs. Overton finished her filing while Mrs. Hathaway affixed the "Closed" sign on the door, unplugged the Christmas lights, and drew the window shades all around. The boys sat silent, watchful.

Said Mrs. Overton, "I told you about those two pre-teens, didn't I?"

"Yes, ma'am, you did."

"Then why did you bring them down with the others?"

"Well, I was hoping, I guess." Mrs. Hathaway glanced at her rejected charges. They gazed guiltily into their laps. "It did no harm to give them at least a chance."

Mrs. Overton regarded her for a moment, then answered calmly, "I suppose not." She was pleased with the day's proceeds, too pleased to argue over a minor transgression. Anyway, she did not want to discourage a certain degree of compassion, believing it was one of the qualities that made Mrs. Hathaway an effective matron.

Outside it was beginning to snow. Before leaving, Mrs. Overton wrapped herself in a muffler and donned a woolen cap. "I'll see you day after tomorrow then."

"Goodnight, ma'am," said Mrs. Hathaway, then turning to the boys. "Come along."

As they slowly ascended the stairs, one of the boys emitted a peculiar nasal sound, a congested sentiment perhaps.

"Quiet, child," said Mrs. Hathaway.

THE PERSONAL TOUCH

SEED CATALOG – TOSS; Acme flier — keep for Mary; *Sports Illustrated* keep; phone bill, electric bill, gas bill keep, keep, keep. Damn it. Subscription-renewal notice to *Snoop* — toss. . . .

Joe Priddy tossed, but the envelope landed face up, balanced on the edge of the wastebasket. He was about to tip it in when he noticed the words PERSONAL MESSAGE INSIDE on the lower-left front.

Personal, my ass, he thought, but he picked it up and read it.

Dear **Mr. Pridy,**

We have not yet received your subscription renewal to SNOOP, the Magazine of Electronic and Personal Surveillance. We trust that, after having been a loyal subscriber for 9 months, you will renew your subscription so that we may continue to send SNOOP to you at **19 Merrydale Drive**.

We do not have to remind you, **Mr. Pridy**, of the constant changes in surveillance technology and techniques. We are sure that in your own town of **Sidewheel, NY**, you have seen the consequences for yourself. So keep up to date on the latest in surveillance, **Mr. Pridy**, by sending **$11.95** in the enclosed prepaid envelope today. As one involved and/or interested in the field of law enforcement, you cannot afford to be without SNOOP, **Mr. Pridy**.

Best Regards,

David Michaelson
Subscription Director

P.S.: If you choose not to resubscribe, **Mr. Pridy**, would you please take a moment and tell us why, using the enclosed post-paid envelope? Thank you, **Mr. Pridy**.

Joe shook his head. Who did they think they were fooling? "Pridy," said Joe to himself. "Jesus."

Mary's brother Hank had given Joe the subscription to *Snoop* for his birthday. "As a joke," he'd said, winking at Joe lasciviously, a reference to the evening he and Hank had watched the Quincy girl undress in the apartment across the courtyard with the aid of Joe's binoculars. It had taken some imagination to satisfy Mary's curiosity about Hank's joke, and Joe still felt uncomfortable each time *Snoop* hit his mailbox. And now they wanted him to resubscribe?

He was about to toss the letter again when he thought about the P.S. "Tell us why." Maybe he'd do just that. It would get all his feelings about *Snoop* out of his system to let them know just how he felt about their "personal message."

> Dear MR. MICHELSON,
>
> I have chosen not to resubscribe to SNOOP after having received it for 9 MONTHS because I am sick and tired of computer-typed messages that try to appear personal. I would much rather receive an honest request to "Dear Subscriber" than the phony garbage that keeps turning up in my mailbox. So do us both a favor and don't send any more subscription-renewal notices to me at 19 MERRYDALE DRIVE in my lovely town of SIDEWHEEL, NY. OK?
>
> Worst regards,
>
> Joseph H. Priddy
>
> P.S.: And it's Priddy, not Pridy. Teach your word processor to spell.

Joe pulled the page out of the typewriter and stuffed it into the postpaid envelope.

Two weeks later, he received another subscription-renewal notice. As before, PERSONAL MESSAGE INSIDE was printed on the envelope. He was about to throw it away without opening it when he noticed his name was spelled correctly. "Small favors," he muttered, sitting on the couch with Mary and tearing the envelope open. Could they, he wondered, be responding to his letter?

Dear **Mr. Priddy**,

Christ, another word-processor job. . . . At least they got the name right. . . .

> We received your recent letter and are sorry that you have chosen not to resubscribe to SNOOP, the Magazine of Electronic and Personal Surveillance. We hope, however, that you will reconsider, for if you resubscribe now at the low price of **$427.85** for the next nine issues

$427.85? What the hell? What happened to $11.95?

> we will be able to continue your subscription uninterrupted, bringing you all the latest news and updates on surveillance technology and techniques. And in today's world, **Mr. Priddy**, such knowledge should not be taken lightly. You'll learn techniques similar to those that led New York City law-enforcement officials to the biggest heroin bust in history, that told members of the FBI of a plan to overthrow the state government of Montana by force, that alerted us to your own four-month affair with **Rayette Squires**.

Wha—Joe could feel the blood leave his face.

> You'll get tips on photographic surveillance, as well, and learn techniques that will let your own efforts equal that of the enclosed 2 by 2 showing you and **Miss Squires** at **The Side-wheel Motel** in the lovely town of **Sidewheel, NY.**

Joe dove for the envelope, which was lying dangerously close to Mary's *McCall's*. He peeked as surreptitiously as possible into the envelope and found, between the slick paper flier and the return envelope, a well-lit color photo of him and Rayette in a compromising and fatiguing position. His wife looked up in response to his high-pitched whine, and he smacked the envelope shut, giggled weakly, and finished the letter.

> We sincerely hope, **Mr. Priddy**, that you'll rejoin our family of informed subscribers by mailing your check for **$427.85** very soon. Shall we say within 10 days?

Regards,

David Michaelson
Subscription Director

Joe got up, envelope and letter in hand, and went to the bedroom to get out the shoe box he'd hidden — the one with the money he'd been squirreling away for an outboard motor, the money even Mary didn't know about.

When he counted it, it totaled $428.05. Which made sense. This time, the return envelope wasn't prepaid.

THE VERTICAL FIELDS

In Memory of C. D. K.

ON CHRISTMAS EVE around 1942, when I was a boy, after having the traditional punch and cookies and after having sung 'round the fire (my Aunty Mary at the piano), I, with my sister, my mother and my aunts, and Emma Jackman and her son, got into Emma Jackman's car and drove down Taylor Avenue to church for the midnight service: I looked out the rear window at passing houses, doors adorned with holly wreaths, I looked into windows — catching glimpses of tinseled trees and men and women and children moving through rooms into my mind and memory forever; the car slowed to the corner stop at Jefferson and the action seemed like a greater action, of Christmas in a cold damp Missouri night; patches of snow lay on the ground and in the car the dark figures of my mother and sister and aunts talked around me and the car began to move along in an air of sky — at bottom dark and cold, seeming to transform the car, my face, and hands, pressed close to the glass as I saw my friends with their parents in their cars take the left turn onto Argonne Drive and look for a parking place near the church; Emma Jackman followed, and I watched heavily coated figures make their exits, and move down the winter walk toward the jewel-like glittering church — up the steps into the full light of the doorway — fathers and sons and mothers and daughters I knew and understood them all, I gazed at them with blazing eyes: light poured from open doors; high arched stained glass windows cast downward slanting shafts of color across the cold churchyard, and the organ boomed inside while we parked and got out and walked along the sidewalk, I holding my mother's right arm, my sister held mother's left arm (mother letting us a little support her) — down the sidewalk to join others at the warmly good noisy familiar threshold:

spirits swirled up the steps into the church and Billy Berthold handed out the Christmas leaflets, I gripped mine. I looked at the dominant blue illustration of Birth in white and yellow rays moving outward to form a circle around the Christ child's skull as Mary downward gazed; Joseph; kneeling wisemen downward gazed; I gazed down the long center aisle at the rising altar's dazzling cross and we moved down the aisle, slipped in front of Mr. and Mrs. Sloan and my buddy Lorry, Mr. and Mrs. Dart and my buddy Charles, Mr. and Mrs. Reid and my buddy Gene and his brother Ed—we then knelt away the conscious realization of our selves among music in the House of the Lord, I conscious of a voice that, slowly, coarsely, wandered—the I (eye) in see, hear me (I), we were on our feet singing, and the choir swept down the aisle, their familiar faces moving side to side as collective voices raised in anthem I held the hymnbook open and my mother and sister and I sang in celebration of God the crowded and brightly decorated—pine boughs and holly wreaths hung round the walls with candles high on each pew, I glanced at the gleaming cross—my spine arched, and far beyond the church, beyond the front door, beyond the land of the last sentence in James Joyce's *Dubliners* a distant door seemed to open away beyond pungent green of pine gathered around rich red hollyberry clusters, red velvet, white-yellow center of candle flame, white of silk, gold of tassle, and gleaming glittering eternally cubistic gold cross and darkness of wooden beams powerfully sweeping upward—apex for the strange smoky pneuma that so exhilarated me, I who smiled and reeled in a vast cold cold gaze down at myself listening to Charles Kean's Christian existentialist sermon in time before the plate was passed and the choir had singing, gone, and we were outside, I standing by my sister; my mother and aunts were shaking Charles's hand, I shook that solid hand warmly, and I walked down the steps, my mother and sister and aunts again, again, once again it rushed through me taking my breath, my spine arched toward trees and streets walking slowly breathing deep I moved down the sidewalk, eyes crystallizing streets yards houses and all lives within; my perception forked upward through treetops into the vertical fields of space, and a moment later, in the crowded back seat of the car, as Emma Jackman started the engine, I breathed vapor on the rear window, and with my finger, I signed my name.

THE VISITATION

No one knows what they are about or, for that matter, where they came from. Not even the mayor knows.

Do you know where they come from? we ask.

No, he says, but our census is working on it.

Today the deities (they told us they are gods) burned down Durango's Drugs.

I hear something clambering on the roof, walk outside barefoot onto the lawn, and shine my flashlight upon the east side's apex where three of them sit on their haunches peeling off shingles and sailing them into the neighbors' yards.

Stop that! I shout.

They turn their faces languorously toward mine, stare for a minute or more, then flip three shingles at my forehead.

I duck, crawl back into the house, make myself a pot of tea.

I stopped one on the street.

Excuse me, I said, but could you tell me why you just laid into that Camaro with a tire iron?

Because I felt like it, it said, and walked on.

What the deities look like: Eyes with a golden tint. Fingers, five per hand, thicker than ours. Bad teeth. Average height: 5' 4". General demeanor: displeased.

Where did you get your godhood? we ask.

From our parents, they reply.

Each of us has our own theory. Some say we have been cursed without just cause, others that we have been cursed with just cause, still others that it's all a blessing in disguise. Mrs. Sepal told me what she believed.

I believe that comparisons are odious, she said, and that the heavenly father is a ghost. I believe in one single unfathomable word and nothing else. I believe intentions are glowing fires, that creatures of idleness are bootblacking the sun, that that slave master contemplation has sunk into a deep swoon. She paused, then concluded with a shout, I believe in the eternal coming of the Bridegroom!

The deities descend upon her in droves.

We call a town meeting, but the wrathful deities show up as a woodwind ensemble and drown out our words with their reedy squeals.

I climb up to the cupola on Town Hall and scream up into the sky meaningless syllables. After an hour or so I climb back down and go home. When I enter the kitchen, I see four of them sitting around my overturned refrigerator, feeding on its remains.

We call on the parish priest and ask him what we can do.
Have you tried reason? he says.
We strap him with our belts to a chair, then deliver him up to them.

Life in our village goes on.

They enter my shop, three of them dressed in dark double-breasted suits with shiny bowlers. We're here to plunder, they say.
I say, Well.
Any objections? they ask.
I say, Some of this curiosa I've had for years.
All the better.
I look around the shop as they go into action, but my eyes refuse to focus, all my books and objects a blur.
You deserved this, they say, brushing the dust off their lapels with the backs of their cream-colored hands. Now thank us.
Thank you.
You're welcome, and good day.
Good day, I say.
They tip their bowlers, file out the door.

.   .   .

Then one morning all is quiet, we step shyly from our homes.

Where are they?

Have they ascended to the clouds?

We crumple on our knees to the pavement; we grin stupidly at one another; we begin to tear out each other's hair.

THE STRONG MAN

CHEER UP," HARRY SAID. "It isn't really a serious matter."

"You don't think so?"

He only smiled. It was a great gift, that smile, sudden, frank, wholly disarming, and, like a child's shaped by secret mischief. It was impossible to talk seriously about anything in the face of such an abrupt and charming defense. She looked at him, studied him as she might have examined a perfect stranger—the close-cut, sandy hair, the small eyes, bland and sad as a dog's, the soft lips and the thrilling brightness of his smile. Harry was almost handsome, certainly, but, she thought, strangely unreal. There was a sense of the alien about him. You never quite thought of him in three dimensions.

"No," he went on, "we'll get over it. And anything you can get over isn't really serious—like the measles."

"Or smallpox."

Harry smiled again and poured some beer into her glass. They were sitting in a little trattoria beside the Arno. It was twilight, the long gold twilight of Tuscany in late summer, and all of the tables were taken. Along the sidewalks on both sides of the street the bright, close-pressed crowds flowed as slowly as the river. They had just arrived in Pisa that afternoon from Rome.

"We'll stay here a couple of days and rest," he said. "It's a restful place. We can sit by the window in the hotel room and have late breakfasts and see the river. In the morning I'll take you over to see the *campanile*. It really does lean, you know."

"Does it?" she said. "I'm not sure I'm going to stay with you. I'm not at all sure I ought to."

"Don't be silly," he said. "Of course you'll stay."

"You're so sure of me. Why are you always so sure?"

She was fumbling in her pocketbook for matches. She thought for a moment that she was going to cry and she didn't want that to happen. He leaned across the table and lit her cigarette with his lighter.

"Where would you go?"

"You bastard," she said.

"No, I'm serious," Harry said. "For once I'm being perfectly serious. Let's try and be rational about this whole thing. Where would you go?"

"Home. I think I'd like to go home."

"Out of the question," he said. "What would you do when you got there — get a divorce?"

"Stop it, Harry. I don't know what I'm going to do."

"I want to know," he said quickly. "Do you want a divorce or don't you? It's just that simple. Either — or."

"I don't know, Harry. I don't know what to do yet. I'm trying to work all this out in my mind. Will you please stop asking me dumb questions?"

"What about the baby? You ought to think about that. Did you ever stop to think about the baby?"

At last she began to cry. He gave her his handkerchief.

"Please," he said. "Even if these people can't understand English, they can't ignore a sobbing woman."

She stiffened a little.

"You care what they think, don't you?"

"There, you see, you've stopped now."

"I could say it in Italian," she said. "I could stand up and say it in very simple Italian. This is my husband who is making me cry. My husband is always making me cry. My husband is always sleeping with other women. When I find out about it we leave. We are always leaving places."

"You know what they'd say? They'd say, why don't you leave him? The logical answer."

"You'd like that, wouldn't you?"

"I don't know," Harry said. "I never really thought of it until just now."

"You can't even imagine it. After all this time, you can't even conceive of my leaving you. Now that I'm pregnant, you're certain."

"Do we have to go through all this?"

"You can't even imagine my leaving you, can you?"

"No," he said. "To tell you the truth I can't."

"All right," she said. "Suppose I don't. Suppose I just stay. Then what?"

"Everything," he said, smiling wonderfully. "Then everything. We'll begin again. No reason why not. We could go up to Paris. I know some people there."

"Why not home?"

"Why not?"

"Are you serious? Would you really go home?"

"I might even go to work," he said. "Idle hands . . ."

"The awful thing," she said, "is that I never know when you're telling the truth. I never know whether I can trust you."

He signaled for the waiter.

"I suppose you'll have to," he said. "I suppose you'll just have to take that chance."

They crossed the street and edged into the crowd walking along the bank of the river. It was getting dark now and the mountains to the north were only a bulk of heavy shadows. The mountains were disappearing and the river was dark. She could smell the river and she could hear it, but she could only see it where light fell. She felt dazed, as if not only Harry but the whole world was unreal, vanishing. It gets dark and the mountains go away.

"Where does everything go in the dark?" she had asked when she was a child.

"Things just goes to sleep," the colored nurse had said. "They just curl up and go to sleep."

They moved across the bridge with the crowd and then they were on a narrow cobbled street with cafés and restaurants and movie theaters. They heard a military band playing faintly somewhere and they heard the laughter and the rich syllables of the language all around them. Farther along the street they entered a small square. At the corner there was a tight circle of people around a single figure. The man was very pale under a light, powerfully built, in bathing trunks and sneakers. He stood relaxed, slump-shouldered, while a short fat man, his bald head shining in the lamplight, walked slowly around the circle of viewers displaying a placard with a picture of the man in bathing trunks.

"What is he?" she asked. "A magician?"

Harry laughed. "No," he said. "He's some kind of a strong man. Do you want to watch?"

"I don't know. I've never seen one."

"Let's."

There was a hush as the man began his performance. He lifted heavy weights over his head, straining, his pale muscles bulging and the sweat glistening all over his body. When he had finished, the short man passed through the crowd taking a few coins in his hat. The strong man leaned against the lamppost breathing heavily. She thought he looked so lonely out there in that zone of light, alone and almost naked. He did not seem to be looking at anyone or anything. He seemed unaware of the crowd. He only rested, breathing hard, tautly aloof like a beast in a cage. She took Harry's hand in hers.

"Let's go," Harry said. "This is a bore."

"Wait," she said. "He's going to do something with ropes."

Two men from the crowd carefully wrapped him in a net of knotted ropes. When they had finished, he could not move his hands or his feet, and they stepped back into the crowd. The strong man remained still for a moment. Then he closed his eyes and began to strain against the ropes. Sweat was slick on his forehead. The large veins in his neck showed blue and swollen against his skin. Very slowly, painfully it seemed, he began a shrugging motion with his shoulders. The ropes left raw red lines where they bit into his flesh. For a desperate moment it seemed to her that he would never be able to free himself, but then he twisted sharply and somehow freed one arm. The crowd clapped, and the short man passed the hat again while the strong man finished wriggling free of the rest of the ropes.

"He's going to try chains next," she said. "Let's see him get out of chains."

"It's just a trick. Don't you see that? Come on."

"I want to see it."

"For Christ's sake!" Harry said. "Oh, all right."

This time he was wrapped tightly in chains. He stood looking blankly into the faces of the crowd while two men wrapped him in chains.

The strong man started with his whole body twisting against the chains. Abruptly he slipped and fell and there was a gasp and the brute sound of iron on stone. He lay as still as a fallen doll on the street.

"Let's go," Harry said.

"I want to watch," she said. "I want you to stay and see it."

"He'll never get loose now. They'll have to set him free."

"I don't think so."

"This is silly," Harry said. "I can't see any earthly reason why we should have to stand here and watch this."

"Look!" she said. "He's moving now."

The strong man began to writhe on the street. He moved along on his back, tense and fluttering like a fish out of water. He rolled over onto his stomach and now they could see blood on his lips and the glazed, fanatic concentration in his eyes.

"You don't have to look," she said. "Close your eyes if you don't want to look at it."

She watched the man in chains and she felt a strange exhilaration. She felt her own body move, tense with the subtle rhythm of his struggle. One arm free, then, slowly, very slowly, the other, and, at last sitting up, he twisted his hurt legs free. While his companion passed the hat, the strong man sat in the street and looked at his legs, smiling a little. She turned away and looked at Harry. Poor Harry would never understand. Whatever she finally decided to do, Harry would never understand.

"Let's go back to the hotel and have dinner," he said.

They walked back the way they had come, and as they crossed the bridge over the Arno she saw that there was a new moon and she could see the dark shape of the mountains. They were still there, and she could feel the strength and flow of the river, and she could feel her child, the secret life struggling in her womb.

IMPORTANT THINGS

For YEARS THE CHILDREN whimpered and tugged. "Tell us, tell us."

You promised to tell the children some other time, later, when they were old enough.

Now the children stand eye to eye with you and show you their teeth. "Tell us."

"Tell you what?" you ask, ingenuous.

"Tell us The Important Things."

You tell your children there are six continents and five oceans, or vice versa.

You tell your children the little you know about sex. Your children tell you there are better words for what you choose to call The Married Embrace.

You tell your children to be true to themselves. They say they are true to themselves. You tell them they're lying, you always know when they're lying. They tell you you're crazy. You tell them to mind their manners. They think you mean it as a joke; they laugh.

There are tears in your eyes. You tell the children the dawn will follow the dark, the tide will come in, the grass will be renewed, every dog will have its day. You tell them the story of The Littlest Soldier whose right arm, which he sacrificed while fighting for a noble cause, grew back again.

You say that if there were no Evil we wouldn't have the satisfaction of choosing The Good. And if there were no pain, you say, we'd never know our greatest joy, relief from pain.

You offer to bake a cake for the children, a fudge cake with chocolate frosting, their favorite.

"Tell us," say the children.

You say to your children, "I am going to die."

"When?"

"Someday."

"Oh."

You tell your children that they, too, are going to die. They already knew it.

You can't think of anything else to tell the children. You say you're sorry. You *are* sorry. But the children have had enough of your excuses.

"A promise is a promise," say the children.

They'll give you one more chance to tell them of your own accord. If you don't, they'll have to resort to torture.

ROTH'S DEADMAN

THE DEADMAN'S HEAD was rotated slightly toward the window; and the desultory afternoon, the sun hard on the trees beside the parking lot and the sprinklers working in the grass, encroached upon the room in unbroken vividness and multiformity. The plastic intravenous tube was still taped at the ankle, the swollen yellow ankle, yellow and swollen as the face and neck of the man, fifty-four years old according to his wristband, now dead, admitted three days previously, alive upon arrival, two days in a coma, and gone now ten minutes before Roth could get to see it happen.

The chart in the nurse's station said the deadman in 117 was: J. B. Houk; business executive; L. R. Downing, Inc.; divorced, two children; possibly alcoholic.

Roth, the new orderly, had often come to stand quietly behind the curtain and watch the phenomenon of J. B. Houk before he died. Roth would stand over the bed and wonder what kind of man J. B. Houk was. The barrel chest of the man heaved irregularly, and his body always appeared to be sucking dextrose from the intravenous tube, drawing in the liquid with ruthless energy. There was something vaguely brutal or unscrupulous in the face, lines about the mouth fixed through time into an automatic hypocritical grimace of benevolence displayed for some selfish end. The hair was pure white above the jaundiced face — some might have called him a distinguished-looking man — and the eyes had been blue, very light blue and surprisingly transparent when Roth first saw them, before J. B. Houk closed his eyes that second day and allowed his body to labor on unburdened by consciousness.

Ray was already stripping clothes out of the closet and folding them up at the foot of the bed. "What should I do?" Roth said.

"I was waiting till you got here to do the body," Ray said. He brought a small suitcase out of the closet and a scarlet-patterned bathrobe on a hanger and placed the clothes he had finished folding into the suitcase, then the bathrobe, exposing the baldspot in his flat-top as he bent down. "We'll have to take care of all these belongings," Ray said, pointing to the nightstand. "I'm supposed to show you how to finish him up so you can do it yourself next time."

"Will we have to take him downstairs?"

"No, Scobie's will be here in a few minutes. They'll take care of him. We don't usually store them here at the hospital." Roth visualized the door to the morgue, identical to the other doors he passed every afternoon on the basement floor after punching his timecard except for the black lettering on it (he might have expected that kind of door to be made of stone or heavy metal).

Ray handed him a paper bag, and Roth went to the nightstand and opened the drawer. Inside was a pair of glasses without a case, a gold wristwatch, wallet, set of car keys, ballpoint pen, four or five packs of matches from a cocktail joint, two large twenty-five cent cigars, and a circular indexed marker for locating appropriate Biblical passages "when in doubt," "when laden with temptation," "when suffering ill-health," etc. Roth placed the articles carefully in the open bag like packed groceries. In the cabinet section of the nightstand was a Gideon's Bible and a dog-eared pile of magazines, a blur of red-margined covers with words like "consumer" and "world" on them — graphs, statistics, and pictures of other businessmen. Roth scooped them up and laid them in the open suitcase with the folded paper bag.

"Miss Trigg said to be sure not to disturb Mr. Tilney," Ray whispered. "He's liable to have another cardiac." Roth reached back and pulled the curtain taut that separated the two beds in the room, wondering for a moment what the frightened unknown little man who lay two yards away might be thinking.

"He's been playing possum, I think," Roth whispered. The bedsprings squeaked at this and Ray chuckled nervously.

"Thinks it might be a bad omen. They're likely to start going three-at-a-time, you know." Roth shrugged.

"Now," Ray said, "the first thing you do is remove any dentures he might have, close his mouth so his jaw won't freeze open, and get his head straight on the pillow, nose up — otherwise you might get a blue cheek."

"Right."

"You can imagine how a blue cheek would go over with the funeral home." Ray quickly inserted his fingers in the half-opened mouth, pushed the tongue back, brought his hand out again almost immediately, and closed the jaw with his palm. Then he gripped the head above the hairline and turned it counterclockwise away from the window. The head stayed where he put it.

"He hasn't got any false teeth."

"Good."

"Notice how I was careful not to touch the skin except where I had to. Wherever you touch him, that part's going to turn color, so you've got to be careful."

"How will they get this yellow out of him? He seems pretty discolored already."

"They have ways. Yellow's easier than blue, and yellow's not our fault. They'll have him laid out looking like the picture of health. Don't worry. He'll be the healthiest-looking man at the funeral."

"Shouldn't we get this intravenous out?" Ray nodded.

"It doesn't matter much if you touch him there because nobody sees that." Ray quickly unraveled the bandage at the ankle and was extracting the needle. Roth unhooked the dextrose bottle to give him slack, scrutinizing the greenish underwater effigy of his face reflected from the glass container, his head weirdly suspended above the starched hospital shirt.

Just then Roth heard a sound of rubber-soled shoes shrieking on the vinyl of the outer hall. The door of the room across the hall was slightly ajar, but nothing was visible but the door itself, surrounded by the immaculate tile walls of the corridor. Then Miss Trigg, the head nurse, came shrieking through the door frame. He and Ray started like grave robbers.

"The family's here to visit," she said. "Have you got him ready? Dr. Shantril hasn't told them yet. He's on his way down."

A brown-haired woman appeared in the hallway, and Miss Trigg blushed and turned to look at the body. The suitcase was still lying open next to it on the bed, and the bony feet and ankles, bruised and purple from the intravenous, were sticking out where the sheet was pulled up. The body was uncovered above the waist.

"He's not quite ready yet," Ray said.

Roth's hand was gripping the iron barrel of the intravenous rack. He could see the woman pause in the doorway and speak to someone out of sight. Miss Trigg yanked the sheet, covering the toes, and quickly tucked it in across the bottom. Ray was reaching toward the suitcase, still clutching the ankle bandage, when Roth saw the woman start to move.

"She's coming in," Roth said.

"I'm sorry," Miss Trigg said, partially blocking the woman at the foot of Mr. Tilney's bed, "you'll have to wait until the doctor arrives." Two girls, one about twelve, one about sixteen, had come in behind the woman. They looked at Miss Trigg expectantly.

"Has there been any change?" the woman said. The sixteen-year-old girl was watching Roth as he wheeled the intravenous rack against the wall. She had brown fluffy hair down to her shoulders. Ray brought out the closed suitcase and crossed behind Miss Trigg and laid it on the chair. Miss Trigg seemed to be at a loss for words. The older girl gave her a frightened look and suddenly stepped around her and planted herself beside the deadman's bed. She seemed to rise up on the balls of her feet.

"The doctor should be here any minute, Mrs. Houk," Miss Trigg said. "I'm sorry." They were all looking at the body now.

The woman's expression was haggard, resigned, immediately resigned, faintly disgusted. "It'll be all right," she said. Then the older girl threw herself upon the swollen, yellow man and desperately kissed the rigid face. Her back heaved up and down.

"Oh, Daddy," she sobbed. "Oh, Daddy, Daddy."

TICKITS

TOBY HECKLER PLACED the slip of yellow paper under the windshield wiper of the black Oldsmobile that straddled two parking spaces. On the yellow paper Toby had printed in red ink "PRAKING MISTEAK" and signed his name "TOBY" in a childish-looking hand. He snapped the cover on his Pilot Razor Point, slipped the pen over his ear, put the pad of yellow papers in his jacket pocket. He moved down Main Street, his chin held high, his sneakers spanking white from Baby's Liquid Shoe Polish.

As Toby passed Thom McAn, he looked in the window, caught the reflection of his sneakers, looked down at them, moved his toes inside. He straightened the pen on his ear, patted the pad of yellow papers in his pocket, moved along. People stared at Toby; he kept his chin high.

Near the First National Bank two elderly ladies waited for the bus. They stood in the middle of the sidewalk away from the curb. Toby pulled out his pad, slipped the pen off his ear, held the cap with his teeth. He printed slowly, meticulously, then handed one of the ladies the slip, "TO MUSH IN WAY" signed "TOBY." He secured his instruments, walked along as before. The two ladies examined the slip of paper, moved closer to the curb.

At the intersection of Main and South the pedestrian crossing light shone bright orange, "DONT WALK." Traffic moved, people stood on the curb. A man with a pin-striped suit and briefcase stepped off the curb, was about to sneak across between cars. Toby began to reach for his pad. The cars closed together; the man stepped back to the curb. Toby brought his hand back. When the green light read "WALK," Toby and the man crossed. The man went into a shop. Toby waited for him, handed him a slip as he came out, "ALLMOST WALKD."

Patrolman McVee stood in front of Charlie's Tobacco Shop; McVee's badge number was 635. Toby stopped, stood next to him. McVee looked over.

"How's it going, Toby?" McVee said.

Toby pulled out his pad, showed it to McVee.

"Lots of business, eh Toby?"

Toby put his pad back, nodded. His eyes rolled, looked tortured.

"Yes, Toby, it's a bitch," McVee said.

Toby looked at McVee's shoes. Except for a single smudge they were shiny, black. Toby bent down, rubbed off the smudge with his hand.

"Thanks Toby," McVee said.

Toby caught McVee's eye, looked down at his own sneakers.

"Very nice, Toby. Spiffy," McVee said.

Toby raised his chin again, moved along.

Before the rain came, Toby had used up half his pad. Near Mario's Grinders there was a dog tied to a parking meter; he had wrapped his leash tightly around the pole. Toby stuck a slip under his collar, "TYED WORNG." Toby walked into the YMCA, handed the man at the desk a slip, "Y BORKEN." On a Park Square bench a man ate a candy bar; he threw his wrapper down. Toby handed him the wrapper and a slip, "PAPUR ON GARSS." The man walked away throwing both papers down. Toby caught up to him, gave him all the papers and another slip, "NOT LISSENING." The man said "Christ," put all the papers in his pocket.

The rain began to wet Toby's slips, blot his ink. He put everything away, looked up at the sky, rolled his eyes.

By the time he got back to Main and South, it was raining hard. A car moved through the intersection, splashed dirty water on his sneakers. Toby walked quickly down South, cut through the alley between Sam's Auto Supplies and Blue Arc Welding, avoided puddles on Mill, moved along the flood control wall on River, came to his bungalow, entered.

Inside there were smells of cabbage, cigarette smoke, spilt alcohol. The entry was dark, lit intermittently with a pale light from the television. He knew his mother lay on the sofa, smoking, drinking, surrounded by TV magazines. The sofa with a large hump cast a shadow on the wall.

Toby took off his sneakers, carried them up the stairs.

His mother turned her head, "Toby, is that you?" Her voice was raspy, tired. But Toby was already in his room, the door closed, Baby's Liquid Shoe Polish in front of him on the floor.

His mother moved to the bottom of the stairs. She coughed, yelled, "Toby!"

Toby opened the door, showed himself to his mother.

She held a cigarette and a drink. "Toby, you could've been a goddamn burglar sneaking around me like that!" Toby closed the door, reached under his bed.

"Toby, you goddamn nut!"

Toby pulled out a shoebox. On the cover it read, "MUTHERS TICKITS."

Toby wrote three slips: "TO MUSH SOMKING," "TO MUSH DIRNKING," "TOO MUSH YELING." He placed the slips in the box. Then, before he put the box away, he wrote one more slip in his largest letters: "ERVYTHING WORNG!"

With the box safely under his bed, Toby sat on the floor, bit his tongue, went to polishing his sneakers spanking white.

THE COGGIOS

I T IS SPRING, AND flamingoes return to the Coggios' lawn, along with the virgin in her sky-blue robe. Inside the miniature picket fence, daisy pinwheels are spinning; a pair of young deer graze and listen. I listen too, imagining the voices of the Coggios calling to me from out behind the house where they take their afternoon leisure.

The Coggio house is lemon yellow, large but not too large. Mr. Coggio is old and bowlegged, and he wears a straw hat when he works outside. In the early days of spring, two of his boys are out with him, hauling manure, mowing, and raking while Mr. Coggio, on his hands and knees, trims the edges and collects clippings, talking softly to himself or maybe to the ground. You never see a dandelion on the Coggio property. No clover, no weeds. The grasses are plush, untangled, as tempting to walk on as those golf courses you see.

As lunchtime approaches, two large Coggio daughters emerge from the house carrying first rags and buckets of soapy water, then linens, china, and silverware. They move across the lawn through sunlight and shade to the screened-in picnic pavilion which has the same yellow roof as the house and birdhouses, perched high over the garden on long poles. Daughters scour the picnic table, the benches, the cement floor. Now they lay out a clean white linen tablecloth. The cloth and the table may be ten, twenty, thirty years old. It's hard to tell the age of things the Coggios own, because they take such good care of them. The white cloth, for instance: if anything is spilled on it the women run boiling water through the stain, soak it, scrub it, and hang it on the clothesline in the sun. I have seen them circle the yard in the evenings gathering up garden tools, lawn chairs. Their knives are sharpened on a stone, their tools oiled, paintbrushes rinsed and rinsed. Rust never forms on the hedge clippers. Nothing is left out in the rain or snow.

It is time to eat, and Mrs. Coggio steps grandly out of the house carrying before her a deep dish pie with an intricate latticework crust on top. The ruffles on her flowered apron, stiff and shiny with starch, are unmoving in the breeze. All the Coggio clothes are crisp, their colors bright with bluing, ironed with great patience by daughters on the sunporch. Tuesday afternoons they take turns at the ironing board, singing with the radio and sipping lemonade while they work. When they sweat, they pat their faces with real handkerchiefs.

The Coggios have settled at the table, crossing themselves and saying the words. Plates are passed and napkins raised and lowered. The boys and their father eat fast, buttering rolls and popping them into their mouths. The women chew steadily, rhythmically, watching the youngest boy as he talks. Mr. Coggio listens but does not look up from his plate.

The ceremony reverses itself, and the women rise to collect remnants of the meal, returning to the house in a silent procession. Now that I know them so well I can almost see the Coggios through the walls of their house, working in the kitchen. They are placing empty soda bottles under the sink in order of size. They are twisting the tops of large plastic trash bags. Someone is bent over the oven replacing the perfectly clean tin foil liner. I can see white, gold-flecked formica countertops, gleaming chrome and stainless steel, a toaster cover made to look like a cat.

Outside Mr. Coggio takes up his bag of clippings. The boys poke each other, returning to their rakes. Then there are sounds: dishes tinkling, a bird that alternates melodies, one high shrill call followed by another that sounds like a crow. The oldest Coggio boy is smoking a cigarette behind the shed, leaning against the wall and staring off into the woods.

It is late afternoon. I can see them from here, taking the sun out back. The girls sit across from one another in the swing, the sun in their hair. The Mr. and Mrs. sit close by in lawn chairs. She knits and he, like his son, gazes toward the woods, smoking his pipe. The girls talk softly. Mr. Coggio nods, is sleepy. The pipe in his lap, he sleeps. The girls whisper. Nothing is moving but the wisps of loose hair that flutter around the faces of the women in the sunlight. This is my favorite way of seeing them.

I survey the house, the grounds, and imagine the Coggios' future. I know the girls will never marry. Why should they? But the boys are restless. They will go, and come back with women carrying babies in white baptismal clothes, and the Coggios will add a high chair, swing sets and a wading pool to their collection. Sunday afternoon gatherings will be bigger and louder. The girls will play with toddlers in the green grass, first urging them to walk, then holding them back as they chase one another in and out among the adults, screaming happily.

At this hour of day, when the sun is low and strong, the Coggios will stand at the end of the driveway waving and smiling as the sons and wives and children back away from them onto the highway and disappear. It is then they will see me. I am patient, knowing that if I wait long enough I will be welcome in this yard. I will be ready, having learned their cleanliness and their order; ready, when I hear them call me from across the yard.

Come to us, the women will sing sweetly. Come, come! The old man will speak roughly but with a hint of a smile. Mrs. Coggio will hold up a peach pie for me to see.

I'm coming! I'll call back, and stepping lightly onto the grass, past the pinwheels, past the virgin and the flamingoes, I will take my place.

HOW J. B. HARTLEY
SAW HIS FATHER

FROM A HEADLAND AIMED west into the sea, Hartley saw the night waves throw themselves against this windless California shore.

Below the headland of granite, the beach was a sickleblade of light disappearing into a fog bank south of Fort Ord.

First as shadow athwart an offshore reef, then as a massive shape rising, Hartley saw it, and at once looked at his wrist watch to note this hour, and the number of seconds passing.

Thinking back, thinking back on it a great many times, Hartley understood those sixty-two seconds to be very much like an X-ray plate he had viewed at a hospital, the plate of a man's head; not a nail or shrapnel, but an irregular piece of steel, mutant, as though moss-covered, lodged without intention or explanation in that brain. The shard of steel seemed adrift yet firm in the effulgence that was that brain's watery tissues. Exactly that way: this massive shadow rising from the reef's corridors was held also in a geographical frame of headland, of the shoreline south. The Bay and the X-ray juxtaposed always came back to Hartley even though not fully understood, those parallels.

When only a boy, Hartley saw himself becoming a draftsman; therefore across the first page of all his textbooks he inscribed either straight, accurate lines, or lines curved exactly, as the edge of a lunch money coin is curved. Later Hartley saw himself becoming an engineer, a Civil Engineer; therefore "Civil" became a word that he repeated to himself often at night.

Later, Hartley's drafting projects were very neat, to scale, but Hartley's solutions to the problems in Pre-Engineering were often wrong—the figures correct, but reversed on the Answer Sheet. Whereupon Hartley became a well-satisfied Programmer.

Hartley worked always until midnight. He imposed his programs-of-order on the surges of paper that flowed from the tellers' stations through the accounting channels of six, chain-owned banks.

If once he had been a foster child, Hartley lived now very well in an apartment complex, alone. Each month he saved one hundred dollars, ate no meat.

Often past midnight after work in the Bank, for no conscious reason, Hartley parked on this headland in order to stare at the sea. This night he was neither extended nor fatigued. Nevertheless, he saw a shadow rise, become substance, become waterborne, saw it rock steadily in the moon's half-light.

From a feeling deeper than any reef, Hartley understood he must come here again, in secret, to stand in this place, to view this thing again. Nor would he bring others, especially none of the divorced women tellers who had children; nor would he photograph it with infrared technology for report to the All-Branch Newsletter. . . .

Without averting his gaze, Hartley kneeled, sighted accurately, and with the point of a fish-sized stone, made a mark on the clay skin of the headland ⟶ the azimuth precise, a mark aimed at the shadow.

Offshore, Hartley saw the forehead shape, then the upthrust crag of its nose, the mouth agape — a head floating, its surface the glitter of wet kelp and slime, the eyes formal, without expression, as in statuary, staring aloft at the sky.

This head afloat tilted upward. Hartley thought the body of a giant must be half-buoyant, half-waterlogged below the surface. The onshore breeze veered. The head of craggy granite came slowly about, drifted toward this headland.

Hartley thought hulk, thought wrecked hull; water cascaded down from the eye and from the nostrils, like water from the scuppers of a rolling ship. Air under great pressure, from some inner cavern, caused one nostril and the mouth to exhale a cloud of mist.

As the head rose, the last water rushed down the cheek and through the kelp that was its beard. The head rolled. One ear took water, then drained white foam back into the sea. It was no giant. It was a head floating.

Neither frightened nor in awe nor moved, Hartley watched the head ride lighter, hold steady in the sea.

Hartley looked directly down into its mouth, agape in the light. He saw strong, battered teeth — like tusks randomly aligned — all the rows of teeth worn smooth by the action of the waves.

The wind blew a stronger gust, a great black wing of a bird rowing the night. The wind strong across the mouth made the mouth's cavern speak.

Hartley listened intently.

From the head adrift and from the undertow of water, he heard . . .

Ordnung . . . Order . . . Ordur . . .

Like a dark sail taking a slow-minded wind, again half-wash, the granite bulk of a head drifted offshore, was again in darkness, went without either grace or ceremony beneath the surface of the Bay.

Hartley was still kneeling, the sharp marker stone in his hand.

Low, as though fleeing, a seabird flew along the cliff's edge, pivoted in a roil of wings, seemed to grow large before Hartley's face — then, screaming, was gone.

Hartley stood. Again he noted the exact time.

Hartley thought ahead, believed his apartment would be quiet at this hour because a great many other night workers, people he did not know, also lived there.

Hartley believed he would sleep very well until late afternoon, a Saturday. And then that night, or for certain on Tuesday, he would return to this headland.

But he never did.

THE NEIGHBOR

THE IDEA WAS TO WATCH his gaunt wife, seated on the sulky, drive the chocolate-colored mare down the dirt road to the general store, to make a small purchase there, and return. He was a black man in his fifties, she a white woman the same age, his children (from a previous marriage) were black, her children (also from a previous marriage) were white. Everyone else in town was white also. Many of them had never seen a black man before this one. That's probably why he had this idea about the sulky and his wife and the store.

On the other hand, he may have had it because he and his wife and all their children were incompetent and, in various ways, a little mad. The madness had got them kicked out of the city, but here, after three years in this small farm community north of the city, it was the incompetence that angered the people around them. Country people can forgive madness, but a week ago, the family's one immediate neighbor, a dour young man in his late twenties, had walked out his back door and had seen, for the tenth time, one of their chickens scratching in his pathway to the woodpile. He'd rushed back into his house, and returning with an Army .45 hand-gun, had fired eight bullets into the chicken, making a feathered, bloody mess of it.

That night, the black man with his two teen-aged daughters and his two teen-aged stepsons and his wife drove to the racetrack and bought for one hundred dollars an unclaimed, chocolate-colored trotter, an eighteen-year-old mare named Jenny Lind. They rented a van and lugged her home and put her in the barn with the goats, sheep, chickens, and the two Jersey heifers. The farm, the huge barn, the animals — except for the mare — were all part of an earlier idea, the idea of living off the land. But the climate had proved harsh, the ground stony and in hills, the neighbors more or less uncooperative — and of course there was that incompetence.

It was the end of the summer, and every morning as the sun rose the black man got up and before his breakfast walked the mare along the side of the dirt road in the low, cold mist. Behind him, in layers, were the brown meadow, the clumpy rows of gold and ruby-colored elm trees, and the dark hills, and the mist-dimmed, orange sun. Every morning he paraded Jenny Lind the length of the route he had planned for his wife and the sulky — his jet black arm raised to the bridle, his face proudly looking straight ahead of him as he walked past his neighbor's house, his mind reeling with delight as he imagined his wife in her frail-wheeled sulky riding to the store, where she would buy him some pipe tobacco and some salt for the table, a small package to be wrapped in brown paper and tied with string, and then returning along the curving dirt road to the house, one of her sons or his daughters would run out, and holding the reins for her, would help her graciously down. In that way, the horse received its daily exercise — for no one in the family knew how to ride, because, as he insisted, no one in the family had been to a riding academy yet, and besides, Jenny Lind was a trotter.

They searched all over the state for a sulky they could afford, but no one would sell it to them. Finally, he phoned the man at the racetrack who had sold them the horse and learned of a good, used sulky for sale in a town in the far southwest corner of the state. That morning, after exercising the mare, he and his wife got into the pickup truck and drove off to see about the used sulky.

All day long, the two teen-aged sons and the two teen-aged daughters rode the mare, bareback, up and down the dirt road, galloping past the neighbor's house, braking to a theatrical stop at the general store, and galloping back again. A hundred times they rode the old horse full-speed along that half-mile route. Silvery waves of sweat covered her heaving sides and neck, and her large, watery eyes bulged from the exertion, and late in the afternoon, as the sun was drifting quickly down behind the pines in back of the house, the mare suddenly veered off the road and collapsed on the front lawn of the neighbor's house and died there. The boy who was riding her was able to leap free of the collapsing bulk, and astonished, terrified, he and his brother and stepsisters ran for their own house and hid in a loft over the barn, where, eating sandwiches and listening to a transistor radio, they awaited the return of their parents.

The neighbor stood in his living room and, as darkness came on, stared unbelieving at the dead horse on his lawn. Finally, when it was completely dark and he couldn't see it anymore, he went out onto his front porch and waited for the black man and his wife to come home.

Around ten o'clock, he heard their pickup clattering along the road. The truck stopped beside the enormous bulk of the horse. With the pale light from the truck splashed across its dark body, the animal seemed of gigantic proportions, a huge, equestrian monument pulled down by vandals. The neighbor left his porch and walked down to where the horse lay. The black man and his wife had got out of their truck and were sitting on the ground, stroking the mare's forehead.

The neighbor was a young man, and while a dead animal was nothing new to him, the sight of a grown man with black skin, weeping, and a white woman sitting next to him, also weeping, both of them slowly stroking the cold nose of a horse ridden to death — that was something he'd never seen before. He patted the woman and the man on their heads, and in a low voice told them how the horse had died. He was able to tell it without judging the children who had killed the animal. Then he suggested that they go on to their own house and he would take a chain and with his tractor would drag the carcass across the road from his lawn to their meadow, where tomorrow they could bury it by digging a pit next to it, close enough, he told them, so that all they would have to do was shove the carcass with a tractor or a pickup truck and it would drop in. They quietly thanked him and got up and climbed back into their truck and drove to their own house.

READING THE PAPER

ALL I WANT TO DO is read the paper, but I've got to do the wash first. There's blood all over everything. Duke and the rest of the family except me and Timmy were killed last night by a drunk driver, run over in a movie line, and this blood is not easy to get out. Most of the fabrics are easy to clean, however, so I don't even bother reading the fine print on the Cheer box. They make this soap to work in all conditions anymore. Then I get Timmy up and ready for school. He eats two Hostess doughnuts and before he's even down the street and I've picked up the paper, I can hear him screaming down there. Somebody's dragging him into a late model Datsun, light brown, the kind of truck Duke, bless his soul, always thought was silly. So, I've got the paper in my hands and there's someone at the door. So few people come to the back door that I know it's going to be something odd, and I'm right. It's that guy in the paper who escaped from the prison yesterday. He wants to know if he can come in and rape me and cut me up a little bit. Well, after he does that, my coffee's cold, so I pour a new cup and am about to sit down when I see Douglas, my brother from Dill, drive in the driveway in his blue Scout, so I pour two cups. Douglas looks a little more blue this morning than a week ago. He started turning blue about a year before they found the bricks in his house were made out of Class Ten caustic poison or something. He's built a nice add-on or he and Irene, bless her soul, would have moved. But at least this morning, he's wearing an extra John Deere hat on the growth on his shoulder, so that's an improvement. He says he's heard about Duke and the three girls and he asks me, "What were you all going to see?" I can barely hear him because I see two greasers backing Duke's new T-bird out the sidelawn. If they're not careful, they're going to hit the mailbox. They miss it and pull away; that car was always the prettiest turquoise in the world. I stir a little more Cremora into my coffee and turn to my blue brother. His left eye is a little worse, bulging more and glowing more often these days. You know, as much as I stir and stir this Cremora, there's always a little left floating on the top.

THIEF

HE IS WAITING at the airline ticket counter when he first notices the young woman. She has glossy black hair pulled tightly into a knot at the back of her head—the man imagines it loosed and cascading to the small of her back—and carries over the shoulder of her leather coat a heavy black purse. She wears black boots of soft leather. He struggles to see her face—she is ahead of him in line—but it is not until she has bought her ticket and turns to walk away that he realizes her beauty, which is pale and dark-eyed and full-mouthed, and which quickens his heartbeat. She seems aware that he is staring at her and lowers her gaze abruptly.

The airline clerk interrupts. The man gives up looking at the woman—he thinks she may be about twenty-five—and buys a round-trip, coach class ticket to an eastern city.

His flight leaves in an hour. To kill time, the man steps into one of the airport cocktail bars and orders a scotch and water. While he sips it he watches the flow of travelers through the terminal— including a remarkable number, he thinks, of unattached pretty women dressed in fashion magazine clothes—until he catches sight of the black-haired girl in the leather coat. She is standing near a Travelers Aid counter, deep in conversation with a second girl, a blonde in a cloth coat trimmed with gray fur. He wants somehow to attract the brunette's attention, to invite her to have a drink with him before her own flight leaves for wherever she is traveling, but even though he believes for a moment she is looking his way he cannot catch her eye from out of the shadows of the bar. In another instant the two women separate; neither of their directions is toward him. He orders a second scotch and water.

When next he sees her, he is buying a magazine to read during the flight and becomes aware that someone is jostling him. At first he is startled that anyone would be so close as to touch him, but when he sees who it is he musters a smile.

"Busy place," he says.

She looks up at him — Is she blushing? — and an odd grimace crosses her mouth and vanishes. She moves away from him and joins the crowds in the terminal.

The man is at the counter with his magazine, but when he reaches into his back pocket for his wallet the pocket is empty. *Where could I have lost it?* he thinks. His mind begins enumerating the credit cards, the currency, the membership and identification cards; his stomach churns with something very like fear. *The girl who was so near to me*, he thinks — and all at once he understands that she has picked his pocket.

What is he to do? He still has his ticket, safely tucked inside his suitcoat — he reaches into the jacket to feel the envelope, to make sure. He can take the flight, call someone to pick him up at his destination — since he cannot even afford bus fare — conduct his business and fly home. But in the meantime he will have to do something about the lost credit cards — call home, have his wife get the numbers out of the top desk drawer, phone the card companies — so difficult a process, the whole thing suffocating. What shall he do?

First: Find a policeman, tell what has happened, describe the young woman; damn her, he thinks, for seeming to be attentive to him, to let herself stand so close to him, to blush prettily when he spoke — and all the time she wanted only to steal from him. And her blush was not shyness but the anxiety of being caught; that was most disturbing of all. *Damned deceitful creatures*. He will spare the policeman the details — just tell what she has done, what is in the wallet. He grits his teeth. He will probably never see his wallet again.

He is trying to decide if he should save time by talking to a guard near the x-ray machines when he is appalled — and elated — to see the black-haired girl. (*Ebony-Tressed Thief*, the newspapers will say.) She is seated against a front window of the terminal, taxis and private cars moving sluggishly beyond her in the gathering darkness; she seems engrossed in a book. A seat beside her is empty, and the man occupies it.

"I've been looking for you," he says.

She glances at him with no sort of recognition. "I don't know you," she says.

"Sure you do."

She sighs and puts the book aside. "Is this all you characters think about — picking up girls like we were stray animals? What do you think I am?"

"You lifted my wallet," he says. He is pleased to have said "lifted," thinking it sounds more wordly than *stole* or *took* or even *ripped off*.

"I beg your pardon?" the girl says.

"I know you did — at the magazine counter. If you'll just give it back, we can forget the whole thing. If you don't, then I'll hand you over to the police."

She studies him, her face serious. "All right," she says. She pulls the black bag onto her lap, reaches into it and draws out a wallet.

He takes it from her. "Wait a minute," he says. "This isn't mine."

The girl runs; he bolts after her. It is like a scene in a movie — bystanders scattering, the girl zig-zagging to avoid collisions, the sound of his own breathing reminding him how old he is — until he hears a woman's voice behind him:

"Stop, thief! Stop that man!"

Ahead of him the brunette disappears around a corner and in the same moment a young man in a marine uniform puts out a foot to trip him up. He falls hard, banging knee and elbow on the tile floor of the terminal, but manages to hang on to the wallet which is not his.

The wallet is a woman's, fat with money and credit cards from places like Sak's and Peck & Peck and Lord & Taylor, and it belongs to the blonde in the fur-trimmed coat — the blonde he has earlier seen in conversation with the criminal brunette. She, too, is breathless, as is the policeman with her.

"That's him," the blonde girl says. "He lifted my billfold."

It occurs to the man that he cannot even prove his own identity to the policeman.

Two weeks later — the embarrassment and rage have diminished, the family lawyer has been paid, the confusion in his household has receded — the wallet turns up without explanation in one morning's mail. It is intact, no money is missing, all the cards are in place. Though he is relieved, the man thinks that for the rest of his life he will feel guilty around policemen, and ashamed in the presence of women.

ISLA

AFTER THE HURRICANE the coral was broken up, floating loose around the reefs. Within a few weeks it became toxic and the fish died when they breathed it, hundreds of them undulating toward the beaches on the waves.

One morning we woke and there were at least forty of them on their sides, lapping the shore with each rush of water, sloshing to rest for a moment and being carried by the current farther down the beach. That morning we filled garbage bags with them and hauled them up the dune to the heap. But after the beach was cleared and we stood talking on the sand we could see more of them coming, their flat bodies bobbing up and down on the waves.

Some of them were still barely alive, opening and closing their mouths, eyes swiveling in their round sockets. We picked them up too, not caring that perhaps it was more painful for them to suffocate on land. Harvey stood with his hands planted on his hips, his sunburned belly hanging over his trunks as he watched the fish float in. He refused to pick them up as we dragged our plastic bags along the shoreline. He complained about the smell and moved only to push his sunglasses back on his face. His forehead under his hat was beaded with sweat.

We gave up in front of the grove where the tide was the strongest. We could not fight the waves, they brought more and more dead fish and bits of the broken coral.

No one walks there except sometimes Ponce, in the evening or morning light. The first person is so difficult. I lean back in my hammock and watch his slow return across the sand.

If you lie long enough in a palm grove you will hear the coconuts dropping, a final thud on the sand. There is nothing that will quench a thirst more than the water inside. We break them open with a pick, using the flat razor end, the pointed end buried in the sand. We stand on the handle and bring them down hard again and again, stabbing the green flesh until we hear it hit against the nut inside. Then we split it with a knife.

Ponce respects the coconut trees. He owns the grove without possessing any of them. They belong to the island and with a stroke of luck or destiny, he says, he lives on the island, a successful man who wants none of his success, who perhaps feels guilty for it, so he stays in the grove, goes out on his boat to fish, or walks to the beach where no one else will go.

No one writes a story of a hammock, he told me, although a hammock will hold your whole body, a Mayan hammock, cradling you into the night more than any lover, the air underneath cooling you more than any bed. If the rope breaks, he said, it is not the fault of the hammock, it is the fault of the rope.

When the boy drowned off the beach Ponce was with us drinking vodka. He went into the sea with his mask and flippers, drunk like the rest of us who paced on the shore. He soon came back, trailing his fins behind him.

Fifteen minutes under water is too long, he told us walking back to the grove. The boy is dead.

The ambulance came, and the men in their fishing boats. Divers leapt into the water to search the caves, taking a little time because they knew it was too late. The islanders had heard the siren and they came running, lining up on the beach, waiting with arms folded in front of them. The body was found stuck under the coral, lungs exploded. He was a boy who had just arrived on the latest ferry. His brother wept on his knees in the sand.

My first day I swam there. The current carried me toward the rocks and I stayed in place, struggling until it let me go.

We whistled when someone went in too far, or we said nothing. None of us believed the sea would kill until the boy who just arrived.

I had a dream last night, says Ponce, that somehow the strings of a hammock were being played like an instrument. It was beautiful and perfect. He picks up his drink and nods toward the red hammock strung between two coconut palms, swaying in the salty breeze.

The hammock was woven by a man, he says. But the music came from the wind.

CROSSBONES

AT THE END OF THE SUMMER, or the year, or when he could do more with his talent than play guitar in a Village strip joint . . . and after considering his talent for commitment and reluctance she found reluctance in her own heart and marriage talk became desultory, specifics dim, ghostly, lost in bed with Myron doing wrong things, "working on" her, discovering epileptic dysrhythmia in her hips, and he asked about it and she said it hurt her someplace but not, she insisted, in her head, and they fought the next morning and the next as if ravenous for intimacy, and disgraced themselves yelling, becoming intimate with neighbors, and the superintendent brought them complaints that would have meant nothing if they hadn't exhausted all desire for loud, broad strokes, but now, conscious of complaints, they thrust along the vital horizontal with silent, stiletto words, and later in the narrowed range of their imaginations could find no adequate mode of retraction, so wounds festered, burgeoning lurid weeds, poisoning thought, dialogue, and the simple air of their two-room apartment (which had seemed with its view of the Jersey cliffs so much larger than now) seemed too thick to breathe, or to see through to one another, but they didn't say a word about breaking up, even experimentally, for whatever their doubts about one another, their doubts about other others and the city— themselves adrift in it among messy one-night stands—were too frightening and at least they had, in one another, what they had: Sarah had Myron Bronsky, gloomy brown eyes, a guitar in his hands as mystical and tearing as, say, Lorca, though Myron's particular hands derived from dancing, clapping Hasidim; and he had Sarah Nilsin, Minnesota blonde, long bones, arctic schizophrenia in the gray infinities of her eyes, and a turn for lyric poems derived from piratical saga masters. Rare, but opposites cleave in the divisive angularities of Manhattan and, as the dialectics of embattled individuation became more intense, these two cleaved more tightly:

if Sarah, out for groceries, hadn't returned in twenty minutes, Myron punched a wall, pulverizing the music in his knuckles, but punched, punched until she flung through the door shrieking stop; and he, twenty minutes late from work, found Sarah in kerchief, coat, and gloves, the knotted cloth beneath her chin a little stone proclaiming wild indifference to what the nighttime street could hold, since it held most for him if she were raped and murdered in it. After work he ran home. Buying a quart of milk and a pack of cigarettes, she suffered stomach cramps.

Then a letter came from St. Cloud, Minnesota. Sarah's father was coming to visit them next week.

She sewed curtains, squinting down into the night, plucking thread with pricked, exquisite fingertips. He painted walls lately punched. She bought plants for the windowsills, framed and hung three Japanese prints, and painted the hall toilet opaque, flat yellow. On his knees until sunrise four days in a row, he sanded, then varnished floorboards until the oak bubbled up its blackest grain, turbulent and petrified, and Monday dawned on Sarah ironing dresses—more than enough to last her father's visit—and Myron already twice shaved, shining all his shoes, urging her to hurry.

In its mute perfection their apartment now had the expressive air of a well-beaten slave, simultaneously alive and dead, and reflected, like an emanation of their nerves, their own hectic, mainly wordless, harmony, but it wouldn't have mattered if the new curtains, pictures, and varnished floors yelled reeking spiritual shambles because Sarah's father wasn't that kind of minister. His sermons alluded more to Heidegger and Sartre than Christ, he lifted weights, smoked two packs of cigarettes a day, drove a green Jaguar and, since the death of Sarah's mother a year ago in a state insane asylum, had seen species of love in all human relations. And probably at this very moment, taking the banked curves of the Pennsylvania Turnpike, knuckles pale on the walnut wheel, came man and machine leaning as one toward Jersey, and beyond that toward love.

Their sense of all this had driven them, wrenched them out of themselves, onto their apartment until nothing more could make it coincident with what he would discover in it anyway, and they had now only their own absolute physical being still to work on, at nine o'clock, when Myron dashed out to the cleaners for shirts, trousers, and jackets, then dressed in fresh clothing while Sarah slammed and smeared the iron down the board as if increasingly sealed in the momentum of brute work, and then Myron, standing behind her, lighting a cigarette, was whispering as if to himself that she must hurry, and she was turning from the board and in the same motion hurled the iron, lunging after it with nails and teeth before it exploded against the wall and Myron, instantly, hideously understood that the iron, had it struck him, had to burn his flesh and break his bones, flew to meet her with a scream and fists banging her mouth as they locked, winding, fusing to one convulsive beast reeling off walls, tables, and chairs, with ashtrays, books, lamps shooting away with pieces of themselves, and he punched out three of her teeth and strangled her until she dissolved in his hands, and she scratched his left eye blind—but there was hope in corneal transplantation that he would see through it again—and they were strapped in bandages, twisted and stiff with pain a week after Sarah's father didn't arrive and they helped one another walk slowly up the steps of the municipal building to buy a marriage license.

ROSARY

HERE IS A MAN WALKING on a road under the half-moon. The trees are tall and well-furred; the light is little. In his left hand, sometimes swinging at his side and sometimes held lightly poised over his heart, he counts the crystal beads of a rosary. After a quarter of a mile of dark road, he passes a large building of some hard to determine kind. In a ground floor wing, one room is brightly lit; near a window sits a woman with glossy black hair, bent to some papers. The man admires the profile, the hair, the air of industriousness. He likes people who work hard. He walks on, dismissing the notion of rapping on window or door and chatting with the woman. It must be frightening to be a woman alone in a building at night, when the building itself is alone in the countryside, nothing for half a mile round except trees and a man with crystal beads in his hand and the young deer he had seen cross the road in front of him a few minutes back. She would be scared if I knocked, he thought, and walked on.

Now it may be that before the man had drawn abreast of the window the woman had seen him coming, had looked out casually from a darkened window in another room and seen this man stepping up the intermittently moonlit road. It may be that the gleam of crystal in his hand seemed to her the gleam of moon on dagger. It may be that she longed for this silent shadowy assassin to come destroy her, to rescue her from hard work or loneliness or her glossy hair. It may be that she posed at the lighted window to woo his attention, and long after he passed still hoped he might be lurking in the rhododendrons. Perhaps ten minutes later she bravely, desperately stepped out of the unbolted door and stood on the lawn and saw no one but the same deer browsing under the fruit trees. Or not the same: who can tell one animal from another?

THE SOCK

MY HUSBAND IS MARRIED to a different woman now, shorter than I am, about five feet tall, solidly built, and of course he looks taller than he used to and narrower, and his head looks smaller. Next to her I feel bony and awkward and she is too short for me to look her in the eye, though I try to stand or sit at the right angle to do that. I once had a clear idea of the sort of woman he should marry when he married again, but none of his girlfriends was quite what I had in mind and this one least of all.

They came out here last summer for a few weeks to see my son, who is his and mine. There were some touchy moments, but there were also some good times, though of course even the good times were a little uneasy. The two of them seemed to expect a lot of accommodation from me, maybe because she was sick — she was in pain and sulky, with circles under her eyes. They used my phone and other things in my house. They would walk up slowly from the beach to my house and shower there, and later walk away clean in the evening with my son between them, hand in hand. I gave a party, and they came and danced with each other, impressed my friends and stayed till the end. I went out of my way for them, mostly because of our boy. I thought we should all get along for his sake. By the end of their visit I was tired.

The night before they went, we had a plan to eat out in a Vietnamese restaurant with his mother. His mother was flying in from another city, and then the three of them were going off together the next day, to the Midwest. His wife's parents were giving them a big wedding party so that all the people she had grown up with, the stout farmers and their families, could meet him.

When I went into the city that night to where they were staying, I took what they had left in my house that I had found so far: a book, next to the closet door, and somewhere else a sock of his. I drove up to the building, and I saw my husband out on the sidewalk flagging me down. He wanted to talk to me before I went inside. He told me his mother was in bad shape and couldn't stay with them, and he asked me if I would please take her home with me later. Without thinking I said I would. I was forgetting the way she would look at the inside of my house and how I would clean the worst of it while she watched.

In the lobby, they were sitting across from each other in two armchairs, these two small women, both beautiful in different ways, both wearing lipstick, different shades, both frail, I thought later, in different ways. The reason they were sitting here was that his mother was afraid to go upstairs. It didn't bother her to fly in an airplane, but she couldn't go up more than one story in an apartment building. It was worse now than it had been. In the old days she could be on the eighth floor if she had to, as long as the windows were tightly shut.

Before we went out to dinner my husband took the book up to the apartment, but he had stuck the sock in his back pocket without thinking when I gave it to him out on the street and it stayed there during the meal in the restaurant, where his mother sat in her black clothes at the end of the table opposite an empty chair, sometimes playing with my son, with his cars, and sometimes asking my husband and then me and then his wife questions about the peppercorns and other strong spices that might be in her food. Then after we all left the restaurant and were standing in the parking lot he pulled the sock out of his pocket and looked at it, wondering how it had got there.

It was a small thing, but later I couldn't forget the sock, because here was this one sock in his back pocket in a strange neighborhood way out in the eastern part of the city in a Vietnamese ghetto, by the massage parlors, and none of us really knew this city but we were all here together and it was odd, because I still felt as though he and I were partners, we had been partners a long time, and I couldn't help thinking of all the other socks of his I had picked up, stiff with his sweat and threadbare on the sole, in all our life together from place to place, and then of his feet in those socks, how the skin shone through at the ball of the foot and the heel where the weave was worn down; how he would lie reading on his back on the bed with his feet crossed at the ankles so that his toes pointed at different corners of the room; how he would then turn on his side with his feet together like two halves of a fruit; how, still reading, he would reach down and pull off his socks and drop them in little balls on the floor and reach down again and pick at his toes while he read; sometimes he shared with me what he was reading and thinking, and sometimes he didn't know whether I was there in the room or somewhere else.

I couldn't forget it later, even though after they were gone I found a few other things they had left, or rather his wife had left them in the pocket of a jacket of mine — a red comb, a red lipstick, and a bottle of pills. For a while these things sat around in a little group of three on one counter of the kitchen and then another, while I thought I'd send them to her, because I thought maybe the medicine was important, but I kept forgetting to ask, until finally I put them away in a drawer to give her when they came out again, because by then it wasn't going to be long, and it made me tired all over again just to think of it.

BILLY'S GIRL

Frst Billy was on the raft and then he was not. Sun shone on the blue water. Carmine looked for him in the bathhouse, at the popcorn stand where he liked to waste time with Camille, then down by the lifeguard station. But nobody had seen him. If I catch that kid, Carmine said to me in the bathhouse, but I hadn't seen him either, what could I see from behind the counter there except a little stretch of open water, the sun bright on the big lake, pines in the distance. Occasionally some queenie would stroll by but I hadn't seen Billy at all, he could still be out there hiding among the big float tanks underneath the boards, his break over, turn up later rake in hand, why, Mr. D'Angelo, I've been clearing up this area like you told me to. It would be just like him.

But after a while they called the sheriff and two guys came into the bathhouse behind me and went into the storeroom where they keep the drag lines, these hooks as big as your head. By then it was late afternoon. The sheriff's guys were out there in their little boat putt-putting around the raft, lines hanging over the stern, when Billy's girlfriend came down that evening for a swim. When it was completely dark they switched on lights and kept at it.

He's only kidding, the way he always does, Billy's girlfriend said to me. She was perched on the edge of my counter swinging her legs, looking real good and knowing it. By then the place was pretty well cleared out. We went behind the rows of wire baskets and started to make out. There was nobody around, it was dark, and we sort of sank down on a pile of wet towels. Right away she stuck her tongue in my mouth. The towels gave off a sour odor. Her suit was still damp around the edges, I noticed. Out on the lake the motor died down again. Every so often they'd had to ease off, something tangled in the lines, seaweed or an old log. But this time it was Billy all right, like a big musky with all the fight gone out of him, hooked right through the eye the deputy said. By then I was into Billy's girlfriend pretty good, and she was liking it.

SPEED OF LIGHT

Things go wrong.

Take Constantine Muzhikovsky. He had everything going for him. Good law practice. Nice secluded house on the outskirts. Sweet little vegetable garden out back that brought him no end of pleasure come springtime. Handsome, devoted wife. Kids grown and gone. The way Muzhikovsky saw things, it was time to ease off and enjoy a tranquil, orderly life.

Then zap.

One night while they lay in bed watching Johnny Carson, Muzhikovsky's wife told him it was over. Johnny's last guest, a religious nut plugging a book, ranted on.

"Did you hear me?" Muzhikovsky's wife said.

"Yes," Muzhikovsky said. He stared at the glowing TV. "What," he said.

A blind man could see it, Johnny's guest assured him. The signs, the portents: all heralding the impending arrival of the blazing glory of our Lord and Savior, you bet. Johnny nodded sagely; then, when his guest wasn't looking, dropped his jaw, mugged dopey credulity.

The audience roared.

"I said I want a divorce."

Her voice sounded tinny, crackly, vaguely unreal. Muzhikovsky turned. She sat stiffly beside him, small breasts wrapped in folded arms, elbows pointing hard angles at the screen. Her narrow chin jerked; thin lips tightened.

"What?" he said.

She shook her head. "You never listen. I'm telling you I want a divorce."

Muzhikovsky opened his mouth, closed it. "When?" he said, finally, because he didn't know what else to say.

She turned her head, silver curls flashing in the television's glow. Fluorescent tears sizzled down her cheeks. "As soon as possible."

Muzhikovsky blinked. "Why?"

"I can't take it anymore. You're driving me crazy." Her voice was high and tight. "I don't love you."

Muzhikovsky felt suddenly light-headed. He stared at the glaring screen before him, tried to make sense of the dizzying rush of brilliant images. The screen flickered; the scene changed, changed again. Muzhikovsky couldn't keep up.

"Do you understand?" the voice beside him asked.

"You're tired," he heard himself say. "Get some sleep. We'll talk tomorrow."

But the next morning Muzhikovsky was awakened by the news on his clock radio, and all thoughts of last night's episode paled in comparison. It was incredible. He dressed and went to the kitchen. His wife poured his coffee, set the newspaper before him. Headlines confirmed what the radio claimed.

The speed of light had increased.

Muzhikovsky took a quick sip, scalded his tongue, scanned the details. It had been disclosed late last night. Scientists all over the world were coming up with the same results. The speed of light, until now constant at 299,792.458 kilometers per second, was speeding up: 301,561.5 k.p.s. last night, over 304,000 k.p.s at press time. The President, awakened early this morning, had called out the National Guard to prevent rioting and looting. The Pope had requested an hour of worldwide prayer.

Muzhikovsky sat stunned. His wife stared out the window. He could see the worry in her face, but mostly she was taking the news calmly. That was her style.

Muzhikovsky folded the paper neatly. "What do we do now?" he said. "Do we take it in stride or panic or what?"

His wife served him a slice of dry, burnt toast. She folded her arms, stood staring at him. Hers would be a fatalistic view, he realized. He hadn't lived with this woman for thirty years without learning her reactions. Her answer would not surprise him.

"There's nothing to do," she said. "It's over."

Muzhikovsky called his office, told his secretary he wouldn't be in.

"You have a meeting this morning," she said.

"Cancel it."

"But it's with the Central Illuminating and Electric representative. You have a hearing next week on their proposed rate increases."

Muzhikovsky laughed bitterly. "It's over. Can't you see? It doesn't matter anymore."

He turned on the TV in the living room. Special reports filled the airwaves. At last confirmed reckoning, the speed of light had reached 311,218.725 k.p.s. Carl Sagan stood before a blackboard inscribed with the equation $E = mc^2$. He smiled reassuringly, spoke at some length — Muzhikovsky couldn't make out what he was saying. the voice crackled and buzzed — then carefully chalked a slash through the equal sign.

So much for relativity. So much for a logical, ordered universe.

Muzhikovsky ran fingers through thinning hair. He could hear his wife puttering about upstairs. Closet doors opened and closed; hangers rattled and chimed. Muzhikovsky shook his head. The most invariable constant known to humankind had become subject to change, laws of physics were becoming obsolete at every turn, all of established existence was bound to fall apart about them, and his wife was housecleaning. He had to smile. She always maintained a marvelous sense of balance, duty, attention to detail: an attribute he'd always loved her for.

And she was right. Nothing to do now but go on doing what you've always done. Muzhikovsky considered weeding and watering his garden, but as he rose from his chair, the latest reading appeared on the screen: 359,028.025 k.p.s. He looked out the window, squinted at the bright, hazy sky, sat back down.

It seemed like a bad day to be out in the sun.

Morning passed quickly, the television a kaleidoscope of conflicting queries, theories, explanations. Evangelists preached apocalypse. Physicians prescribed caution. Scientists scratched their heads, shrugged, chattered helplessly of leptons and quarks and other mysterious entities of various flavors and colors. Perhaps, one physicist said, this was a natural electromagnetic phenomenon that occurred at regular intervals, somewhat like the earth's ice ages. Maybe, another argued, they'd been measuring wrong all along.

Who could tell? Layman and scientist alike were stumped. Anybody's opinion was worth as much as anybody else's.

Sitting, watching, waiting to see just how fast light could go, Constantine Muzhikovsky was formulating his own hypothesis.

Things change. That's all. Things you count on. Things you take for granted. Things you never imagined could change. They change.

And, Muzhikovsky thought, there was nothing he could do to change this random changing. Nothing but change his attitude toward change.

Muzhikovsky's wife stood before him, blocking the screen. Sunlight streaked from the window behind her, gave her a burnished silver nimbus.

"What are you doing?" she said.

Muzhikovsky shaded his eyes, smiled. "Nothing. Trying to take this as calmly as you, I guess."

"How are you doing?"

He shook his head. "It's not easy. You expect things to go on like always, then all of a sudden something you've always taken as given. . . ." He stopped. She was biting her lip, on the verge of tears. "I'm sorry," Muzhikovsky said. "Since there's nothing we can do about it, I guess there's no sense dwelling on it."

She switched off the TV. Muzhikovsky caught an update before the screen winked out: 374,243.999 k.p.s. and climbing, still climbing, getting faster and faster. Where would it stop? Would it stop at all? What would happen if it didn't? Would the universe simply fibrillate itself out of existence? Who could tell?

"I'm sorry it had to happen," his wife said. "I know it came as a shock."

"Shock," Muzhikovsky echoed. "Yes."

But you couldn't lose your frame of reference, no matter what. One final measure of control. He was sitting in his own home. His garden was growing out back. His wife was at hand, talking to him, soothing him.

"I'm not just doing this on a whim," she was saying. "I want you to know that. I've thought about it for years, but there were the kids to think about. And then there was habit, too, I suppose. I always hoped things might get better."

"What?" Muzhikovsky said. She was sitting on the arm of the chair, touching his hand. Her fingers felt hot.

"Maybe I'm not being fair," she said. "I just can't go on, that's all."

Muzhikovsky stared at the blank screen. It seemed to brighten. Slowly at first, then faster and faster.

"Do you understand?" she said, gripping his arm.

He pulled his gaze from the television, looked up at her, astonished by her sudden urgency, but the glare from behind her slashed at his eyes, blurred his vision.

"My bags are packed. I've called a cab. We can work out the details later." She was crying now. "Just tell me you understand why I'm doing this."

Things were far too bright. Everything was going faster and faster. Muzhikovsky couldn't think, couldn't look at her anymore. He lowered his eyes, blinked.

"Doing what?" he said.

Her grip tightened on his arm. He heard sobbing; his heart quickened. He patted her hand.

"Would it help to talk?" he said.

GERALD'S SONG

MY STOCKS HAVE DESCENDED, my stocks are in pottery and my stocks have descended. The soldiers destroy all the pottery where they are fighting, my stocks are in the company that imports that pottery, other things are up but my stocks are down. Down because of the war in that country where there is pottery.

Once I said the boys are giving up their lives so I should not complain. I did not start the war, I did not like the war, I put my money in pottery not bullets, but I should not complain. The fighting boys have a right to complain but I should not complain. It didn't work.

I have my mother to think of. I live with her, I buy her things, she is tiny and pale and moves with a creak. She worries that I will have nothing when she dies. She says, *how is the pottery,* I say *down,* she bends and she whistles and she says, *O Gerald.*

The pottery looked good, the pottery had a future, the pottery was a sure thing. I put all of my money, the money my father left me, in the pottery. The pottery has gone down to a dollar, has nearly vanished.

O Gerald.

O Mother.

I have wanted to do something, I have wanted to write to the stock exchange, I have wanted to write to the newspaper, I have wanted to write to the President. It is not good, this war, it is not good for any of us, but what can I do, what can I say, I can only fret and what does that change?

O Mother.

O Gerald.

People can love each other, it was in the hope of people loving each other that I picked pottery, pottery could let us know about other people, civilization is to be found in pottery, I was hopeful when I put my money into it, I thought of poor families eating better because of the market for their pottery. I did not invest solely to make a profit. He who does that would be sinful.

O Gerald.

O Mother.

We look in the shops on Sunday, my mother and I, we look in the windows and pick out things for each other. My mother does not walk well, I stop with her for tea, she says, *Gerald, you will look divine in that cravat.* O, my heart is heavy. O, my soul is heavy. Soon there will be no more cravats. *It's the war, Mother, I have put everything in pottery and now there is the war.*

The war the war.

O Mother.

The war is taking everything away.

I did not want to be a soldier, I could never have been a soldier. Her cousin helped us, he was on the draft board, it was not unfair, she was getting old, I could not go to the Army with my mother getting old, I did not go. I stayed home and we played chess. She said, *what are you going to do with your father's money?* I said, *put it in pottery.* She said, *are you sure that's wise?* I said, *pottery can't lose.*

O the war the war. What am I to do?

The President said we have to be there, I believed him, then the Secretary of State said we have to stay there, and I believed him, then our congressman said we have to bring this to a successful conclusion or we can't show our faces anywhere in the world, and I believed him. I believed them all. But the pottery is down and my mother is getting older.

Gerald, you must do something.

What can I do?

You must do something. I will worry myself sick if you don't.

What can I do?

Don't let me down now.

What can I do?

O Gerald.

O Mother.

She threw her teacup. It struck me on the forehead. *Do something, you stupid boy,* she said, *do something.*

I called our congressman and wired the Secretary of State and wrote a letter to the President. They all told me in one way or another that the war can't be stopped. I said to her, *they can't stop it.* I said, *once in it's hard to get out. I know that from the pottery.*

You are as stupid as the government, she said.

No one could have predicted.

As stupid as the government.

I'm sorry, Mother.

What did you want with pottery anyway?

I wanted to help the people in other countries.

Let the sons-of-bitches help themselves.

I'm sorry, Mother.

In your father's day we let them help themselves. It was better.

Yes, Mother.

O Gerald, why can't they stop the stupid war?

I wish they would.

We'll be poor if they don't stop the war.

Yes, Mother.

I went to my broker. I said, *what can I do?*

He said, *you shouldn't have invested in pottery.*

I said, *but you told me to.*

He said, *brokers make mistakes too. We are only human.*

I said, *do you have money in pottery?*

He said, *my money is in bullets. I was lucky.*

I said, *what can I do?*

He said, *wait and hope. When the pottery goes up we'll sell and put the money in bullets.*

The pottery didn't go up.

My mother kicked the coffee table. She said, *I have always lived well. I don't intend to live any other way now. I am old. My arthritis is acting up. How could you do this to me, Gerald?*

I'm sorry, Mother.

She spit at me. She wiggled her arms in the air. *How could anyone be so stupid?* She cursed and tried to get up. I think she was going to attack me. She fell back. She nearly fell to the floor.

Take it easy, Mother.

Who can take it easy on the way to the poorhouse?

O Mother.

I am used to comfort, Gerald, and you are taking it from me.

O Mother.

O Gerald.

. . .

They didn't stop the war, my pottery is down to thirty cents, I have taken to not coming straight home after my work at the library, I have taken to stopping for a drink, I have another drink and then another and then I worry that my mother has fallen off her chair and I go home. She is always awake, sitting, rigid, staring down my shirt front, saying *Gerald, you were always a dope.*

I can't bear the looks she gives me, that's why I drink, I didn't try to lose my money, I didn't ask for the war, it is too late to get my money out now, I feel I am going down, we are all going down, I don't want to go down, this is my life and I want to live it, I don't understand the war, politics bore me, speeches bore me, I want more interesting things, I like books, I read about pottery when it's not busy in the reference room, I used to enjoy reading about pottery, now it makes me sick, but it is my interest, I read about it, pottery is made all over the world, there are different kinds of pottery for different countries, pottery is one of the oldest things made, Mexican pottery is very pretty, my mother is old and dying, I didn't start this war, it was a happy country before the war, people could pursue their interests, pottery was mine, it still is, I don't enjoy it as much as I used to, the war makes it less interesting, the war makes my mother irritable, the war is taking my money away, we have a hard time getting page boys at the library, they are all going into the Army, why must they go, why must we fight, who knows why we are fighting, who knows what's important about that little country, what has happened that we don't know, what has happened that the congressman and the senator and the president can't help us, why is there war, who are those people we are fighting, what do they want with us. I would have gone on investing in their pottery, they could have made lots of money selling their pottery in this country, did they sell it in another country, is that why we are fighting them.

There is a war and I don't understand it, there is a war and I don't understand it, there is a war and I don't understand it.

O Mother.

O Gerald.

MOVING PICTURES

Y OU SIT IN THE NEPTUNE Theatre waiting for the thin, overhead lights to dim with a sense of respect, perhaps even reverence, for American movie houses are, as everyone knows, the new cathedrals, their stories better remembered than legends, totems, or mythologies, their directors more popular than novelists, more influential than saints — enough people, you've been told, have seen the James Bond adventures to fill the entire country of Argentina. Perhaps you have written this movie. Perhaps not. Regardless, you come to it as everyone does, as a seeker groping in the darkness for light, hoping something magical will be beamed from above, and no matter how bad this matinee is, or silly, something deep and maybe even too dangerous to talk loudly about will indeed happen to you and the others before this drama reels to its last transparent frame.

Naturally, you have left your life outside the door. Like any life, it's a messy thing, hardly as orderly as art, what some call life in the fast lane —: the Sanka and sugar-donut breakfasts, bumper-to-bumper traffic downtown, the business lunches, and a breakneck schedule not to get ahead but simply to stay in one place, which is peculiar, because you grew up in the sixties speeding on Methadone and despising all this, knowing your Age (Aquarian) was made for finer stuff. But no matter. Outside, across town, you have put away for ninety minutes the tedious, repetitive job that is, obviously, beneath your talents, sensitivity, and education (a degree in English), the once beautiful woman — or wife — a former model (local), college dancer, or semiprofessional actress named Megan or Daphne, who has grown tired of you, or you of her, and talks now of legal separation and finding herself, the children from a former, frighteningly brief marriage whom you don't want to lose, the mortgage, alimony, IRS audit, the aging, gin-fattened face that once favored a rock star's but now frowns back at you in the

bathroom mirror, the young woman at work, born in 1960 and unable to recall John Kennedy, who after the Christmas party took you
to bed in her spacious downtown loft, perhaps out of pity because
your mother, God bless her, died and left you with a thousand dollars in debt before you could get the old family house clear — all that
shelved, mercifully, as the film starts: first that frosty mountaintop
ringed by stars, or a lion roaring, or floodlights bathing the tips of
buildings in a Hollywood skyline: stable trademarks in a world of
flux, you think, sure-fire signs that whatever follows — tragedy or
farce — is made by people who are accomplished dream-merchants.
Perhaps more: masters of vision, geniuses of the epistemological
Murphy.

If you have written this film, which is possible, you look for your
name in the credits, and probably frown at the names of the Crew,
each recalling some disaster during the production, first at the
studio, then later on location for five weeks in Oklahoma cowtowns
during the winter, which was worse than living on the moon, the
days boiling and nights so cold. Nevertheless, you'd seen it as a miracle, an act of God when the director, having read your novel, called,
offering you the project — a historical romance — then walked you
patiently through the first eight drafts, suspicious of you at first
(there was real money riding on this, it wasn't poetry), of your
dreary, novelistic pretensions to Deep Profundity, and you equally
suspicious of him, his background in sitcoms, obsession with "keeping it sexy," and love of Laurel and Hardy films. For this you wrote
a dissertation on Derrida? Yet, you'd listened. He was right, in the
end. He was good, you admitted, grudgingly. He knew, as you —
with your liberal arts degree — didn't, the meaning of Entertainment.
You'd learned. With his help, you got good, too. You gloated. And
lost friends. "A movie?" said your poet friends, "that's wonderful,
it's happening for you," and then they avoided you as if you had
AIDS. What *was* happening was this:

You'd shelved the novel, the Big Book, for bucks monitored by
the Writers Guild (West), threw yourself into fast-and-dirty scripts,
the instant gratification of quick deadlines and fat checks because
the Book, with its complexity and promise of critical praise, the Book
with its long-distance demands and no financial reward whatsoever,
was impossible, and besides, you didn't have it anymore, not really,
the gift for narrative or language, while the scripts were easy, like
writing shorthand, and soon — way sooner than you thought — the

films, with their lifespan shorter than a mayfly's, were all you could do. It's a living, you said. Nothing lasts forever. And you pushed on.

The credits crawl up against a montage of Oklahoma farmlife, and in this you read a story, too, even before the film begins. For the audience, the actors are stars, the new Olympians, but oh, you know them, this one—the male lead—whose range is boundless, who could be a Brando, but who hadn't seen work in two years before this role and survived by doing voice-overs for a cartoon villain in *The Smurfs*; that one—the female supporting role—who can play the full scale of emotions, but whose last memorable performance was a commercial for Rolaids, all of them; all, including you, fighting for life in a city where the air is so corrupt joggers spit black after a two-mile run; failing, trying desperately to keep up the front of doing-well, these actors, treating you shabbily sometimes because your salary was bigger than theirs, even larger than the producer's, though he wasn't exactly hurting—no, he was richer than a medieval king, a complex man of remarkable charm and cunning, someone to both admire for his Horatio Alger orphan-boy success and fear for his worship at the altar of power. You won't forget the evening he asked you to his home after a long conference, served you Scotch, and then, from inside a drawer in his desk removed an envelope, dumped its contents out, and you saw maybe fifty snapshots of beautiful, naked women on his bed—all of them second-rate actresses, though the female supporting role was there, too—and he watched you closely for your reaction, sipping his drink, smiling, then asked, "You ever sleep with a woman like that?" No, you hadn't. And, no, you didn't trust him either. You didn't turn your back. But, then again, nobody in this business did, and in some ways he was, you knew, better than most.

You'd compromised, given up ground, won a few artistic points, but generally you agreed to the producer's ideas—it *was* his show—and then the small army of badly-paid performers and production people took over, you trailing behind them in Oklahoma, trying to look writerly, wearing a Panama hat, holding your notepad ready for rewrites, surviving the tedium of eight or nine takes for difficult scenes, the fights, fallings-out, bad catered food, and midnight affairs, watching your script change at each level of interpretation—director, actor—until it was unrecognizable, a new thing entirely, a celebration of the Crew. Not you. Does anyone suspect how bad this thing really looked in roughcut? How miraculous it is that its rags of shots, conflicting ideas, and scraps of footage actually cohere? You sneak a look around at the audience, the faces lit by the glow of the screen. No one suspects. You've managed to fool them again, you old fox.

No matter whether the film is yours or not, it pulls you in, reels in your perception like a trout. On the narrow screen, the story begins with an establishing wideshot of an Oklahoma farm, then in close-up shows the face of a big towheaded, brown-freckled boy named Bret, and finally settles on a two-shot of Bret and his blonde, bosomy girlfriend, Bess. No margin for failure in a formula like that. In the opening funeral scene at a tiny, whitewashed church, camera favors Bret, whose father has died. Our hero must seek his fortune in the city. Bess just hates to see him go. Dissolve to cemetery gate. As they leave the cemetery, and the coffin is lowered, she squeezes his hand, and something inside you shivers, the sense of ruin you felt at your own mother's funeral, the irreversible feeling of abandonment. There was no girl with you, but you wished to heaven there had been, the one named Sondra you knew in high school who wouldn't see you for squat, preferring basketball players to weird little wimps and geeks, which is pretty much what you were back then, a washout to those who knew you, but you give all that to Bret and Bess, the pain of parental loss, the hopeless, quiet love never to be, which thickens the screen so thoroughly that when Bess kisses Bret your nose is clogged with tears and mucus, and then you have your handkerchief out, honking shamelessly, your eyes streaming, locked — even you — in a cycle of emotion (yours), which their images have borrowed, intensified, then given back to you, not because the images or sensations are sad, but because, at bottom, all you have known these last few minutes are the workings of your own nervous system. You yourself have been supplying the grief and satisfaction all along, from within. But even that is not the true magic of film.

As Bret rides away, you remember sitting in the studio's tiny editing room amidst reels of film hanging like stockings in a bathroom, the editor, a fat, friendly man named Coates, tolerating your curiosity, letting you peer into his viewer as he patched the first reel together, figuring he owed you, a semifamous scriptwriter, that much. Each frame, you recall, was a single, frozen image, like an individual thought, complete in itself, with no connection to the others, as if time stood still; but then the frames came faster as the viewer sped up, chasing each other, surging forward and creating a linear, continuous motion that outstripped your perception, and presto: a sensuously rich world erupted and took such nerve-knocking reality that you shielded your eyes when the harpsichord music came up and Bret stepped into a darkened Oklahoma shed seen only from his point-of-view — oh yes, at times even your body responded, the sweat glands swaling, but it was lunchtime then and Coates wanted to go to the cafeteria for coffee and clicked off his viewer; the images flipped less quickly, slowed finally to a stop, the drama disappearing again into frames, and you saw, pulling on your coat, the nerve-wracking, heart-thumping vision for what it really was: the illusion of speed.

But is even that the magic of film? Sitting back in your seat, aware of your right leg falling asleep, you think so, for the film has no capacity to fool you anymore. You do not give it your feelings to transfigure. All that you see with godlike detachment are your own decisions, the lines that were dropped, and the microphone just visible in a corner of one scene. Nevertheless, it's gratifying to see the audience laugh out loud at the funny parts, and blubber when Bret rides home at last to marry Bess (actually, they hated each other on the set), believing, as you can't, in a dream spun from accelerated imagery. It almost makes a man feel superior, like knowing how Uri Geller bends all those spoons.

And then it is done, the theatre emptying, the hour and a half of illusion over. You file out with the others, amazed by how so much can be projected onto the *tabula rasa* of the Big Screen — grief, passion, fire, death — yet it remains, in the end, untouched. Dragging on your overcoat, the images still an afterglow in your thoughts, you step outside to the street. It takes your eyes, still in low gear, a moment to adjust to the light of late afternoon, traffic noise, and the things around you as you walk to your Fiat, feeling good, the objects on the street as flat and dimensionless at first as props on a stage. And then you stop.

The Fiat, you notice, has been broken into. The glove compartment has been rifled, and this is where you keep a checkbook, an extra key to the house, and where — you remember — you put the report due tomorrow at nine sharp. The glove compartment, how does it look? Like a part of your body, yes? A wound? From it spills a crumpled photo of your wife, who has asked you to move out so she can have the house, and another one of the children, who haven't the faintest idea how empty you feel getting up every morning to finance their lives at a job that is a ghastly joke, given your talents, where you can't slow down and at least four competitors stand waiting for you to step aside, fall on your face, or die, and the injustice of all this, what you see in the narrow range of radiation you call vision, in the velocity of ideation, is necessary and sufficient — as some logicians say — to bring your fists down again and again on the Fiat's roof. You climb inside, sit, furiously cranking the starter, then swear and lower your forehead to the steering wheel, which is, as anyone in Hollywood can tell you, conduct unbecoming a triple-threat talent like yourself: producer, star, and director in the longest, most fabulous show of all.

ANY MINUTE
MOM SHOULD COME
BLASTING THROUGH THE DOOR

MOM DIED IN THE MIDDLE of making me a sandwich. If I had known it was going to kill her, I never would have asked. It never killed her before to make me a sandwich, so why all of a sudden? My dad didn't understand it, either. But we don't talk about it too much. We don't talk about it too much at all. Sometimes we try. Sometimes it's just the two of us at dinner, and things are almost good.

But only sometimes.

Most of the time it's different. Most of the time I do things like forget to leave her place out at the table. And then we don't know what to do. Then we don't even try to talk. Three plates. Three glasses. The kitchen shines. A bright, shiny kitchen, Mom used to say. And there we are—my dad, her place, and me. And any minute Mom should come blasting through the door, all bundles and boxes, my big winter coat squaring her off at the shoulders and hips, her face smiling and wrinkled like a plant.

I should have known better.

I should have known about these things.

Come on, Mom, what do you say? Is it going to kill you to make me one sandwich? Is it really going to kill you? Remember how you used to play with me? Remember? And then I snuck up behind her chair, undid her curlers, and ran my fingers through her hair until she said all right already, what kind did I want? Then she stood up, turned to my dad, and opened her bathrobe so he could get a peek just to see if the old interest was still there. But I don't think it was. What? he said. He hasn't seen this before? Make the sandwich, he said. And he let his body melt like pudding into the easy chair.

That was it. That was the last thing he said to her. Mom turned up the TV, went into the kitchen, and the next thing we knew, she was calling out for help.

Well, my dad didn't know what was going on anymore than I did, so he got up from his chair, trudged across the room — making sure to scrape his feet on the carpet all the way so he could really shock her good this time — and that was it. Mom was dead on the floor of the kitchen, her bathrobe open at the waist.

And I thought, Well, there's Mom dead, what now? No one thinks about that. No one thinks about what happens after you find your mother dead like that, all over the kitchen floor. But I'm telling you, that's when the real fun starts. That's when you have to try mouth-to-mouth on her — on your mother, for God's sake — knowing that if she does come around she'll spit up in your face, because that's what happens, but praying for it, anyway, because if she doesn't, then it's all over. That's when you've got to call an ambulance and wait for them to throw a sheet over her head so they can take her away from you. That's when you've got to sit there and watch them put their hands all over her body and know they'll never believe you even tried to save her. That's when the neighbors see the flashing red light in your driveway and wonder what kind of rotten son you are that you couldn't save your mother. That's when you've got your whole life to live, and all it's going to be is one excuse after another for why you didn't save her. What do you do? We didn't know, so my dad poured her on the couch, and we waited. We waited and watched TV.

It was on.

But like I said, we don't talk about it too much. How can we? Mom was the talker. That's what she used to say. She used to say, "Boys, what would you do without me?" And here we are, without her. My dad and I wouldn't know how to talk to each other if you paid us, so we don't even try. Not much, anyway. What am I going to say? How's your love life? What's it like to sleep alone? He doesn't want that. He doesn't want that at all. He wants me out of the house. But he doesn't really want that, either, you know. What would he do then? Six rooms can be too many if you're not careful. I tell him this at dinner sometimes. I tell him how much he needs me. How much he cares. But he doesn't care. He cares about the kitchen, the robe, the things I did to try to save his wife. My hands. Her body. My lips. Her mouth.

"Tell me," he says, "is that really how you want to remember your mother?"

THE BLACK QUEEN

HUGHES AND McCRAE were fastidious men who took pride in their old colonial house, the clean simple lines and stucco walls and the painted pale blue picket fence. They were surrounded by houses converted into small warehouses, trucking yards where houses had been torn down, and along the street, a school filled with foreign children, but they didn't mind. It gave them an embattled sense of holding on to something important, a tattered remnant of good taste in an area of waste overrun by rootless olive-skinned children.

McCrae wore his hair a little too long now that he was going gray, and while Hughes with his clipped moustache seemed to be a serious man intent only on his work, which was costume design, McCrae wore Cuban heels and lacquered his nails. When they'd met ten years ago Hughes had said, "You keep walking around like that and you'll need a body to keep you from getting poked in the eye." McCrae did all the cooking and drove the car.

But they were not getting along these days. Hughes blamed his bursitis, but they were both silently unsettled by how old they had suddenly become, how loose in the thighs, and their feet, when they were showering in the morning, seemed bonier, the toes longer, the nails yellow and hard, and what they wanted was tenderness, to be able to yield almost tearfully, full of a pity for themselves that would not be belittled or laughed at, and when they stood alone in their separate bedrooms they wanted that tenderness from each other, but when they were having their bedtime tea in the kitchen, as they had done for years using lovely green and white Limoges cups, if one touched the other's hand then suddenly they both withdrew into an unspoken, smiling aloofness, as if some line of privacy had been crossed. Neither could bear their thinning wrists and the little pouches of darkening flesh under the chin. They spoke of being with younger people and even joked slyly about bringing a young man home, but that seemed such a betrayal of everything that they had believed had set them apart from others, everything they believed had kept them together, that they sulked and nettled away at each other, and though nothing had apparently changed in their lives, they were always on edge, Hughes more than McCrae.

One of their pleasures was collecting stamps, rare and mint-perfect, with no creases or smudges on the gum. Their collection, carefully mounted in a leatherbound blue book with seven little plastic windows per page, was worth several thousand dollars. They had passed many pleasant evenings together on the Directoire settee arranging the old ochre and carmine colored stamps. They agreed there was something almost sensual about holding a perfectly preserved piece of the past, unsullied, as if everything didn't have to change, didn't have to end up swamped by decline and decay. They disapproved of the new stamps and dismissed them as crude and wouldn't have them in their book. The pages for the recent years remained empty and they liked that; the emptiness was their statement about themselves and their values, and Hughes, holding a stamp up into the light between his tweezers, would say, "None of that rough trade for us."

One afternoon they went down to the philatelic shops around Adelaide and Richmond Streets and saw a stamp they had been after for a long time, a large and elegant black stamp of Queen Victoria in her widow's weeds. It was rare and expensive, a dead-letter stamp from the turn of the century. They stood side-by-side over the glass countercase admiring it, their hands spread on the glass, but when McCrae, the overhead fluorescent light catching his lacquered nails, said, "Well, I certainly would like that little black sweetheart," the owner, who had sold stamps to them for several years, looked up and smirked, and Hughes suddenly snorted, "You old queen, I mean why don't you just quit wearing those goddamn Cuban heels, eh? I mean why not?" He walked out leaving McCrae embarrassed and hurt and when the owner said, "So what was wrong?" McCrae cried, "Screw you," and strutted out.

Through the rest of the week they were deferential around the house, offering each other every consideration, trying to avoid any squabble before Mother's Day at the end of the week when they were going to hold their annual supper for friends, three other male couples. Over the years it had always been an elegant, slightly mocking evening that often ended bitter-sweetly and left them feeling close, comforting each other.

McCrae, wearing a white, linen shirt, starch in the cuffs and mother-of-pearl cuff links, worked all Sunday afternoon in the kitchen, and through the window he could see the crab apple tree in bloom and he thought how in previous years he would have begun planning to put down some jelly in the old pressed glass jars they kept in the cellar, but instead, head down, he went on stuffing and tying the pork loin roast. Then in the early evening he heard Hughes at the door, and there was laughter from the front room and someone cried out, "What do you do with an elephant who has three balls on him . . . you don't know silly, well you walk him and pitch to the giraffe," and there were howls of laughter and the clinking of glasses. It had been the same every year, eight men sitting down to a fine supper with expensive wines, the table set with their best silver under the antique carved wooden candelabra.

Having prepared all the raw vegetables, the cauliflower and carrots, the avocados and finger-sized miniature corns-on-the-cob, and placed porcelain bowls of homemade dip in the center of a pewter tray, McCrae stared at his reflection for a moment in the window over the kitchen sink and then he took a plastic slipcase out of the knives-and-forks drawer. The case contained the dead-letter stamp. He licked it all over and pasted it on his forehead and then slipped on the jacket of his charcoal brown crushed velvet suit, took hold of the tray, and stepped out into the front room.

The other men, sitting in a circle around the coffee table, looked up and one of them giggled. Hughes cried, "Oh my God." McCrae, as if nothing were the matter, said, "My dears, time for the crudités." He was in his silk stocking feet, and as he passed the tray he winked at Hughes who sat staring at the black queen.

SENSE OF WONDER,
SENSE OF AWE

MOTHER WOULD HAVE found my magazine. If the final shape of the experience was Father's responsibility, my mother's was its initiation. Had I hidden the magazine carefully, she would have found it.

I did not hide it carefully. Second desk drawer to the right, second from the top, cover up in a stack of *Classics Illustrated* comic books weighted with a thirty-sixty-ninety triangle. An easy matter for Mother, who had deduced my first prophylactic from the impression it made against the hidden bill slot of my wallet.

It was the sort of magazine that was offered by any drugstore shelf. It had not represented a challenge to procure, nor would it have been difficult to replace. The flush had been long thumbed from its pages. Yet it was a cache of secret wealth which commanded much of my attention. An evening of homework at my desk was punctuated with security breaks. In the midst of a sentence I set down my pencil, opened the drawer, checked the positioning of the triangle, carefully lifted out my copy of *Ivanhoe*. I remember rising in the dark to reassure myself. Once, on the pretext of frostbite, I left an afternoon of tobogganing to run home through the snow.

I did not expect tears from my mother for this one. I did fully expect her to confiscate the evidence, though. I thought about the way she would discover the magazine, watched her reaction to it. In my bed at night I had her slip it under her apron and carry it to her own room, where she looked at the pictures of the women and what they were doing to themselves, read slowly about what the men and women did to each other. It was on one such night that I realized she had already found my magazine. If she had read it, she had returned it neatly to the drawer.

For many days thereafter I gave special significance to my relationship with Mother. I watched with great interest and saw in each of her actions a meaning that I could not fully comprehend. If she drove me to school or insisted that I walk, should she be exasperated or content, consistent or inconsistent, any change or lack of change had its importance. One spring morning I was dismissed from Spanish class to retrieve a message from home at the front office. I had forgotten my lunch, and Mother made a special trip to leave it with the school receptionist. On my return to class through the narrow, thickly waxed hallways, chilled and empty now at the mid-period, I opened the bag and read the simple note she had included with my lunch. "For my absent-minded son." There was a bar of my favorite chocolate. Back in Spanish I placed her in the chair at my desk. Her long legs were crossed against my unmade bed. My second drawer stood out at her side, and the magazine lay folded open into her lap, offering in the highest gloss every secret it could think to uncover.

Days gathered, weekends loomed and faded, and my understanding of the situation grew more complex. I awaited my father's entrance. He would be almost unnoticeably ill at ease, I knew. His knock would come twice as I sat at my homework. His sleeves would be up and he would carry a newspaper or rolled magazine that he would swing, at times, like a bat, or sight along like the barrel of a rifle, or delicately cast as if he were fly-fishing a strong, clear, cold stream. He had elevated the matter of the phrophylactic to a position of new status. I was to be understood in my need to experiment. I was to be congratulated for protecting myself. Perhaps, though, I could take better care to insure my privacy.

Father would enter, I knew. Yet he did not. The storm window at my desk was replaced by its screen; each night the darkness was more hesitant to fill my bedroom. Still the magazine lay perfectly arranged in its hiding place. And as the warm evenings passed I was forced to consider the possibility that Mother had withheld from him her discovery.

My own discovery greatly complicated the affair. When we three met at the dinner table every question had a second edge. To each interplay, whether it concerned history tests or mashed potatoes, was assigned an intricate set of motivations. My assessment of my parents' understanding was constantly changing. I was awed by their gestures of dignity and composure.

It was over dinner that my father finally spoke. The sun was spread across the table in stripes that ran at an angle onto Mother's chest and face. Had he told us, he asked, of Miss Kalfeon, his seventh grade teacher. I watched Mother; she nodded and smiled.

Miss Kalfeon chewed gum in class and carried a pencil behind her ear. She was wry and quick, solid in her maths, brilliant with literature. She was not unlovely. A wealth of bronze hair tossed and kicked against her shoulders, her legs were long and firm. When she lectured she stood with a manner that Father could yet see. Feet spread wide before the class, knees locked, her strong back arched, her fingers straightened at her hips.

Mother began to clear and asked hadn't there been a book. Yes. For Miss Kalfeon it was the most famous book in the English language, the most important creative work of the modern mind. It was large and old and worn, and she turned it in her hand as if it were a thing of great value and great wonder. She said that it put into beautiful words the thoughts that normal people had about themselves and others in the course of a day. Sometimes, as my father and his classmates could well imagine, the thoughts were quite racy. Father could never read the last chapter without thinking of Miss Kalfeon.

Mother offered the title of the book. She stood slowly rocking by the sink, her arms straightened into the pockets of her apron. The ribbons of sunlight that came in low across the room slipped and rolled across her body. She smiled. Hadn't there been a picture, she asked. Yes.

When the spring arrived, Miss Kalfeon put away her nylons and wore sleeveless cottons of yellow and green. Sometimes, at her desk, or when she turned at the board, Father was able to see the white of her underwear at her breast. He had begun to draw her likeness. Alone in his room, at the study carrels in the library, eventually at his desk in class, he pictured Miss Kalfeon as he felt she would look when uncovered from her cotton and silks. If not altogether accurate, his concept of female anatomy was highly imaginative. Many of the poses that he shaped for her were shameful, some small and mindless, yet none captured so well the sense of mystery about her as her lecturing stance. Father was deeply involved in a picture one day at the back of the classroom when he looked up to discover Miss Kalfeon standing over him. He flushed. She reached down and turned the tablet to her angle. She smiled and touched his shoulder lightly and walked to the front.

Mother asked did he know where she was now. Yes, he said, she was before the class, dressed in sleeveless cotton, her bare legs planted firmly on the waxed floor.

At my own desk that same night I could not concentrate on homework. At impulsive moments I opened my second drawer, and when darkness finally took the room I lay in bed and pictured Miss Kalfeon.

BLIND GIRLS

SHE KNEW IT WAS only boys in the field, come to watch them drunk on first wine. A radio in the little shack poured out promises of black love and lips. Jesse watched Sally paint her hair with grenadine, dotting the sticky syrup on her arms. The party was in a shack down the hill from her house, beside a field of tall grass where black snakes lay like flat belts. The Ripple bottles were empty and Jesse told pornographic stories about various adults while everyone laughed; about Miss Hicks the home-ec teacher whose hands were dimpled and moist and always touching them. It got darker and the stories got scarier. Finally she told their favorite, the one about the girl and her boyfriend parked on a country road on a night like this, with the wind blowing and then rain, the whole sky sobbing potato juice. Please let's leave, pleads girlie, It sounds like something scratching at the car. For God's sake, grumbles boyfriend, and takes off squealing. At home they find the hook of a crazed amputee caught in the door. Jesse described his yellow face, putrid, and his blotchy stump. She described him panting in the grass, crying and looking for something. She could feel him smelling of raw vegetables, a rejected bleeding cowboy with wheat hair, and she was unfocused. Moaning in the dark and falsetto voices. Don't don't please don't. Nervous laughter. Sally looked out the window of the shack. The grass is moving, she said, Something's crawling in it. No, it's nothing. Yes, there's something coming, and her voice went up at the end. It's just boys trying to scare us. But Sally whined and flailed her arms. On her knees she hugged Jesse's legs and mumbled into her thighs. It's all right, I'll take you up to the house. Sally was stiff, her nails digging the skin. She wouldn't move. Jesse tied a scarf around her eyes and led her like a horse through fire up the hill to the house, one poison light soft in a window. Boys ran out of the field squawling.

THE SIGNING

My WIFE DIES. Now I'm alone. I kiss her hands and leave the hospital room. A nurse runs after me as I walk down the hall.

"Are you going to make arrangements now for the deceased?" he says.

"No."

"Then what do you want us to do with the body?"

"Burn it."

"That's not our job."

"Give it to science."

"You'll have to sign the proper legal papers."

"Give me them."

"They take a while to draw up. Why don't you wait in the guest lounge?"

"I haven't time."

"And her toilet things and radio and clothes."

"I have to go." I ring for the elevator.

"You can't do that."

"I am."

The elevator comes.

"Doctor, doctor," he yells to a doctor going through some files at the nurses' station. She stands up. "What is it nurse?" she says. The elevator door closes. It opens on several floors before it reaches the lobby. I head for the outside. There's a security guard sitting beside the revolving door. He looks like a regular city policeman other than for his hair, which hangs down past his shoulders, and he also has a beard. Most city policemen don't; maybe all. He gets a call on his portable two-way set as I step into one of the quarters of the revolving door. "Laslo," he says into it. I'm outside. "Hey you," he says. I turn around. He's nodding and pointing to me and waves for me to come back. I cross the avenue to get to the bus stop. He comes outside and slips the two-way into his back pocket and walks up to me as I wait for the bus.

"They want you back upstairs to sign some papers," he says.

"Too late. She's dead. I'm alone. I kissed her hands. You can have the body. I just want to be far away from here and as soon as I can."

"They asked me to bring you back."

"You can't. This is a public street. You need a city policeman to take me back, and even then I don't think he or she would be in their rights."

"I'm going to get one."

The bus comes. Its door opens. I have the required exact fare. I step up and put my change in the coin box.

"Don't take this man," the guard says to the bus driver. "They want him back at the hospital there. Something about his wife who was or is a patient, though I don't know the actual reason they want him for."

"I've done nothing," I tell the driver and take a seat in the rear of the bus. A woman sitting in front of me says, "What's holding him up? This isn't a red light."

"Listen," the driver says to the guard, "if you have no specific charge or warrant against this guy, I think I better go."

"Will you please get this bus rolling again?" a passenger says.

"Yes," I say, disguising my voice so they won't think it's me but some other passenger, "I've an important appointment and your slowpokey driving and intermittent dawdling has already made me ten minutes late."

The driver shrugs at the guard. "In or out, friend, but unless you can come up with some official authority to stop this bus, I got to finish my run."

The guard steps into the bus, pays his fare, and sits beside me as the bus pulls out.

"I'll have to stick with you and check in if you don't mind," he says to me. He pushes a button in his two-way set and says "Laslo here."

"Laslo," a voice says. "Where the hell are you?"

"On a bus."

"What are you doing there? You're not through yet."

"I'm with the man you told me to grab at the door. Well, he got past the door. I tried to stop him outside, but he said I needed a city patrolman for that because it was a public street."

"You could've gotten him on the sidewalk in front."

"This was at the bus stop across the street."

"Then he's right. We don't want a suit."

"That's what I thought. So I tried to convince him to come back. He wouldn't. He said he'd kissed some woman's hands and we can have the body. I don't know what that means but want to get it all in before I get too far away from you and lose radio contact. He got on this bus. The driver was sympathetic to my argument about the bus not leaving, but said it would be illegal his helping to restrain the man and that he also had to complete his run. So I got on the bus and am now sitting beside the man and will get off at the next stop if that's what you want me to do. I just didn't know what was the correct way to carry out my orders in this situation, so I thought I'd stick with him till I found out from you."

"You did the right thing. Let me speak to him now."

Laslo holds the two-way in front of my mouth. "Hello," I say.

"The papers to donate your wife's body to the hospital for research and possible transplants are ready now, sir, so could you return with Officer Laslo?"

"No."

"If you think it'll be too trying an emotional experience to return here, could we meet someplace else where you could sign?"

"Do what you want with her body. There's nothing I ever want to have to do with her again. I'll never speak her name. Never go back to our apartment. Our car I'm going to let rot in the street till it's towed away. This wristwatch. She bought it for me and wore it a few times herself." I throw it out the window.

"Why didn't you just pass it on back here?" the man behind me says.

"These clothes. She bought some of them, mended them all." I take off my jacket, tie, shirt and pants and toss them out the window.

"Lookit," Laslo says, "I'm just a hospital security guard with a pair of handcuffs I'm not going to use on you because we're in a public bus and all you've just gone through, but please calm down."

"This underwear I bought myself yesterday," I say to him. "I needed a new pair. She never touched or saw them, so I don't mind still wearing them. The shoes go, though. She even put on these heels with a shoe-repair kit she bought at the five-and-dime." I take off my shoes and drop them out the window.

The bus has stopped. All the other passengers have left except Laslo. The driver is on the street looking for what I'm sure is a patrolman or police car.

I look at my socks. "I'm not sure about the socks."

"Leave them on," Laslo says. "They look good, and I like brown."

"But did she buy them? I think they were a gift from her two birthdays ago when she gave me a cane picnic basket with a dozen-and-a-half pairs of different-colored socks inside. Yes, this is one of them," and I take them off and throw them out the window. "That's why I tried and still have to get out of this city fast as I can."

"You hear that?" Laslo says into the two-way radio, and the man on the other end says, "I still don't understand."

"You see," I say into it, "we spent too many years here together, my beloved and I — all our adult lives. These streets. That bridge. Those buildings." I spit out the window. "Perhaps even this bus. We took so many rides up and down this line." I try to uproot the seat in front of me but it won't budge. Laslo claps the cuffs on my wrists. "This life," I say and I smash my head through the window.

An ambulance comes and takes me back to the same hospital. I'm brought to Emergency and put on a cot in the same examining room she was taken to this last time before they moved her to a semi-private room. A hospital official comes in while the doctors and nurses are tweezing the remaining glass splinters out of my head and stitching me up. "If you're still interested in donating your wife's body," he says, "then we'd like to get the matter out of the way while some of her organs can still be reused by several of the patients upstairs."

I say, "No, I don't want anyone walking around with my wife's parts where I can bump into him and maybe recognize them any day of the year," but he takes my writing hand and guides it till I've signed.

THE QUAIL

THE QUAIL CAME just before the lilacs bloomed in the green time of their first spring married. The morning was the first warm morning with no frost, only dew. Feeling sun on the bed she rose earlier than usual; when she saw the quail in the back yard she woke him. He saw eight birds scratching earth and pecking in the landlord's garden.

He told her they were California Quail. The hens were like dowager women, plump and impeccably arrayed in brown and gray. They were escorted by three portly males with gray-vested chests and an ascot of black plumage at their throats. Each bird had one black plume feather bobbing on the forehead. They wandered the garden like a tour group, stopping to peck in the earth, gliding, aimless and individual but coveyed together.

The couple dressed, whispering about the birds and watching them peck breakfast from the lawn. He made coffee, warmed rolls, and they ate at the kitchen table where they could watch the covey. He opened the window; they could smell the morning dampness and apple blossoms. Sun came through the window; the rolls were sweet with raisins, and they did not have to say anything to each other.

That evening, on his way home from work, he stopped at a feed store and bought cracked corn. He explained to her that the quail would stay as long as they were fed and well-treated. He scattered the corn near the kitchen window, and at sunset the birds returned. They came very close to the window, pecked at the corn, and took rolling dirt baths in the landlord's garden. She asked him if the birds would eat the landlord's seeds and plantings. He told her that the garden was in no danger as long as they fed the birds cracked corn.

After the birds came, they began to set the alarm clock early. At first it was to give them more time for coffee, rolls and watching the covey. When the lilacs bloomed and the tulips came out they set the alarm earlier still and made love before rising. She would bathe after and he would make breakfast, put out more corn for the birds.

It was best watching the covey just after sunrise, before the traffic noises, before the landlord let his poodle out. The landlord lived next door with a chicken wire fence dividing the two yards. When he let the poodle out, it would be crazy to get at the quail, charging the fence, yapping the insane little dog's bark. The covey would rise, flailing air, then settle in the apple tree's low branches waiting for the dog to calm himself and drop back to the corn.

Before long he could put corn on the windowsill and the quail would join them for breakfast. If they were quiet and ate without sudden movement, the birds would flutter to the windowsill a foot from the coffeepot and roll basket. The birds pecked at the corn, eating one piece at a time. Their beaks tapped the sill and their eyes gleamed. He removed the screen to see if they would come inside.

The four cocks were bold, sometimes walking onto the table, preening, ruffling feathers, shaking their plumes. For weeks she tried to feed them sweet roll crumbs from her fingers. The males looked at it, but it was a hen who finally ran to the offered scrap, eyed it sideways with her plume like a hat feather cocked over one eye, and took the crumb. There was the touch of the hen's beak on her fingers. She laughed aloud; the covey exploded from the windowsill. When a week passed and the birds finally began coming to the windowsill again, the hen always took one crumb.

Evenings they would sit in lawn chairs and watch the covey feed. When the early roses bloomed and the landlord's garden sprouted, they saw a hen mated. It was in the garden and they did not see the courtship, only the act when the cock, all gray and brown feathered with black throat feathers, twisted the hen's neck down with his bill. The hen writhed in the soil as the cock mounted her and beat her sides with his wings.

And the landlord's wife railed from inside the landlord's house, "Tom! They're in the garden again, TOM!" The landlord ran from the house, waving his arms, hissing, his neck wrinkled and old, his hair white stubble.

The birds rose flailing air.

His wife held the screen door open, leaned out screeching, "Tom you *got* to do something about them birds! We got to eat that damn garden this winter, now you want to eat this winter you *do* something."

The screen door made a whacking slam and she was out, stooped, her poodle at her feet, her legs splayed, her dress a gray farm woman's dress with a stained apron. She sounded like the poodle.

"Dammit, *Tom!* You going to do something about them birds?"

The tenant and his wife sat in the lawn chairs watching, thinking *they* should do something. Tell the old woman, maybe, that the birds wouldn't bother the seedlings. But they thought she would fight with them, scream at them because she was angry and old. They thought it best to say something later, when she calmed herself.

The next day the landlord said he liked the birds and said the garden had grown enough to be out of danger. He said he had always liked quail. Even when he was a boy he had thought them beautiful and fine eating, but there was his wife. The landlord said his wife would most likely be better in a day or two and the garden was always a sore spot with her because they canned for winter.

When the poppies bloomed and the sweet peas came in, three broods were hatched. The first chicks appeared at breakfast with the hen leading a weaving path to the corn and the cock running half-circles behind them keeping the chicks in line. They counted ten new birds in the three families and they rose even earlier so they could linger over breakfast and smell the drying mustard weed behind the garden.

One hen led her chicks for evening strolls down the front sidewalk. She would promenade her family punctually at five-thirty. The landlord and his wife sat on the front porch one night not believing the hen would show as the tenant had described. They all laughed when the hen strutted by on cue. The landlord and his wife drank beer and told them about the Depression when there was drought and they had to save everything. The old woman said she still had those habits and also said she had been overly concerned about the garden. The tenant couple thought the landlord's wife would be just fine.

When it was autumn, they canned apples and applesauce. The landlord took in his squash, carrots, tomatoes, beets. The landlord's wife traded canned cherries for their canned apples. The landlord cut back the garden, and the tenant helped the old man put up storms, turn the garden, and clean the garage. He bought a fifty pound bag of cracked corn and built a feeding trough of redwood. With the trough on the windowsill there was enough room for all eighteen quail even with the window closed.

The covey was in good shape for the winter. He told her the birds would have an easy winter with the cracked corn and said they would stay near food. The chicks had grown, they were well fed, sleek with new adult plumage. The original eight were rotund, fattened by the summer's corn. He assured her the birds would be fine for the winter.

When the leaves turned and there was frost again they closed the kitchen window. She could not feed the hen crumbs but they could talk now without frightening the birds. They talked about the summer with the quail waking them early. He told her he had hoped all his life that it would someday be like it had been that summer.

When there was hard frost and cold mornings they lingered in bed, awake, warm next to each other, thinking of the quail, thinking of the warmth.

The morning after the first snowfall, the quail were gone. He brushed the snow out of the feeding trough and replaced the wet corn. The covey did not come back that night and the corn had not been touched the next morning. He told her the quail had probably gone to the hills outside town for winter. He told her there was better cover in the hills and that the hunting season was over, so they would be fine. He told her the birds would be back in the spring and it would be the same again.

The tenant and his wife slept late and hard through the winter. The winter was dry, bleak, and cold. There was talk of drought for summer; the landlord hoarded water for his garden by storing it in old oil drums.

The tenant changed the corn often, spreading some on the frozen ground. But the quail did not return and sparrows and jays ate the corn. His wife said she knew the quail would be back in the spring and it would be the same.

When the ground thawed and there was the mud and dirt smell outside, the tenant saw the landlord cleaning his garage and went to help. When he saw the plastic bag full of gray and brown feathers: down feathers, plume feathers, some with bits of dried skin; when he saw that sack and the large chicken wire trap that had not been in the garage before, he asked the landlord how he had managed to catch all the birds at once. The landlord said it had been his wife's idea. They had waited for the first winter storm and trapped the birds when they were huddled together. He said they had been fine eating.

The tenant did not tell his wife about the bag or trap but it was as if she knew. After a while he quit putting out the corn and when the fifty pound bag began to rot, he threw it on the trash.

SLEEPY TIME GAL

In THE SMALL TOWN in northern Michigan where my father lived as a young man, he had an Italian friend who worked in a restaurant. I will call his friend Phil. Phil's job in the restaurant was as ordinary as you can imagine — from making coffee in the morning to sweeping up at night. But what was not ordinary about Phil was his piano playing. On Saturday nights my father and Phil and their girlfriends would drive ten or fifteen miles to a roadhouse by a lake where they would drink beer from schoopers and dance and Phil would play an old beat-up piano. He could play any song you named, my father said, but the song everyone waited for was the one he wrote, which he would always play at the end before they left to go back to the town. And everyone knew of course that he had written the song for his girl, who was as pretty as she was rich. Her father was the banker in their town, and he was a tough old German, and he didn't like Phil going around with his daughter.

My father, when he told the story, which was not often, would tell it in an offhand way and emphasize the Depression and not having much, instead of the important parts. I will try to tell it the way he did, if I can.

So they would go to the roadhouse by the lake, and finally Phil would play his song, and everyone would say, Phil, that's a great song, you could make a lot of money from it. But Phil would only shake his head and smile and look at his girl. I have to break in here and say that my father, a gentle but practical man, was not inclined to emphasize the part about Phil looking at his girl. It was my mother who said the girl would rest her head on Phil's shoulder while he played, and that he got the idea for the song from the pretty way she looked when she got sleepy. My mother was not part of the story, but she had heard it when she and my father were younger and therefore had that information. I would like to intrude further and add something about Phil writing the song, maybe show him whistling the tune and going over the words slowly and carefully to get the best ones, while peeling onions or potatoes in the restaurant; but my father is already driving them home from the roadhouse, and saying how patched up his tires were, and how his car's engine was a gingerbread of parts from different makes, and some parts were his own invention as well. And my mother is saying that the old German had made his daughter promise not to get involved with any man until after college, and they couldn't be late. Also my mother likes the sad parts and is eager to get to their last night before the girl goes away to college.

So they all went out to the roadhouse, and it was sad. The women got tears in their eyes when Phil played her song, my mother said. My father said that Phil spent his week's pay on a new shirt and tie, the first tie he ever owned, and people kidded him. Somebody piped up and said, Phil, you ought to take that song down to Bay City—which was like saying New York City to them, only more realistic—and sell it and take the money and go to college too. Which was not meant to be cruel, but that was the result because Phil had never even got to high school. But you can see people were trying to cheer him up, my mother said.

Well, she'd come home for Thanksgiving and Christmas and Easter and they'd all sneak out to the roadhouse and drink beer from schoopers and dance and everything would be like always. And of course there were the summers. And everyone knew Phil and the girl would get married after she made good her promise to her father because you could see it in their eyes when he sat at the old beat-up piano and played her song.

That last part about their eyes was not, of course, in my father's telling, but I couldn't help putting it in there even though I know it is making some of you impatient. Remember that this happened many years ago in the woods by a lake in northern Michigan, before television. I wish I could put more in, especially about the song and how it felt to Phil to sing it and how the girl felt when hearing it and knowing it was hers, but I've already intruded too much in a simple story that isn't even mine.

Well, here's the kicker part. Probably by now many of you have guessed that one vacation near the end she doesn't come home to see Phil, because she meets some guy at college who is good-looking and as rich as she is and, because her father knew about Phil all along and was pressuring her into forgetting about him, she gives in to this new guy and goes to his hometown during the vacation and falls in love with him. That's how the people in town figured it, because after she graduates they turn up, already married, and right away he takes over the old German's bank — and buys a new Pontiac at the place where my father is the mechanic and pays cash for it. The paying cash always made my father pause and shake his head and mention again that times were tough, but here comes this guy in a spiffy white shirt (with French cuffs, my mother said) and pays the full price in cash.

And this made my father shake his head too: Phil took the song down to Bay City and sold it for twenty-five dollars, the only money he ever got for it. It was the same song we'd just heard on the radio and which reminded my father of the story I just told you. What happened to Phil? Well, he stayed in Bay City and got a job managing a movie theater. My father saw him there after the Depression when he was on his way to Detroit to work for Ford. He stopped and Phil gave him a box of popcorn. The song he wrote for the girl has sold many millions of records, and if I told you the name of it you could probably sing it, or at least whistle the tune. I wonder what the girl thinks when she hears it. Oh yes, my father met Phil's wife too. She worked in the movie theater with him, selling tickets and cleaning the carpet after the show with one of those sweepers you push. She was also big and loud and nothing like the other one, my mother said.

THE ARTICHOKE

. . . until we take into account his most personal views
about the artichoke, the glove, the cookie, or the spool.
— Breton, *Nadja*

IT WILL HAPPEN on a train to Banff, both of us thinking we're
on a vacation. We'll be in the dining car, smoking and discussing
Baudelaire or discussing Gulf Oil or discussing inflation, while we
wait for the waiter. While we wait for the waiter, in no hurry, and
not really very hungry. And in this discussion we'll use the expres-
sions *GNP* and *market value* and *idea of evil*. And it will be you and
I talking, not somebody else somewhere else, and not some fake
couple got up for fiction.

The waiter comes to take our order. He's black, in a white
jacket. He'll be black because that's how waiters on trains to Banff
are, it's the decision of the railroad to conduct its business in this
way. We'll wish he weren't our waiter, but there you are. And there
we will be while the waiter waits as he's paid just enough but not
too much to do, until I've made my point about Baudelaire and we
break off this discussion to order.

The tablecloth will be starched white linen. Not because we
want starched white linen, but because if you take a train to Banff
you get a white linen tablecloth. And we're taking this train through
these mountains. The mountains won't be there for us, of course,
but they'll be there.

And we'll order an artichoke. Because we like them. We like
them, and there they are on the menu.

We know we can change some things but not others, and we
know which ones we can change, when you kick a rock you break
your toe, and now we're hungry. By this time we've dispensed with
the waiter's blackness, the starch in the linen, the mountainous

mountains, we've adjusted our feelings about them to this fact. We're also bored with these feelings that insist on hanging around like tedious children who have nothing to do, but mostly we're hungry. And everyone of course gets hungry, we can gather together around this point as around a table. Right now I could easily dispense with high-toned moral phrases and sit down with the Chairman of the Board of Gulf, as long as each of us had an artichoke.

Here comes the waiter with a white platter. I see the artichoke's rows of spiked leaves, leaves shaped like feathers, and closer now, rounded to a point like feathers, much closer, and are those feathers coming closer, those are really feathers — and now my hunger backs all the way up from my belly into my mouth, a heart that wants to fly out and away — it's feathers, it's a feathered headdress, it's a head — and the waiter sets before me the purple head of Quetzalcoatl on a tray.

I want to say *No*, you've mixed up my order with someone else's, I'm not the one who asked for this, take it away. *But Madame*, he says, *you ordered it*. And I want to say "Don't call me Madame!" But there is Quetzalcoatl's head on my tray.

What we ordered isn't what we want, you'd think any fool could see that. We've always assumed our gentle intentions excuse our imperial way of life. But we still haven't got used to a waiter bringing Quetzalcoatl's head on a platter, whose head we'd forgotten we were supposed to ask for, having gone on this vacation through mountains forested rugged amazing though no longer virgin, leaving the kids in school studying how to manage the Corportion, whose managers we'd comfortably managed to forget we are.

A LOST GRAVE

H ECHT WAS A BORN late bloomer.

One night he woke hearing rain on his windows and thought of his young wife in her wet grave. This was something new, because he hadn't thought of her in too many years to be comfortable about. He saw her in her uncovered grave, rivulets of water streaming in every direction, and Celia, whom he had married when they were of unequal ages, lying alone in the deepening wet. Not so much as a flower grew on her grave, though he could have sworn he had arranged perpetual care.

He stepped into his thoughts perhaps to cover her with a plastic sheet, and though he searched in the cemetery under dripping trees and among many wet plots, he was unable to locate her. The dream he was into offered no tombstone name, row, or plot number, and though he searched for hours, he had nothing to show for it but his wet self. The grave had taken off. How can you cover a woman who isn't where she is supposed to be? That's Celia.

The next morning, Hecht eventually got himself out of bed and into a subway train to Jamaica to see where she was buried. He hadn't been to the cemetery in many years, no particular surprise to anybody considering past circumstances. Life with Celia wasn't exactly predictable. Yet things change in a lifetime, or seem to. Hecht had lately been remembering his life more vividly, for whatever reason. After you hit sixty-five, some things that have two distinguishable sides seem to pick up another that complicates the picture as you look or count. Hecht counted.

Now, though Hecht had been more or less in business all his life, he kept few personal papers, and though he had riffled through a small pile of them that morning, he had found nothing to help him establish Celia's present whereabouts; and after a random looking at gravestones for an hour he felt the need to call it off and spent another hour with a young secretary in the main office, who fruitlessly tapped his name and Celia's into a computer and came up with a scramble of interment dates, grave plots and counter plots, that exasperated him.

"Look, my dear," Hecht said to the flustered young secretary, "if that's how far you can go on this machine, we have to find another way to go further, or I will run out of patience. This grave is lost territory as far as I am concerned, and we have to do something practical to find it."

"What do you think I'm doing, if I might ask?"

"Whatever you are doing doesn't seem to be much help. This computer is supposed to have a good mechanical memory, but it's either out of order or rusty in its parts. I admit I didn't bring any papers with me but so far the only thing your computer has informed us is that it has nothing much to inform us."

"It has informed us it is having trouble locating the information you want."

"Which adds up to zero minus zero," Hecht said. "I wish to remind you that a lost grave isn't a missing wedding ring we are talking about. It is a lost cemetery plot of the lady who was once my wife that I wish to recover."

The pretty young woman he was dealing with had a tight-lipped conversation with an unknown person, then the buzzer on her desk sounded, and Hecht was given permission to go into the director's office.

"Mr. Goodman will now see you."

He resisted "Good for Mr. Goodman." Hecht nodded only and followed the young woman to an inner office. She knocked once and disappeared, as a friendly voice talked through the door.

"Come in, come in."

"Why should I worry if it's not my fault?" Hecht told himself.

Mr. Goodman pointed to a chair in front of his desk and Hecht was soon seated, watching him pour orange juice from a quart container into a small green glass.

"Will you join me in a sweet mouthful?" he asked, nodding at the container. "I usually take refreshment this time of the morning. It keeps me balanced."

"Thanks," said Hecht, meaning he had more serious problems. "Why I am here is that I am looking for my wife's grave, so far with no success." He cleared his throat, surprised at the emotion that had gathered there.

Mr. Goodman observed Hecht with interest.

"Your outside secretary couldn't find it," Hecht went on, regretting he hadn't found the necessary documents that would identify the grave site. "Your young lady tried her computer in every combination but couldn't produce anything. What was lost is still lost, in other words, a woman's grave."

"*Lost* is premature," Goodman offered. "*Displaced* might be better. In my twenty-eight years in my present capacity, I don't believe we have lost a single grave."

The director tapped lightly on the keys of his desk computer, studied the screen with a squint, and shrugged. "I am afraid that we now draw a blank. The letter *H* volume of our ledgers that we used before we were computerized seems to be missing. I assure you this can't be more than a temporary condition."

"That's what your young lady already informed me."

"She's not my young lady, she's my secretarial assistant."

"I stand corrected," Hecht said. "This meant no offense."

"Likewise," said Goodman. "But we will go on looking. Could you kindly tell me, if you don't mind, what was the status of your relationship to your wife at the time of her death?" He peered over half-moon glasses to check the computer reading.

"There was no status. We were separated. What has that got to do with her burial plot?"

"The reason I inquire is, I thought it might refresh your memory. For example, is this the correct cemetery, the one you are looking in — Mount Jereboam? Some people confuse us with Mount Hebron."

"I guarantee you it was Mount Jereboam."

Hecht, after a hesitant moment, gave these facts: "My wife wasn't the most stable woman. She left me twice and disappeared for months. Although I took her back twice, we weren't together at the time of her death. Once she threatened to take her life, though eventually she didn't. In the end she died of a normal sickness, not cancer. This was years later, when we weren't living together anymore, but I carried out her burial, to the best of my knowledge, in this exact cemetery. I also heard she had lived for a short time with some guy she met somewhere, but when she died, I was the one who buried her. Now I am sixty-five, and lately I have had this urge to visit the grave of someone who lived with me when I was a young man. This is a grave that everybody now tells me they can't locate."

Goodman rose at his desk, a short man, five feet tall. "I will institute a careful research."

"The quicker, the better," Hecht replied. "I am still curious what happened to her grave."

Goodman almost guffawed, but caught himself and thrust out his hand. "I will keep you well informed, don't worry."

Hecht left irritated. On the train back to the city he thought of Celia and her various unhappinesses. He wished he had told Goodman she had spoiled his life.

That night it rained. To his surprise he found a wet spot on his pillow.

The next day Hecht again went to the graveyard. "What did I forget that I ought to remember?" he asked himself. Obviously the grave plot, row, and number. Though he sought it diligently he could not find it. Who can remember something he has once and for all put out of his mind? It's like trying to grow beans out of a bag of birdseed.

"But I must be patient and I will find out. As time goes by I am bound to recall. When my memory says yes, I won't argue no."

But weeks passed and Hecht still could not remember what he was trying to. "Maybe I have reached a dead end?"

Another month went by and at last the cemetery called him. It was Mr. Goodman clearing his throat. Hecht pictured him at his desk sipping orange juice.

"Mr. Hecht?"

"The same."

"This is Mr. Goodman. A happy Rosh-ha-shonah."

"A happy Rosh-ha-shonah to you."

"Mr. Hecht, I wish to report progress. Are you prepared for an insight?"

"You name it," Hecht said.

"So let me use a better word. We have tracked your wife, and it turns out she isn't in the grave there where the computer couldn't find her. To be frank, we found her in a grave with another gentleman."

"What kind of gentleman? Who in God's name is he? I am her legal husband."

"This one, if you will pardon me, is the man who lived with your wife after she left you. They lived together on and off, so don't blame yourself too much. After she died he got a court order, and they removed her to a different grave, where we also laid him after his death. The judge gave him the court order because he convinced him that he had loved her for many years."

Hecht was embarrassed. "What are you talking about? How could he transfer her grave anywhere if it wasn't his legal property? Her grave belonged to me. I paid cash for it."

"That grave is still there," Goodman explained, "but the names were mixed up. His name was Kaplan but the workmen buried her under Caplan. Your grave is still in the cemetery, though we had it under Kaplan and not Hecht. I apologize to you for this inconvenience but I think we now have got the mystery cleared up."

"So thanks," said Hecht. He felt he had lost a wife but was no longer a widower.

"Also," Goodman reminded him, "don't forget you gained an empty grave for future use. Nobody is there and you own the plot."

Hecht said that was obviously true.

The story had astounded him. Yet whenever he felt like telling it to someone he knew, or had just met, he wasn't sure he wanted to.

AFTERWORDS

THE TRADITION

WHILE SOME WRITERS in this section implicitly or explicitly treat the short-short story within the strictures of the larger short story (Peden), others grant the short-short not only a multiplicity of modes (Chappell) but a much longer history (Matthews). They examine the short-short in terms of the fundamental elements of fiction (Weaver, Baxter); its effects on those elements and on both reader and writer (Baxter, Davis, Francis); its aims (L'Heureux, Chappell); the materials from which it comes (Greenberg, Johnson); and the larger world which it implies (Chappell, Theroux). They sometimes find resemblances between the short-short and poetry, as do the writers in Section II, but more often draw strong distinctions between them (Johnson, Weaver, Michaels). Finally, some order can be brought to the diversity of these opinions by understanding that short-shorts derive not from one but from "at least five different traditions" (Minot).

Fred Chappell

The short-short story can take as many shapes and moods as the larger short story can manage. It is not necessarily limited to reminiscence, it is not constrained to cover a very brief period of time, it can be voiced in almost any known mode: realism, naturalism, fantasy, allegory, parable, anecdote.

Its two requirements are that it be quite short — two thousand words are almost too many — and that it be troubling. *Unease*, whether humorous or sad, is the effect the short-short aims at. Even if the story achieves resolution, it cannot be a simple resolution and it should not give the impression of permanence. The self-containment of the short-short is incomplete; this form does not create a world in the way that a poem or short story may do; rather, it inhabits a larger world which it must take pains to imply. And the underscored knowledge that a larger world may obtrude upon it lends to the short-short both its inherent fragility and its peculiar toughness.

My favorite short-short story is Heinrich von Kleist's "The Madwoman of Locarno" which, now that I consider it, probably negates all the generalizations I have set down here.

Paul Theroux

It is prose fiction of a certain length—about four pages, I guess. It should not be mistaken for an anecdote; it is highly calculated—its effects, its timing. In most cases it contains a novel.

John L'Heureux

What I like about the term "short-short story" is its easy inclusiveness. Any four or five pages will qualify for entrance. But to get in and stay in, a short-short must stop time and make it timeless, or anatomize a character, or confer form on a small corner of chaos.

It should disturb us with its not quite homely or acceptable truths, like *Ecclesiastes*, like the Parables.

Ontologically, the short-short story is an exercise in virtuosity that tightens the circle of mystery surrounding what we know, or what we think we know.

If all this sounds too grand or airy, I would say that a really good short-short, whatever else it may be, is a story we can't help reading fast, and then re-reading, and again, but no matter how many times we read it, we're not quite through it yet.

Gordon Weaver

Fiction, I believe, is narrative. All fictions exhibit a narrative (not so with poetry), however incidental that factor might be in a particular story's equation, however distorted the chronology of narrative that can be found in many works.

Thus, the short-short presents a fiction writer a very profound challenge: in how small a space can he create the felt presences that animate successful stories? Any writer can evoke a memorable, persuasive persona—a living voice—in a sentence or two; most of us require a modicum of sheer bulk to achieve the (however fragile it might be) sufficient narrative. I do not agree with Faulkner that failed poets write short stories, failed short story writers write novels

. . . if this were so, then those who write epic poems must logically be those who failed when they essayed the haiku, right?

But I would argue that the shorter the fiction, the greater become the odds against the success of the endeavor. That is why, I think, most short-shorts fail — most are no more than vignettes (much less anecdotes), about as satisfying in their effect as the examples of that bastard genre, the "prose-poem" (talk about a contradiction in terms!), that I have read.

So any serious writer can test himself against this limited and limiting form; it might be a good idea for any writer to try one every so often just to see what kind of shape he's in. Readers of this anthology will, I assume, check the contents out and assign judgement with respect to a pretty simple standard: is it a "story" or not?

Charles Baxter

In the abruptly short-short story, familiar material takes the place of detail. Oh yes, the reader says: a couple quarreling in a sidewalk restaurant, a nine-year-old boy stealing a Scripto in Woolworth's, a woman crying in the bathtub. We've seen that before. We know where we are. Don't give us details; we don't need them. What we need is surprise, a quick turning of the wrist toward texture, or wisdom, something suddenly broken or quickly repaired. Yes, we know these people. Now just tell us that they do.

A small cast of familiar characters, non-exotic locations, pet themes: to work these materials in a short space is to balance one's own virtuosity as a writer against the reader's ability to anticipate. The tune is usually thin, played on one instrument, and lasts anywhere from thirty seconds to about four minutes. Like Debussy's "Syrinx" (two minutes, thirty-eight seconds), its intervals are unexpected and must continue to resonate when the piece is over. It's a test of the reader's ability to fly, using minimal materials.

Why these things, now? Well, who is notable for making plans anymore? Who feels like the hero of an epic? These are tunes for the end of time, for those in an information age who are sick of data. The future has narrowed, become so small a tunnel that no one feels like crawling into it. It's not that people don't have attention spans. They just don't believe in the future, and they're tired of information. Ask the kids: anything worth doing isn't worth doing for long.

Lydia Davis

People who do not themselves write have told me they like reading short stories and especially very short stories because they don't have much time and like to finish what they read soon after they start reading it. It seems true that many people are more distracted than ever before and find it harder than ever to concentrate on a single thing for a long time unless it has to do with something essential to them, like earning money or examining and adjusting their various relationships with other people. It is also harder for anyone to be calm now.

The very short story is certainly good for that, being a nervous form of story. You don't have time to get used to it (forget it) as you read. It keeps itself more separate from you than a longer story, maybe because it is more recently begun, and so it is more demanding of your attention.

Fables and parables have for thousands of years found brevity a good way to make a point. Kafka's paradoxes and those of immediate predecessors of his initiate the parable that doesn't have a moral, and other writers go on with that.

People write parables about a world that has nothing to do with the modern world, or parables that do partake of this modern world, or more realistic very brief stories, and these last often begin and end in the middle of things and present us with unheroic characters, reflecting our willingness, now, not to aggrandize our lives, in which if something happens it always begins and ends in the middle of something else and in which there are also, or maybe only, conjunctions of the ridiculous and less ridiculous over and over again.

What is certain, in any case, is that we are more aware of the great precariousness and the possible brevity of our lives than we were in the past, our lives being actually more precarious than they used to be, and for this reason, perhaps, we express not only more despair but also more urgency in some of our literature now, this urgency also being expressed as brevity itself.

Alvin Greenberg

Why Is the Short Story Short & the Short-Short Even Shorter?

Brevity. Brevity is the face of mortality. No one blathers at the edge of the grave, except clergymen (and some writers), whose minds are on immortality, which gives them more time because it's presumed to go on forever — just as they often seem to. For the rest, staring into that open hole, brevity, till we become as concise as the Unnameable at (where else?) the end (or Beckett himself, forever paring it down): "I must go on, I can't go on, I'll go on."

In short, mortality. And for the shorts, mortality, as we have been assured by no less an authority than the man who fathered the modern short story: "There are certain themes of which the interest is all absorbing, but which are too entirely horrible for the purposes of legitimate fiction. . . . To be buried alive is, beyond question the most terrific of those extremes which has ever fallen to the lot of mere mortality." So we will bypass "legitimate fiction" (the novel) and see what we can do with our suffocating lives in brief. Briefer yet, now, given the irony of an age in which life expectancy expands (Finally, time to read all those huge Russian novels!) while the chance of enjoying that expanded lifetime rapidly shrinks (Quick, tell me a story!).

I am reminded of a project I once had: to collect the last words of the famous and maybe even less-than-famous, having heard a number of interesting examples, all of them brief and intriguing — a project put to an end by my being brought face-to-face with death on a personal level and therefore no longer able to trivialize it with aphorism and anecdote. But what I want to say about those last words is simply this: there are always very few of them. At the end, I suppose, there is not really all that much to say, and certainly not much time to say it in. We are already a writer's generation beyond Flannery O'Connor, whose mind, like Poe's, was always on last things, and the time, like our fiction, is getting shorter.

"For the love of God, Montresor," I only wanted enough time to finish this novel.

H. E. Francis

They are hardly new. Writers have always challenged themselves to absolute reduction, skeletons. They tempt death. If a perspective shifts, certainly we have a story. But the form costs — it sacrifices most of itself. Experience borders perilously on nothing. We are saved from *nothing* by an abrupt turn to encounter a few assembled straws. Stress may fall on any story element: characters approach anonymity, setting nears irrelevance, situation (however flimsy) almost invariably presides, or tone. Tone and situation are the prima donnas.

They are where story and poem meet, though only some rare marvels (a Hemingway, say) share most aspects of poetry. *Can* our time achieve the one-to-one density of parts (each with multiple meanings) in a density of the whole (with multiple interpretations) of earlier parable and allegory? Kafka—the most valiant—tries.

Perhaps the recent proliferation (?) suggests the honest search, which yields glitters of truth (the form must fit the glitter) or the search for originality, which dead-ends at technique. Ours is a necessarily self-conscious age.

Maybe brevity—on sight—alerts a reader's expectancy: he collaborates. The impact is O. Henry without the cheating—all gears grind to that "inevitable" last line.

For me there is this distinction—that great an(pro?)tagonist *Time* is sacrificed. Time becomes the *writer's* antagonist. He has caught perception in a dead interval. The form matches the instant's perception. That brevity is the joy, the Roman candle thrust, burst—*Ahhh!*—and darkness. As a too frequent experience, they bore. I seldom find one which bears re-reading. Time in a story offers, in its fuller play over parts, in a growing density, a rich experience which bears constant re-reading because it brings more of the reader's self into play and, long after, expands, expands, expands—

Charles Johnson

The likely father of the unusual form called the contemporary short-short story is, I'd wager, Edgar Allan Poe who, in his classic essay called "On the Aim and Technique of the Short Story" (1842), emphasized for modern fiction the virtues of brevity, priority of "effect," and the unity achieved by a work short enough to be read in a single sitting. Of course, the blame for fathering this form can't be placed on Poe alone. Editors like it because it means we can publish several titles in a single issue, thereby creating the illusion of diversity on the contents page. Writers who don't feel, as I often don't, up to the long-distance demands of a complex novel can spend a few days on a short-short and still feel, by God, that they're accomplishing *something*. Readers, who are doubtlessly the real culprits here, can digest the short-short in a few minutes as they sit in the bathroom, ride the bus, or wait in the checkout line at Safeway—if nothing else, the short-short is symptomatic of an Age where speed is everything, the Concorde is admired because it saves time, and where our rhythms have been conditioned by sitcoms that stop at twelve-minute intervals for commercial breaks; an Age of "digests" that churns out three-minute music-videos for adolescents with short attention spans, fast-food restaurants, and the twenty-four-hour divorce. Can anyone doubt that for a tired, time-harried reader, who has dozens of things competing for his or her attention, the short-short is fiction's version of the quick-fix?

Yet, it can be a powerful fix, like poetry which it resembles because the short-short demands compression and economy. It usually relies on narration (dramatic scenes classically structured on Aristotelian lines take too long), a bewitching voice and, given its brevity, it often achieves the lasting wallop carried by Japanese haiku and koans, as in the fiction of Jim Heynen and Barry Lopez. It is strangely pure. And all of a piece. Moreover, it is protean, assuming any shape — the sketch, fable, parable, a transcript of dialogue, a list — and, adding to its appeal, it gives writers a vehicle for expressing all those scraps of experience that are fascinating but too thin for a traditional "rising-conflict-to-resolution" story or novella. Only a fool would rigidly define the short-short because, above all else, it must be an innovative, attention-grabbing exploration of that perennial mystery that is the origin and end of expression itself: language.

Leonard Michaels

A short story has value insofar as it comes close, in one or another way, to being a poem. Short-short stories can seem to come very close to being poems, since they depend immensely on implication, but there is always a peculiar danger. In suggesting a poem, and not being a poem, a short-short can seem merely disgraceful.

William Peden

Skinny Fiction, or Mini-Fiction: a single-episode narrative with a single setting, a brief time span, and a limited number of speaking characters (three or four at the most); a revelation-epiphany: the click of a camera, the opening or closing of a window, a moment of insight.

James B. Hall

The form's origins are obscure, but always there were commercial implications: short-short fiction fit easily into magazine space surrounded by higher-priority advertisements. Early editorial (and reader) popularity of the form is to be closely associated with the advent of rotary-steam presses and the mass-circulation newspapers and magazines of the late nineteenth century, especially in America.

Because its roots were in popular culture, the intention of the short-short story was to entertain. Because its language was largely journalistic, the early short-short story presented a characteristic weakness. The combination of brief scope and truncated language precluded complex comment on the nature of human life, and yet this order of comment is of central value in prose fiction. The short stories of O. Henry, with their melodramatic reverse-endings, were a kind of artistic success which seldom overcame the form's regressive conventions.

Presently, the writer views the short-short form more urbanely, for some things about this extreme form changed, while other conventions remained.

For example, word count (1,000–2,000 words) still has editorial appeal. Nevertheless, we now see the form not as minimalist art, but as miniaturist art; the appeal is similar to the fugue, cloissoné, ivory carving, the couplet. Among the popular arts, the short-short form suggests the appeal of a clever vaudeville turn. If circus is a popular art, the short-short form suggests the appeal of the very small person, the dwarf. In circus terms, we appreciate the short-short form and take it seriously; we do not confuse the short-short form with either the geek or the strong man. Handled imaginatively, the form now claims a specialized literary audience, and rewards variously both the writer and the reader.

In any event, the short-short is clearly a subgenre of the short story, but there are notable distinctions, mostly of degree.

For example, the unit of artistic composition in the short story is the full scene; the short-short genre presents half-scenes and, proportionally, uses far less foreshortened material. The opening passages of the shorter form take the reader farther — more forcefully — into the shadow of the fiction; the closing passages are often more resonant, more suggestive.

Because of its miniaturist commitment, the short-short form is not notable for bold actions, even though something always happens; the short-short fiction tends to be a story of manners, of key moments in the relationship of two protagonists, the vehicle for modern myth, fable, or excursions into horror.

Because the writer's executive control of the materials of a short-short story must be at once absolute and delicate, the artistic failure rate is high. What might have been illuminating and suggestive about life itself often remains merely an episode; materials and themes of personal importance to the author resist the shaping impulse, and the quick, intense, well-controlled piece becomes 10,000 words and no end in sight. The ability of a writer to get the reader's interest, get a limited effect, and get out, requires much more literary and artistic background than at the onset seems reasonable.

A literary commentator recently averred that short story writers are the "heroes" of contemporary literature — a proposition which may be argued. If there is any truth at all to the short story writer as hero, then the short-short story writer in that identical landscape stands exceedingly tall.

Jack Matthews

The short story is many things, and many different sorts of things, but it seems to me that, at its most effective, it provides a philosophical model of potential human actions, therefore meanings. Most of its natural forms are determined by dialectic progression; like the Platonic dialogues (many of which are of short story length), they play out the implications of a certain idea or set of events.

There is a sort of very short story that is so pointed, so highly focused, that its pointedness (not quite the same as point) is uniquely realized. Petronius' "The Widow of Ephesus" is a classic example, and any addition, or "enrichment" in texture or characterization, would weaken and impoverish the story as it now stands. There are many ways for the very short story to function well; but the precise forms and details of this function will be intrinsic to the story itself, whatever it may be.

Stephen Minot

Why are there so many conflicting definitions of so simple a form as the short-short story? Because it is rooted in at least five different traditions. As writers we're partial to the form we enjoy the most. Favoritism is natural enough among opinionated people, but it doesn't do credit to the richness of the subgenre.

Some short-shorts, for example, announce themselves as *true experience*. They are sudden, abrupt, personal. We improvise oral versions all the time. We start off with "Hey, listen to this!" or "I still can't get over it!" Even, "Here's one for the books!" Exclamation marks grab attention. Heads turn our way. We're on stage. We've been doing this ever since we discovered that talking is more fun than grunting. Writers merely make deliberate and intricate what talkers do carelessly and intuitively. Short-shorts in this tradition are vivid, intense, dramatic. They seem highly personal even when they're made up. Writers lie a lot.

The *anecdote* is less personal and more structured. Some critics are down on anecdotal fiction because the shape is often more important than the feeling. More classical than romantic. We think of O. Henry, but Saki is more subtle, Maupassant more sophisticated, Brautigan more skewed and hence more contemporary. Americans who were raised in the South or, like me, in New England recall listening to anecdotes told by nonwriters who were masters of the told tale. We never said, "Hey, I've heard that before." We savored the form, recognizing beginnings, repetitions, and endings. We never asked, "And then what happened?"

When anecdotes surprise us into laughter they are called jokes. When they deliver lessons, they become parables. Parables are not in vogue right now unless steeped in irony. When anecdotal tales deal with animals and endure for centuries they become fables. But no matter what form an anecdote takes, it is carefully crafted and structured.

More analytical yet is the *speculation*. What kind of building would house a library which contains every single piece of knowledge? Borges asks. What's it like for a sperm struggling upstream in a highly competitive race toward an ill-defined goal? Barth asks. What would it be like to herd a flock of au pair girls across the plains? Barthelme asks. Idea is everything; ingenuity reigns. Character and even plot become subservient to theme. There's often no narrative build-up, sometimes no plot whatever. That's a story? Sure it is, but it's also first cousin to a highly illustrated essay.

Speculative stories are close to *dream stories* except that dreams don't always offer easily defined concepts. Mood is stressed more than theme. Joyce Carol Oates, for example, often presents short dream accounts which defy precise thematic analysis. Tone is everything. With her, the mood is often dark, vaguely threatening, Kafkaesque. But when Brautigan draws on this tradition the tone is gentle and light. What they share is the intensity and the vividness of those dreams even our analysts can't pick apart.

Finally, there is the *poetic story*. These are not to be confused with prose poems which are often prosaic fragments written in short lines for no apparent reason. Poetic stories like Dylan Thomas' "August Bank Holiday" are rich in auditory effects — alliteration, assonance, rhythms of syntax and repetition. When read aloud, poetic stories usually offer more to the ear than many prose poems. Imagery is more highly valued than narrative structure. They remain prose, however, because line length is left to chance; it is not a part of the art form.

As fiction gets longer — story, novella, novel — the emphasis tends to be placed on a different set of concerns: complexities of plotting, subtleties of characterization, and the portrayal of social scene. The short-short, then, is something distinct in nature as well as in length. It is truly a subgenre.

Not every story in this collection will fit neatly into a single category, but each work is indebted to one or more of these five distinct traditions. This multiplicity of influences is what gives short-shorts such richness and variety.

TOWARD A NEW FORM

WHILE SOME OF THESE WRITERS acknowledge tradition even more broadly and thoroughly than those in the previous section, they differ in seeing a closer alliance between poetry and the prose of many short-shorts, and in their view of our times less as causing a reshaping of the old than allowing the new to emerge (Kelly, Banks, Bellamy, Oates) — or at least to contend against traditionally necessary expansions of description and character (Stevick). If the way of the short-short is "erasure," its "aim is restorative, to keep us young" (Strand). Departures from form are celebrated (Dybek), or demonstrated within fiction itself (Gildner). Arriving at a new form may be bound to the search for its name (Heller, O'Connor, Banks).

Joe David Bellamy

Compression and concision have always been part of the aesthetic of the American short story form. Some writers, perhaps spurred on by the information overload of our time, began to experiment with just how far these values could be pushed without losing the minimal weight needed for a memorable dramatic statement. Though readers may have shorter attention spans than previously, they are also well-equipped to process information quickly; and many have responded enthusiastically to these compressed, tightly wound new forms.

Robert Kelly

Sudden Fiction: Notes on Fiction That Knows Its Proper Space

In 1973 the Stone Wall Press in Iowa City published the beautifully printed *Stone Wall Book of Short Fictions*, edited by Robert Coover and Kent Dixon. Coover had written to me a year or two before, inviting me to send along something for that collection, which I did — a piece called "Opera," which at the time could hardly have been published anywhere except in such an adventure. I had great hopes for short fiction (which I call usually just fiction — leave it to the individual conscience how long the lovely lie is kept going), hopes which are pretty well realized, especially now that the genre (if it is one) has become the great fertile plain where, for once, poets and novelists can meet together as equals, and each produce effective work, funded by their separate dispositions and preparations.

In that Stone Wall collection, we find some of the names that will continue to dominate our sense of curt fiction: Borges, Barthelme, Brautigan, Coover, Edson, Oates. Looking at those names, and pondering those who came later, along with the poets (Merwin and Anderson and Benedickt are in that collection too), I begin to realize that what short fiction really is is a rebirth of the complementary notions of Deed and Telling.

In all the years of psychological fiction that extended the hegemony of Henry James through a writership and readership far less subtle and less skillful than the master, the feeling for event, for action, had died out of mainstream fiction. And for all their wondrous milking of the minimal, Joyce and Proust did nothing to restore it. Off in the despised limelight of no-better-than-journalism were Kipling and Haggard and Buchan, with the enigmatic Conrad uneasily poised, in flight, between the two orders of what-there-is-to-tell. His colleague and deep friend Ford was ever too much of James's party to be a reliable teller (though he may have the best short novel of all), and may be at his best in the tiny fictions of his autobiographical reflections — a little boy in a velvet suit on Franz Liszt's lap.

So there were writers of eternal boys' stories swotting away at their clear workable prose, busy with sensible clichés, and on the other hand the aesthetes were venturing fragile beauty in the willful splendors of the ordinary, with all telling and nothing told.

In the short fiction of our day, the perfections of telling and of memorable deed are, for once and at last, capable of simultaneous resurrection. There are still microclimates of the Jamesian ordinary versus the Shakespearean grandiose, fantaisie-celtique vying with the acerbic quotidian, as in Ed Dorn's classic, "CB&Q," which may be the richest short-short I've read. We are not struck only with the vaporish prose-poem, the languid uncoiling water snakes in purple wash that the turn of the century welcomed as its shortest prose form — though we can have that too, when it's needed, and there are periods in Michael Palmer as hushed and violaceous as anything in Mallarmé.

What excites me is just this coincidence of poetry and prose, the two extraordinarily different vocations of poet and novelist (who are worlds apart not just in craft but in society, economics, religion), both capable of renewed work in this, for us, new form, neither poetic prose nor prosy verse, but the energy and clarity typical of prose coincident in the scope and rhythm of the poem. [Modest aside: Our Latest Miracle.] And this rhythmic scope, this focus on the *time of the experience of the text*, is what exactly characterizes the form we're talking about. And this scope must be accounted for by any critic who hereafter proposes formally to define short fiction.

Our time has made this succinct fiction possible, and necessary. People who grew up, ourselves, with movies and television had less and less *need* for descriptive exposition, though at the same time a sustained hunger for instantaneous entrainment of place, mood, scene, atmosphere. The coup d'oeil that movies gave us is what short fiction has learned to enact. And many a subtle child in a kiddie matinee has noticed that the coming attractions are more exciting, and more formally alert, than the sprawling ninety-minute B-movies they prefigure. This is the short fiction, the insidious, sudden, alarming, stabbing, tantalizing, annihilating form; and it is this that reminds us that *short* is a misnomer; the fiction we're talking about is *just*, as intonation is just, or a sentence at law — neither too long nor too short. It is meant to be lived out, experienced. Writing, at its best, has always been an enactment, a deed for readers.

One way of telling our fiction has is *erasure*, the deft excision of what the reader expects, but does not need, to be told. Usually stories (especially the infamous "short story") are actually the diffuse shadows cast by an ardent *narreme*, the deed-as-tellable. When this deed is sparely told, the telling is the grace, the told come home.

The best precepts I know derive from the practice of the best writers who wrote curtly, and justly — Gertrude Stein, Mary Butts, W. C. Williams, Joyce's raw epiphanies (especially as published in the early sixties as a text in themselves) — and those who right now are bringing *multum in parvo* to new levels rich, intricate meaningfulness — Lydia Davis, Spencer Holst, Mary Caponegro (whose first collection identified her genre as "microfictions," a word I like), Leslie Scalapino. (So many of them are women, always more courageous in the exploration of new formal domains.) There are older instances — the seventeenth-century genre of "character," the brilliant experiments in chapter length in the later Melville (*Billy Budd* has the smartest structure in the world). These are preceptors, the frontiers I sense of our movement from and to, what makes this, a form.

I remind myself of the reciprocal: that short pithy fiction is possible only in a time and culture that affords also leisure for the longest sustained attention; haiku grows up in a land where the Tale of Genji is classic. If you want to write great microfiction, start with a three volume novel. If you can hold a reader's interest for a week, you can be trusted to hold it for one rapt minute.

The kind of work our small, our *sudden* fiction is celebrates the new audience we have, we are. We see and hear quickly, and are capable of feats of comprehending, grasping the subtlest. The electronic media we're always grumbling about have raised our skills and our hopes, and by themselves they have not curtailed our attention spans. We have become an audience able to wield long and short, see fast and dwell long. It is a privilege to be alive and writing when people are so smart.

Stuart Dybek

Blasters, short-shorts, fictions, prose poems, sketches, American *haibun. . . .*

I hope the debate as to what to call these short prose pieces continues, and that we'll never reach consensus, or feel we've figured it out and categorized them at last. Their elusive quality is part of what makes them attractive. If we can't even name them, how can we be sure what they're supposed to do?

A form carries with it certain built-in expectations, certain predictable possibilities for both reader and writer. But the short prose piece so frequently inhabits a No-Man's Land between prose and poetry, narrative and lyric, story and fable, joke and meditation, fragment and whole, that one of its identifying characteristics has been its protean shapes.

Part of the fun of writing them is the sense of slipping between the seams. Within the constraint of their small boundaries the writer discovers great freedom. In fact, their very limitations of scale often *demand* unconventional strategies.

There is no theory such as Poe's idea of single effect to appraise them by; there is no traditional model or reference standard to judge them against.

Each writer makes up the form. Each piece is another departure. A departure — but from what?

Philip Stevick

Very short stories are, of course, the ur-form of narration. A parable or an exemplum is a short-short story. So is an anecdote. So is a recollected dream. So is a joke. But something happens when the artistic motive enters. Watch Twain telling a frog joke. It grows into a comic monologue of substantial size, no longer a joke or an anecdote, and part of the pleasure is in its prolixity. As we read it, we imagine it being told. But it's all trick. Nobody ever told a frog story at such length. Writing it down, trying to make some substance of it, some artistic gravity, Twain lets it grow. One remembers James, overhearing the barest anecdote at a dinner party, closing his mind to the speaker's elaboration, going home to write a story of eight thousand words. The motives for expanding are obvious: a writer has people; he needs motivational texture; he has place; he needs descriptive density; he has ephemeral slightness; he needs, as Aristotle is customarily translated, "a certain magnitude." Our dailiness, our aural/oral world is made up of short-short stories. But everything militates against translating that shortness into print. A writer who would write short does not merely choose; he strains, resists, contends against the compulsion to write long.

There are writers, to be sure, for whom short comes more easily and they are invariably writers with one foot in the tradition of modern art fiction and one foot in a wholly different tradition, the Hassidic tale, the wonder of the Latin-American pre-literate folk. For most writers of short fiction, however, there was, obviously, for a long time, no point in contending against development. That the possibility of resisting bulk, making a whole out of fifteen hundred words, seems a more available option now than it used to, owes something to the fact that those signs of magnitude of the recent past mean so much less to us now: "character development," "a sense of place." It owes something to our pleasure in the fusion of the extremes of fact and fantasy. And it owes something to our extraordinary sense of sport and play.

Barth wrote the ultimate short fiction, a Moebius strip which reads "Once upon a time there was a story that began . . ." It gives me pleasure, that little story. I have read it many times, even though I know the words. I have held it in my hands. Thirty years ago neither I nor anyone else would have known what to do with it.

Philip F. O'Connor

1960. Graduate student at San Francisco State College hears professor, Herbert Wilner, tell class why the old short-short story is no longer being written. It has a rigid formula, requiring that clue be set into story producing surprise ending. Most notable practitioners were de Maupassant and O. Henry. Offers little opportunity for character development. Character development very important in modern short story.

1963-1971. Writing obsessively, former graduate student, now professor, finds emerging from typewriter along with traditional stories another kind that is more evocative than narrative. To wife and friends he describes new stories as "mood pieces," "experimental" stories, or "non-traditional" stories. He really doesn't know what they are. Except for size, they don't resemble the "short-short story" Herbert Wilner described. They, however, seem a comfortable kin to occasional other very short stories he has begun to see in print.

1983. Writer/professor is asked to serve as judge for Associated Writing Programs short-short fiction awards. Within weeks he begins looking forward to the time he's given each evening to reading several of the hundreds of manuscripts he's been sent. He doesn't find any of the old-fashioned kind of short-shorts. Yet these are not just condensed short stories.

1984. Professor reflects on stories. They are about individuals struggling to maintain dignity in a culture which does not threaten so much with guns as with reasonableness. There are few dramatic resolutions because the antagonists, which are often conditions, not people, engage the character stealthily, like cancer, not tornadoes. It no longer seems to be enough that they hang on like schlemiels but that, in hanging on, they assert and even act on their singular vision of things as they are, attempting to change the changeable in those small ways relatively powerless individuals now and then find possible.

1986. On further reflection, professor believes a new fictional form has arisen. The name "short-short" is not suitable because of unfortunate associations with older form of same name. He proposes this:

1. Sto (new form)
2. Story
3. Stovella (long story or short novella)
4. Novella
5. Novel

Gary Gildner

Henry is the narrator of a recent fiction of mine. Thinking about the short-short story, I am reminded of something he said:

"Living in a small seaside town you forget a lot and, paradoxically, remember a lot. What you forget are the big chunks that go in the middle. The little pieces around the edges are what suddenly surprise you. They surface like driftwood, like shells and jellyfish, they are brilliant and want to mean something. 'I'm a *good* woman,' Margaret once cried out in her soft bed under a skylight dizzy with stars. Who could begin to understand the full range, the body of that opinion? I held her close. I wanted to reassure her. Of course she was a good woman, whatever that meant, and it meant a lot, I know, but what, finally, could you do with it? I don't mean to sound cynical or morose or uncaring. We had roasted a fine chicken; we had had a lovely walk on the beach; we had brought our bodies one to the other and popped extravagantly at the same moment. Now in the aftermath she was expressing — without warning — what sounded like part of a difficult history. And I? I was recalling a scene, years before, in which I had rounded third and was determined to get home. A girl named Joyce Dudzek was leaping in the stands. She had long blonde hair and buck teeth and her father, an usher in our church, tooted his trumpet after I crossed the plate. Oh yes, that did happen. And so did this: lying down in those long-ago gardens, sucking tomatoes, rolling peas, moon-white, straight from the pod."

Russell Banks

In terms of form, we're still at the earliest stages of learning how to talk about the conventional short story. It would seem impossible, then, to speak intelligently about something called the "short-short" story. The very absurdity of the term, however, gives it away, literally, since it's clear that the thing at hand is not a diminutive version of anything. It's its own self, and it's intrinsically different from the short story and more like the sonnet or ghazal — two quick moves in opposite directions, dialectical moves, perhaps, and then a leap to a radical resolution that leaves the reader anxious in a particularly satisfying way. The source, the need, for the form seems to me to be the same need that created Norse kennings, Zen koans, Sufi tales, where language and metaphysics grapple for holds like Greek wrestlers, and not the need that created the novel or the short story, even, where language and the social sciences sleep peacefully inside one another like bourgeois spoons. When physicists locate a new particle, they start by giving it a new name, which helps them identify its properties more reliably and leads more easily to the identification of still newer particles. Naming is how the world enlarges itself. We might try the same with the thing at hand, calling it *poe*, for instance. "Me, I write poes," one could say.

Steven Heller

Sudden Fiction: What's in a Name?

Naming anything, old or new, is the writer's special burden. For as any writer — anyone who strikes a keyboard or puts pen to paper with the intention of creating something worthy enough to bear his own name — surely believes, we cannot know a thing, cannot truly possess it, until we call it by its right name.

What then do we have in this collection of "sudden fiction"?

The title suggests that we shall have fictions, but not necessarily stories. A distinction without a difference? Not for me, since fictions that do not tell stories — do not express changes that somehow matter — do not themselves matter very much to me, whatever their other virtues of language, invention, etc. The fictions I most admire in this volume all tell stories, though some of them, such as Jack Matthews' "A Questionnaire for Rudolph Gordon," are strikingly unconventional.

Aside from the nationality of their authors, the only obvious constraint involved in selecting the fictions for this volume was their length. Beyond this, however, the title *Sudden Fiction* suggests a possible bias toward highly dramatic prose. One finds examples of such fiction in this volume, but a reading of the entire collection disproves the bias. Alongside the quick and wrenching action of Raymond Carver's "Popular Mechanics" (perhaps the ultimate in "sudden" short-short fiction) we find the funny, ironic, eloquently narrated story of "civilized" estrangement of father and son in John Cheever's "Reunion." Likewise, the pell-mell, rhapsodically bitchy voice of Gordon Lish's narrator in "The Merry Chase" is balanced by Tennessee Williams' leisurely paced, heavily plotted narrative in "Tent Worms." Overall, the fictions in this anthology display considerable range of forms and styles. Sudden fiction, it seems, can be anything, as long as it is short and delivers an impact that is both significant and lasting.

I remain a bit uncomfortable with the term, but am intrigued by another question the publication of this collection raises: Will the increasing popularity of very short fiction (a development largely determined less by writers than by editors and audience) ultimately produce a more definable form — one we can rightly name — a form that, like the short story itself, will at some point transcend its seeming limits and produce fictions that are not only very good, like the contents of this volume, but great?

The next two decades may well provide the answer.

Joyce Carol Oates

Very short fictions are nearly always experimental, exquisitely calibrated, reminiscent of Frost's definition of a poem — a structure of words that consumes itself as it unfolds, like ice melting on a stove. The form is sometimes mythical, sometimes merely anecdotal, but it ends with its final sentence, often with its final word. We who love prose fiction love these miniature tales both to read and to write because they are so finite; so highly compressed and highly charged. The tension is that of — one might say — Hagler's eight minutes against Hearns, an epic writ so small one can hardly bear to watch it.

Of course the form, while being contemporary, is also timeless. As old as the human instinct to combine power and brevity in a structure of words. Consider words as disparate as these:

> These are the seductive voices of the night; the Sirens, too, sang that way. It would be doing them an injustice to think that they wanted to seduce; they knew they had claws and sterile wombs, and they lamented this aloud. They could not help it if their laments sounded so beautiful.
>
> Kafka, "The Sirens"

and

> The competitions of the sky
> Corrodeless ply.
>
> Emily Dickinson

and

> Western Wind, when wilt thou blow,
> That the small rain down may rain?
> Christ, that my love were in my arms
> And I in my bed again!

Anonymous

As these selections suggest, the rhythmic form of the short-short story is often more temperamentally akin to poetry than to conventional prose, which generally opens out to dramatize experience and to evoke emotion; in the smallest, tightest spaces, experience can only be suggested. Voice is everything, the melting of the ice on the stove, consuming itself as we watch. There are those for whom one of Chopin's brilliant little Preludes is worth an entire symphony by one or another "classic" composer whose method is to build upon repetition and contrast. . .

It may well be, however, that all the short fictions in existence cannot match a single great novel: Hardy's *Tess*, for instance. But, fortunately, works of art are not in competition. And surely should not be judged as if they were.

Mark Strand

It is condensed, even curt; its rhythms are fleeting, its languor quick, its majesty diminutive. It discredits accretions, honors reduction, and refuses to ramble. Its identity is exceptional, its appetite exclusive. It is refractory, rapid, runtish. It reverses, refutes, revises. It can do in a page what a novel does in two hundred. It covers years in less time, time in almost no time. It wants to deliver us where we were before we began. Its aim is restorative, to keep us young. It thrives on self-effacement, and generates statements, on its own behalf, that are shorn or short. Its end is erasure.

A PRACTICUM

TARGAN SETS OUT the uses of short-shorts for creative writing students and classes, and for professional writers. Also briefly noted here are some of the practical demands, and risks, of length (Dixon, Vivante, Calisher, Curtis). Writers in other sections have spoken of the scraps of experience the short-short often uses (Johnson, Gildner); here, Wolff gives them form in a powerful, personal narrative. Finally, a writer's own development is traced through his experience with short-shorts (Fox).

Barry Targan

The Short-Short Story: Étude

In writing, the short-short story rather than the more common short story comes closer to the classic *étude,* and for this reason is better suited to some of the initial (and longer lasting) needs of the creative writing student. Particularly, the main advantage is this: the writer can get a great deal of specific practice with various elements while staying within a true fiction form. He can pose specific technical problems of characterization, tone, mood, or whatever, and solve the problems in the terms of real stories. Using the short-short story, he avoids the artificiality of the set piece of assignment ("describe a man who has just heard that . . . .") while at the same time he protects himself from an uncertain commitment of energy and time entailed in the short story, for a short story is open-ended in the way a short-short story is not. That is the beauty of it. The short-short story can no more get out of hand, go beyond its *natural* aim, than could Leonardo have drawn more on one sheet than size and design would allow.

And the *étude* presents the artist with an accomplishment, a thing done, always a comforting experience for an artist to have.

In an actual teaching situation the short-short story takes on another value. Rather than talking abstractly about writing problems — or waiting for them to occur in the students' stories — the teacher can suggest that short-short stories be written which address themselves to the anticipated problems. If, after all, all that can really be taught, at least directly, in a creative writing course is *craft*, then to teach craft head-on seems to me to be the thing to do. Not, of course, at the expense of anything else. But the short-short story, because it is *both* story and exercise, respects the larger creative necessity in a young writer even as it teaches him his needed skills. Also, a self-confidence begins to develop as the writer succeeds with the more manageable short-short story where he might have stumbled about with the more difficult short story.

And, too, there are obvious advantages in having shorter works to deal with in the joint conference sessions in which students listen to and discuss each other's work. You can deal with three or more short-short stories sometimes whereas you might stay for hours on one conventional short story. More stories in a class session make for a more involved class. More stories also provide the class with its own problem of making rapid critical shifts and immediate comparisons, an excellent practice in its own right, for a good writer should be a fairly good *practical* critic (as distinct from the *philosophical* critic).

Lastly, and briefly, there are the advantages that the short-short story might have for the "graduate" or professional writer. Naturally, these are more a matter of personal attitude, but the short-short story can sometimes serve nicely as a way to work on a new and separate idea while in the middle of a longer work. To give some fictional shape to an idea is always more satisfying than to merely record the idea in a journal, but time is seldom so easily available, and to risk breaking from a long work isn't a happy thought to most writers. The short-short story, with its compelling *limitedness*, can partially resolve the dilemma. The short-short story can also be used as a testing ground for any number of thoughts, theories, interests that a writer might have. But by now I had better not presume to instruct further.

Stephen Dixon

Each story determines its own style and length. Once the first draft is written and I see what style and length that story is, I try to stay faithful to it. I don't determine the length, it does. If I don't follow the story's demands for length, as well as its demands for voice, I ruin that story, by overwriting, underwriting, not listening to it, and other reasons.

Arturo Vivante

Brief and bright. As Shelley says: "Lightning that mocks the night, / brief even as bright." The flight of sparrows from field to field, across a hedge, as compared to the flight of geese from Newfoundland to Florida. In other words, not just a difference in length, but in pace too.

Like any other living form, it resists and resents being divided, or added onto, for that matter. It clings to every part of itself, and is self-sustaining.

Its peculiarity is its brevity, but its fundamental quality is life, something that it shares with any other form of art.

It needs to be convincing and unpredictable. And it needs a certain spiritual lightness. To borrow terms from cooks, it needs to whip, bind, jell, crystallize, rise; or, from brewers, ferment. This it can't do with all life's details: life has something which art is glad to do without.

Hortense Calisher

I'm not much for limiting statements on the technique or category of anything. All these do is limit — and sooner or later somebody will come along and defy that, or bypass what supposedly couldn't be. Length surely has relevance, but only to the piece of work at hand. To me a story is as long as its inner dictates persuade it to be. Ditto a novel — or a poem. Once, when I was just beginning, I was challenged publicly — "How long should a short story be?" someone in the audience said. "I am writing too — and I want to be sure not to waste time." I quavered back: "As long as a piece of string." When that didn't go well, I added: "I mean — to tie up the package with."

C. Michael Curtis

The shorter the story, the more both writer and reader have to depend on hard moments of discovery, flashes of illumination that provide, in their suggestiveness and aptness, what other writers struggle for pages to make clear. Very short stories need to be free of dithering, or false starts, of shallow exposition or commonplace dialogue. They require a writer to know just where he or she is going, and to be there swiftly. The risks are considerable, and very short stories often appear to be products of impoverished rather than decisive minds. When they work, I think they're wonderful. When they don't, one can at least move on, swiftly, to something better.

Tobias Wolff

I was on a bus to Washington, D.C. Two days I'd been traveling and I was tired, tired, tired. The woman sitting next to me, a German with a ticket good for anywhere, never stopped yakking. I understood little of what she said but what I did understand led me to believe that she was utterly deranged.

She finally took a breather when we hit Richmond. It was late at night. The bus threaded its way through dismal streets toward the bus station. We rounded a corner and there beneath a streetlight stood a white man and black woman. The woman wore a yellow dress and held a baby. Her head was thrown back in laughter. The man was red-haired, rough looking, and naked to the waist. His skin seemed luminous. He was grinning at the woman, who watched him closely even as she laughed. Broken glass glittered at their feet.

There is something between them, something in the instant itself, that makes me sit up and stare. What is it, what's going on here? Why can't I ever forget them? Tell me, for God's sake, but make it snappy—I'm tired, and the bus is picking up speed, and the lunatic beside me is getting ready to say something.

Robert Fox

Who Writes Short-Shorts?

I started writing short-shorts when I dropped out of college, the point at which I became a writer. Turning from William York Tyndall's Lawrence and Joyce to Saroyan's *Daring Young Man on the Flying Trapeze* freed me. I no longer needed character, plot, conflict, resolution, and phallic symbolism. Saroyan's work made me less serious as well. I enjoyed myself in a new way, improvising on ideas. My stories ranged from fantasies like "A Fable" to "She Wrote:", a story by a member of the Rock Hudson Fan Club, a take on

Saroyan's "Dear Greto Garbo." I don't think Saroyan thought about form — what I learned from him was tone. Short-shorts can be tone pieces, much like poems.

Several years later Borges, Cortazar and Juan Jose Arreola turned me back to the form. Borges especially was a natural for me. "He's a great liar," poet Sergio Mondragon said to me. After a couple of years in grad school I needed to play once again.

My interest lay primarily in using dreams as metaphor or as comment on physical reality. I also wrote satires, parodies, mythical memoirs, realistic anecdotal pieces as well, like the early Frito stories. The economy of the form is a great challenge and a quick fulfillment.

I conceive short-shorts as I do poems, seeing the structure of the work in its entirety. But I still don't know if the piece will work until I put words on paper. The fun lies in the tightness and precision necessary to make a short-short work. I've had many conceptions fail — characters who needed development or ideas that just weren't adequate.

Often when I read, listeners can't distinguish between a short-short and a poem. I know the difference because I've chosen the form deliberately, instinctively. But I'm intrigued by many of the prose poems I've been reading in magazines lately, and by the blurring of distinctions between the forms.

SKIPPERS, SNAPPERS,
AND BLASTERS

W E BEGIN AND END with the best of common sense: Paley divides readers into two kinds, those who skip and those who don't, and Garrett has the last word in the matter of literary theory. On the matter of names, Turner prefers a special brand of short-shorts, which might be called "snappers." The rest of these writers and editors (Henry, Busch, Lish, Camoin, Williams and Penner) provide a sampling of reactions to the original working title of this book.

Grace Paley

The truth is people are kind of scared by very very short stories—just as they are by long poems.

A short story is closer to the poem than to the novel (I've said that a million times) and when it's very very short—1, 2, $2^{1}/_{2}$ pages—should be read like a poem. That is slowly. People who like to skip can't skip in a 3-page story.

Alice K. Turner

"Short-shorts" is what we call them at *Playboy* as in, "We love short-shorts," which we certainly do.

Just because we love them doesn't mean we can find them. Every time I talk to students or writers in groups or idle kibitzers, I put in a pitch for short-shorts. "Send them to us," I say. "We *need* them. Make them deft, snappy and breathtaking, and we will send you money for them." Does this do any good? Don't make me laugh. Only half a dozen people in the world can write short-shorts.

I am talking, of course, about our own brand of short-shorts, which would not include many of those printed in this book—those I would call vignettes, or prose poems, or the indefinable "fictions" (isn't that some term?—just makes you want to run out and read a bunch of 'em, doesn't it?). The editors have sneered at the *Good*

Housekeeping short-shorts, too [in an early version of the introduction], and I have to admit that to me those read more like vignettes with suds than real short-shorts.

When I try to define our short-shorts, I often say that they have more to do with the art of anecdote than that of writing. Pacing has everything to do with it — and the snap at the end. Richard Pryor and Lily Tomlin, they understand the short-short instinctively, and I wish one of them would send me something. "Well, *damn!*" I want to say at the end of a short-short, while figuratively slapping my thigh. Otherwise, why not read something long enough to get your teeth into?

A snap, also called a "twist" or a "zinger," is the sort of surprise ending that O. Henry used to put on his stories. It's out of fashion now, considered dated and a bit corny. Still, it satisfies. See, for example, John Updike's "Pygmalion," which could not be more traditional in form, but which, executed with the author's customary eloquence, is a model of economy and wit. Our own short-shorts tend to be broader. Still, in my opinion, if it doesn't have that snapper at the end, it isn't a short-short, just a very short story. The twist can be funny, it can be shocking or touching, but it must be unexpected.

As I say, almost no one can write these little honeys. Either you've got the knack or you haven't. If you don't have it, don't sweat it, as there isn't much market for them anyway. Except, of course, with us.— and, as you may have gathered, we're not exactly an open market.

DeWitt Henry

I don't know that I have anything special to say about the short-short *form*. It exists, clearly. It is fiction and not "prose poetry." I prefer the old-fashioned word "vignette" to "blasters." But the point is that whatever you call the form, it does have validity. Just as a short story is not an episode or excerpt from a novel, the "vignette" is not a "fragment" from a short story. There is completeness, and when it is achieved, a fullness of reference that is self-sufficient.

Frederick Busch

I know a lot of very short stories that *don't* blast: they hum, or whimper a little, or sing, snort, chuckle, sigh, just plain die out — but a blast? Reminds me of a radio station, cheering for a "blast from the past," those golden-oldies kids think are so dated but which *I* remember dancing dirty to just a little while ago.

Gordon Lish

Lucky darned thing for the two fellers which are compiling this compilation that when they were on the lookout for the right citizen to offer them the legitimization of this here term they think so gorgeously apt by way of its being so heftily descriptive of what it is they say they are compiling, which term is the term "blaster," that they had the smart thought to (A) come (go?) to Gordon "The Legitimizer" Lish, and (B) to first think before coming (going?) to him to first put one of Gordon "The Blaster" Lish's own blasters in their compilation so as to (C) therefore enhance the prospect of the Old Legitimizer's doing his stuff, because (D, E, F, G) it just so happens that I, Gordon Lish, am, almost miraculously (but certainly amazingly) in possession of the one particular piece of information for which these two fellers have set themselves the task of turning up — to wit, that it was in my workshop at Columbia University, this in maybe 1982 or 1983, that a boy name of David Ordan (I say "boy" because that is what he was, a nineteen-year-old who got into the room through some sort of sneaky nineteen-year-oldish-type-of dissembling) wrote himself a little bitty story called "Any Minute Mom Should Come Blasting Through the Door," and, boy ("boy" in an epithetish sort of way and not as some sort of expression of address to Ordan, because I would definitely not call Ordan a boy anymore), was it a pisser. I mean a blaster. It blasted all of us who heard Ordan read it aloud and then it blasted the editors of *TriQuarterly*, where it got printed and gave a tremendous blasting to *TriQuarterly*'s readers, and now it's going to go on (come on?) to blast the brave readers of this here compilation of . . . well, of blasters, right? Good. Except the only thing is I hope nobody gets the idea that Ordan's blaster is a better blaster than his teacher's blaster is. I mean, come (go?) on, I'm fifty-one, okay?

[Editors' note: informed that the title Blasters *was out, Mr. Lish sent the following.]*

The two fellers (compilers both) just allowed as how they're going to change the whole deal on me and *not* call these ditties blasters. So I guess none of the above applies. Which is sort of Didion's point, isn't it? Well, okay, I just thought up the term ditty, didn't I?

François Camoin

Minute Fictions (As in Minute Waltz)

This whole business of labeling, of naming, is a vexing enterprise. Why do we do it at all? Aristotle would say to learn more about the world, in this case the world of fiction. But right away we run the risk of making false moves, of creating, as someone said of the legal system, distinctions without differences. In other words is this a collection of short short stories, or of short-short stories? What have we here, a small horse — or a jackass, which is a different species?

And is this a question of reading strategy, or writing strategy? Do I label this a short-short ahead of time, so that I have a different set of criteria in mind when I sit down to write? Or do I label it a short-short afterward so that the reader will know how he should read it? Naming as a sort of instruction to the reader seems more interesting, somehow.

But then what do we do with all the other terms thrown around in our talk about fictions? *Anecdote. Character sketch. Incident.* Not to mention, God help us, *prose poem.* Throw them away, I think. We need a new vocabulary to think about fiction with.

Practical matters intrude as soon as we sit down to write one of these things, however. What about *proportions*? Alice Turner says that short stories should be like Fabergé eggs. What about short-shorts? Tiny Fabergé eggs? Studded with emeralds the size of pinheads? If every short story should have beginning, middle and end, should every short-short have them too, only smaller? Can we subdivide indefinitely, or is there some sort of quantum law at work here, so that a beginning, say, can be only so small before it becomes something else? Maybe short-shorts should be only *ends.* Or *beginnings.* The way that microscopic animals are sometimes only mouths.

Or we could be prescriptive about all this. A minute fiction (let's call them that — *blasters* sounds like a brand of industrial strength laxative, and *short-short* is an abominable coinage) must be no longer than one thousand words. It should not be a miniature anything — short story, novel, Fabergé egg, whatever. Like a well-cut and well-prepared electron microscope slide (do they call them slides? probably not) it should be a slice that is in some wonderful manner emblematic of a whole. An expanded metaphor? Sure. Its small size should be its glory, not its limitation. It should, like Calvino's playful sentence written by the tribesman in the forest, be disturbing enough to get the writer ostracized from polite society.

God help me, but I love them, these *shoulds*, these *musts*. Where would civilization be without them? Without form and void, that's where. But that's the critic speaking, the latent editor. Why don't we just write something, long or short, and let Alice Turner and Michael Curtis and their colleagues decide what to call it? They're full of terminology as an egg is of meat, those people. That's what they *do*. After all someone has to, or we couldn't talk about fiction. So I'm going to get out of their way and go do what *I* do. Even if I don't know what to call it.

Joy Williams

I like the name and the notion very much. I don't think that all your stories do the idea justice. The best ones are Carver's and Cooper's and Lish's and Cheever's and Hannah's. That's what I think, anyway.

Nadine Gordimer once said a great thing about the short story. She said, "A short story occurs in the imaginative sense. To write one is to express from a situation in the exterior or interior world the life-giving drop—sweat, tear, semen, saliva—that will spread an intensity on the page, burn a whole in it."

I think, maybe, she might have said *hole* rather than *whole*, but maybe not, in any case *whole* is better.

You might think a blaster would provide the life-giving drop more readily than a short story but this isn't the case. On these snowy pages lie rather unidentifiable, mostly unimportant yet nonetheless troubling . . . spots.

Jonathan Penner

I think the best answer to the problem of what to call extremely short stories is simply to call them stories. Subsidiary classification, I think, is unnecessary, and tends to demean the works of art being sorted and separated. To name *anything* is to claim a kind of power over it ("I know what they are"), and I would, if I could, defend all these tiny kingdoms against the imposition of that power.

George Garrett

By hook or by crook, by pure luck and whimsical fortune, I have managed to arrive at an age where almost all literary theory bores me to tears. Of course, I eagerly scan the theoretical statements of others. I read those of my friends here (you know who you are), because I admire them and their works and ways and because I seek to know them better and to learn from their good examples. I read the work of my enemies (guess who) with strong conviction that all that they have to say, no matter how honeyed with wit and charm, is at heart bitter with arrogance, absolutely selfish and self-serving and without merit or value except insofar as what they may pretend and profess seems to confirm my worst opinion of them. For myself I can say only this much. Although craft may be, maybe must be, as closed as a clenched fist, art is always open — an eloquently open palm. Art is open doors and windows with wide views. Most theories are *No Trespassing* signs. Don't pick these flowers, they also insist. There are, in truth, more kinds of short-short stories than I ever knew of or imagined. Wonderful! I would now like to be allowed to live long enough to try them all on. Like new hats. I rejoice in the richness and variety of all these voices, or the sundry ways and means, even of the theories, wholesome and half-assed alike.

ACKNOWLEDGMENTS

"A Sudden Story," by Robert Coover, copyright © 1986 by Robert Coover, with permission of the author.

"Mother," from *Later The Same Day* by Grace Paley, copyright © 1985 by Grace Paley, reprinted with permission of Farrar, Straus and Giroux, Inc.

"Even Greenland," by Barry Hannah, as printed in *Carolina Quarterly*, Winter 1985, with permission of the author.

"Reunion," by John Cheever, copyright © 1962 by John Cheever, reprinted from *The Stories of John Cheever*, with permission of Alfred A. Knopf, Inc.

"Twirler," by Jane Martin, as printed in *Esquire*, November 1982, with permission of Alexander Speer, trustee, Jane Martin estate.

"Sunday in the Park," by Bel Kaufman, as printed in *The Available Press/PEN Short Story Collection*, Ballantine, 1985, with permission of the author.

"Five Ives," by Roy Blount, Jr., as printed in *Esquire*, July 1982, with permission of the author.

"Song on Royal Street," by Richard Blessing, reprinted from *Poems & Stories*, Dragon Gate, 1983, with permission of Marlene Blessing.

"Pygmalion," by John Updike, as printed in *The Atlantic*, July 1981, with permission of the author.

"A Fable," by Robert Fox, with permission of the author.

"The Moving," by James Still, reprinted from *The Run For the Elbertas*, with permission of the University Press of Kentucky, 1953, and the author.

"The Cliff," by Charles Baxter, reprinted from *Harmony of the World*, copyright © 1984 by Charles Baxter, with permission of the University of Missouri Press.

"No One's a Mystery," by Elizabeth Tallent, as printed in *Harper's*, August 1985 and reprinted in *The Available Press/PEN Short Story Collection*, Ballantine, 1985, with permission of PEN Syndicated Fiction Project, and the author.

"The Merry Chase," by Gordon Lish, as printed in *Antioch*, Winter 1985, with permission of the author.

"Yours," by Mary Robison, reprinted from *An Amateur's Guide to the Night*, copyright © 1981, 1982, 1983, with permission of Alfred A. Knopf, Inc.

"A Walled Garden," by Peter Taylor, from *The Old Forest and Other Stories*, copyright © 1941 by Peter Taylor, with permission of Doubleday & Company, Inc.

"Heart Attack," by Max Apple, as printed in *TriQuarterly*, Winter 1976, with permission of the author.

ABOUT THE EDITORS

ROBERT SHAPARD, Ph.D., is a former managing editor of *Western Humanities Review*. His short fiction has been published in literary magazines, and he has received a G.E./C.C.L.M. Award for Younger Writers. He teaches literature and fiction writing at the University of Hawaii.

JAMES THOMAS, Ph.D., is the founding editor of *Quarterly West* and the author of *Pictures, Moving,* a collection of stories. For his fiction he has received two N.E.A. Fellowships, a Wallace Stegner Fellowship, and a James Michener Fellowship. He teaches fiction writing at the University of Utah, and is the director of Writers at Work, a summer writers' conference.